Crécy: The age of the archer

Book 1 in the Sir John Hawkwood Series

By

Griff Hosker

SWORD
BOOKS

Published by Sword Books Ltd 2020

Copyright ©Griff Hosker First Edition

*The author has asserted their moral right under the Copyright, Designs and Patents Act, 1988, to be identified as the author of this work.
All Rights reserved. No part of this publication may be reproduced, copied, stored in a retrieval system, or transmitted, in any form or by any means, without the prior written consent of the copyright holder, nor be otherwise circulated in any form of binding or cover other than that in which it is published and without a similar condition being imposed on the subsequent purchaser.
A CIP catalogue record for this title is available from the British Library.
Cover by Design for Writers*

Dedication

To Michael Joseph Hosker, my latest grandson. Welcome to the family!

Contents

Crécy: The age of the archer 1
Dedication 3
Prologue 6
Chapter 1 15
Chapter 2 29
Chapter 3 42
Chapter 4 55
Chapter 5 67
Chapter 6 82
Chapter 7 96
Chapter 8 107
Chapter 9 124
Chapter 10 140
Chapter 11 153
Chapter 12 166
Chapter 13 175
Chapter 14 190
Chapter 15 201
Chapter 16 210
Epilogue 228
Glossary 229
Historical note 230
Other books by Griff Hosker 232

Real People Used In The Book

King Edward Plantagenet
Prince Edward of Wales and Duke of Cornwall- his son
Lord Henry Plantagenet- Earl of Derby, later Earl of Lancaster and Duke of Lancaster
Ralph, Earl of Stafford
Earl Ralph Neville
King Philip of France
Charles Count of Alençon – His brother
Blind King John of Bohemia
Étienne de la Baume- Grandmaster of Crossbows and Constable of Cambrai

Prologue

Essex 1335

My father was a rich and prosperous man, and I should have had an easy life. I should have had a choice of the sword, the church or the family business but he did not like me, and, instead, I had a living hell. He preferred my elder brother Gilbert who was named after him and it was obvious that I was not wanted. I constantly wondered what I had done wrong. My brother would do something for which he would receive a shake of the head and when I committed the same infraction then I would be beaten. I could never please my father and whatever I did was wrong. Had it not been for my mother, whom I loved and who loved me in return, I think that I would have run away from home long before I did. My mother, who was a gentle born lady from a high-born family, tried to protect me, and I think that aggravated the situation for my father was a brute of a man. Whilst I was in the family home or within her sight then I was safe, and I would not be harmed. Once I was with my father and my brother then ill-treatment would follow; at best it was a clip or a blow but sometimes it involved a serious beating which would leave me bleeding with bones which felt cracked. It toughened me up and made my body hard. When my sisters were born then it became harder for, oft times, my mother would be busy with them and I would be subject to the wrath of my father and brother. I was lucky in that my father's business became so successful that he spent increasing lengths of time away from the family home in Sible Hedingham in Essex. I never knew exactly what his businesses were, for he had a number, but I knew he had a tannery and his tenants raised cattle on the lands he owned. To be honest, I was just happy that half of my pain ended when he was not there.

My mother tried to help me all she could, but I had younger sisters who demanded her time and Gilbert was two years older than I and, at that time, much bigger. She helped me by sending me to work with my uncle, her brother and my namesake, John. It seemed to satisfy everyone. I only came home each evening to sleep. I had some peace and my brother and father were rid of me. My uncle was a kind man and I often wished that he was my father. He was a simple farmer but the days I spent with him changed me. I helped him on the farm and his sons were understanding. I begged my mother to allow me to live with him, but she dared not cross my father who seemed determined to punish me. I never discovered the reason for that antipathy towards me.

I became bigger and stronger. Even by the time I had seen ten summers I was the same size as Gilbert but working with my uncle had made me stronger. Not only that, but he had also taught me to use a bow and that exercise broadened my chest. When I visited my home, Gilbert was no longer able to bully me, and I was able to run fast enough to evade my father. The result was that I was thrown out of the family home. I think my father began to fear me. I was getting so big and my arms and hands were so strong that I think he thought I would be violent towards him. There were tears from my mother and my sisters when I left the family home and went to live full-time with my uncle.

I suppose if I had had a more reasonable father then I would have continued to live with my uncle and to enjoy life as a farmer. That was not meant to be. When I had seen more than twelve summers, perhaps even thirteen, I was not sure, my uncle, who was a tenant of my father's was ordered to throw me from the land. That he did not wish to do so was immaterial. I did not know what prompted this although the fact that at the Sunday morning archery practice I had been seen to have a real skill, perhaps made him fear me and that I would do him or my brother some harm. Uncle John and my aunt, not to mention my cousins, were all angry and distraught in equal measure. They did their best for me and I had clothes, a longbow and arrows, a dagger and four pennies not to mention a cloak and blanket when I took the road from my family home. There was but one place to head, London.

I did not intend to become a tailor's apprentice. That decision was taken for me by Fate or God, or I know not who. When I reached London, having spent three days walking there, I was so hungry and exhausted that after walking around the Chepe, London's market seeking food I took the first kindness that I could. The fact that it was not true kindness was, perhaps, the story of my life. I walked from the Chepe down Needlers Lane and saw the tailor sitting outside his shop, sewing. He looked up and when I had eye contact, I begged him for some food. I am not sure if he would have offered me any had Megs, his wife not been emptying the night slops into the pot outside.

He lifted his hand and said, "Away with you gutter rat! Find charity with the monks!"

His wife emptied the last of the slops into the pot on the corner and pointed the vessel at him like some sort of weapon, "Stephen the Tailor, you cannot let the poor bairn wander into the Chepe alone and starving! There are villains there and gangs, as you well know!"

Stephen the Tailor shrugged. He was a runt of a man and rarely smiled. I never like him, but I liked his wife. "We have little enough as it is, wife!" She stared at him and he wilted a little before her baleful look. "If you feed him then he does a day's work for me!"

I nodded for I was eager to please and food would be welcome. "Yes, master! I will work for food!" I knew not what I would do in London, but it seemed to me that food and a roof over my head were priorities. "I will work hard, Master Tailor, for I am not afraid of labour and I am strong!"

Stephen the Tailor spat into the street and said, "Aye, and hands like shovels! Still, you can lift, and you can fetch. Feed him!"

Megs put her arm around me, shaking her head at her husband, "Come with. What is your name?"

"John Hawkwood."

"Well John, I am Megs and the creature you spoke to was my husband. He is not a pleasant man and I know not why I stay with him except that the men who live in London are, by and large, worse than he is. Had not the plague killed my family then I would be in the country still. Put your things in the corner by the fire and sit you at the table. We have little enough, but you shall share it."

As she ladled the food into my wooden bowl, I examined the room. It was just one room. There was a table and two chairs and a bed. The fire was on one wall and the bulk of the room was taken up with bolts of cloth. I could see why the tailor sat under the awning outside. I deduced that there were no children for I saw just the one bed and no sign of them. Megs looked to be too old to have children and I thought to ask her why she had no children and then thought better of it.

As I ate the thin stew and barley bread she chattered like a magpie and I discovered that she stayed with her husband because he was a good tailor and made money. She was the brains behind the business, and she was the one who saved the money and made plans. "One day we shall move from here and travel closer to Windsor. The King and his court spend more time there and it is his lords and courtiers who will pay good money for John's clothes. He is a magician with the needle." She rambled on at length about her husband's skill and having gone two days without food I nodded and ate three bowls of the bean stew. It might have had meat in it at one time but not recently.

Even as I was finished, the tailor put me to work and I was taken to Candlewick Street and the drapers there. Megs took me and she explained, "My husband pays his bills at the end of the week; Friday night is when every purse is full in Chepe Side. The Draper, Tom Robinson is paid then. I will introduce you so that you can go on your own. I confess that having you in the house will make my life easier." I realised that she was telling me then that I would just be carrying the goods back to the workshop and I would not be handling money. It also told me that the Chepe would be full, on a Friday night, of men with full purses!

I suddenly realised that, for good or ill, I now had an employer. I think he saw me as cheap labour and Megs? Perhaps I was the child she had never had. Coins had not been discussed and so I decided to work for two days and fill my belly. Then, if there was to be no payment, I would leave and find employment elsewhere. The Draper seemed unworried that I was not even a youth and when I saw the bolts of cloth I would have to carry my heart sank, for they looked heavy and cumbersome. Looking on the bright side. It would make me stronger.

I made four journeys on that long afternoon but I must have impressed Stephen the Tailor for he said, after we had eaten and he had shown me the corner of the room where I could lay my blanket, that he would offer me an apprenticeship. He said it as though he was making me a knight and he put the papers of indenture before me.

"Seven years you shall study with me and then you will be a master tailor." His rat-like face grew what appeared to be an affliction, but I later discovered was what passed for a smile. "My wife has told me how hard you work and if you work hard then we shall feed you, clothe you and give you a roof over your head. If that is not Christian, then I do not know what is!"

I did not relish the prospect of a life as a tailor but, equally, I did not want to sleep rough anymore and so I nodded and signed; thankful that my mother had taught me to read. I knew that a runaway apprentice could be severely punished, but I was young, and I was confident. My father had created me and given me my faults. My uncle had given me skills and values but my whole life was made complicated by my start in life and I did not know why people seemed to like me for I never liked myself.

That first night gave me a taste of my future. Stephen the Tailor might have had neat hands when it came to tailoring but there was nothing neat about the way he shovelled food into his mouth and spoke while he did so. There was no chair for me, and I sat on a stool which meant my head was at mouth level and I became very adept at dodging gobbets of food. I think that when I became a swordsman those early skills helped me for I learned to avoid objects flying towards me. I was exhausted and I looked forward to a warm dry night but after half an hour of grunting, groaning, heaving and shouting from Megs and her husband as they coupled in their bed, I was ready to go back to the road!

My first half-year in London was an education and I learned skills which would stand me in good stead when I was older. I learned to cut cloth and to sew. The stitches I learned were the simple ones. I would never be able to make the fancy clothes demanded by people who paid but I could make breeks, shirts and tunics. The poor of London would trade for them and my work brought in eggs, fowl, cabbages, beans and the like. I made them from Stephen the Tailor's offcuts. There were also other skills which I learned and they were nothing to do with sewing. I found other apprentices. Some I liked and some I did not. The ones I did not like soon learned to respect my fists and the ones I liked became part of a gang which I led. I did not plan to be a leader, but it happened that way. I fell in with Robert who was a cordwainer's apprentice and lived not far away in Cordwainer Street. I had often seen him coming from the skinners on Rudge Row. Both of us were normally burdened. It seemed to me that apprentice was a sort of human beast of burden and in six months all I had been taught was how to sew and rough cut. I think Stephen the Tailor planned on eking out the skills over the whole seven years.

 I had learned that the happy couple with whom I lived liked to retire early and indulge themselves. Once that was done then they fell into a noisy sleep. I took to slipping silently out during the initial, noisy manoeuvres and I would wander the streets of Chepe Side. Again, those skills helped me when I became a warrior. I had no money and so I just wandered the streets looking for the odd coin or drunk lying in the gutter. If I was lucky then the drunk might have a purse with a few coins in. On the rare occasions that happened, I saved half and spent the other half on ale that was better than that served in the tailor shop. It was one such night when I had been unlucky and not seen any opportunities that I heard an altercation. I crept closer as it did not do to interfere unless there was something in it for me.

 It was down Old Fish Street, which thanks to the smell was always empty at night, that I spied Robert. As I said I had seen him before, and we had waved to each other. I knew his name and he knew mine. He was half my size and more fitted to his apprenticeship than I was. Two bigger youths had him pinned to the wall and were, for some reason, attacking him. I might have walked on had not one of the youths said, "Go on, Gilbert, stick him!"

 Gilbert! My father's and brother's name! It was not my brother but it mattered not and was enough; I bent down to pick up a broken piece of wood which had come off a fish crate. I ran up to the nearest youth and smacked him hard on the side of the head with the wood. He fell in a heap. The other made the mistake of looking down at his companion and I turned him by his tunic and head-butted him. As he fell at my feet, I stamped hard on his hand. I heard the bones break. I did the same with the other. I said nothing to Robert, but I searched the two of them. I found two long and narrow knives; they were the kind used for filleting fish and I found a few coins. I put them in my purse and stood.

"Thank you!"

I turned to Robert. It was almost as though I had not seen him.

I smiled, "That is all right. What was that about?"

If he wanted to tell me he could follow me.

I began to walk back to Needlers Lane, and he hurried after me. Cordwainers Street was on the way. "They work at the fish quay and gut fish. They asked me to steal a pair of shoes for them. I had not managed to do it yet, and they were punishing me. I shall stay indoors from now on." I nodded. "Of course, if you came with me, I wouldn't be afraid."

I laughed, "And why should I do that?"

"I can pay you."

"But you are an apprentice! You don't get paid, do you?"

It was his turn to laugh, "You don't need to be paid to get money."

He then proceeded to tell me the tricks of the trade and how all apprentices learned to make money. Some of them were unique to shoemakers but I saw how they could be adapted to me. I also agreed to protect him from those like the fish boys. I was not worried about the likes of them for I had beaten them once and I was bigger, but I decided to gather other apprentices to become members of my own guild, the guild of self-preservation! After two months had passed, I had six others in my unofficial guild and we met at night and, sometimes, during the day. The other event which enhanced my reputation was the Sunday morning archery practice on the common ground north of the Aldersgate. Apprentices, along with everyone else, were given Sunday off but the men had to attend archery practice after church while the boys were forced to watch. I did not relish that and so I took my bow and joined the men for practice.

When I first appeared, some men laughed. I saw the two fish boys, both still showing the mangled hands which had resulted from my attack and they laughed and jeered too. I did not mind for I knew that I had skill. The captain of the London archers was a huge man called Philip of Lincoln and he did not jeer like the others. He glared at the men near to him and then said, "Come here, boy, and stand next to me. Let me see you string your own bow!" My uncle had taught me to do that. The bow, while not as long as one used by a fully grown man, was made of yew and was as long as me. It would not be long before I needed a longer one. I did so to Philip's satisfaction, for there is a right way and a wrong way to do so. He said, "Choose an arrow." Again, my uncle had taught me that the first arrow should always be the best and I carefully picked the best. I licked the fletch to smooth it and nocked it. "Good, so far." He glowered at some of the men who had laughed, "I can remember some who could neither string a bow nor choose an arrow when first they came to me." He pointed at the butts which were a hundred paces from us. "Now let me see how close you can get to that!"

I was suddenly aware that every eye was on me and that silence had fallen over the practice ground. I went through the routine Uncle John had taught me. I tested the wind, I pulled the bowstring and I focussed on the target. Then, with a comfortable stance, I drew the arrow back until it touched my right ear. As I released, I breathed out and watched the arrow soar. I was lucky and I knew it for my arrow managed to strike the bottom of the butt. My gang all cheered and even some of the men murmured their approval.

Philip leaned down, "You were a little lucky for the wind changed, did it not? When you have the experience, you will wait but you have potential." He stood and said, loudly, to the others, "Now that the nonsense is over then practice can begin. I shall watch when I have had a word with…?"

"John Hawkwood, sir."

"John Hawkwood, the newest member of the London archers!" As arrows flew towards the butts he continued, "You address me as Captain. I serve King Edward and when he goes to war, I lead some of his archers. What is your trade?"

"Apprentice tailor."

I saw him suppress a laugh, "Then you have chosen the wrong trade. Nonetheless, I will make you into an archer for I like your courage. Not many your age would have come here to be mocked and your arrow was well aimed. Even if the wind had taken it you would still have been closer than half of these apologies for men and archers. Now, let us see if we can add to the work already done."

I looked forward to Sunday more than any other day of the week. Megs thought I must be very religious; little did she know. The fact that I could use a bow so well, acted as a deterrent to any who thought to challenge me or my gang and I found that my life, for the first time, was good and Philip of Lincoln had made the difference. I learned much from Philip, who seemed to take me under his wing. He told me how wars were fought and the organisation of wings of men. I learned of the wars against the Scots, the Welsh and the French. He told me that it was rare for him to be in one place so long but the only wars at the moment were between the Northern lords and the Scots. King Edward was enjoying a rare time of peace.

I will not say my time with Stephen the Tailor was wasted for it was not. I was not always fetching, carrying and labouring. I was learning to cut and to sew. He sometimes gave me the task of rough stitching garments. It was not easy for me to learn but my clumsy fingers actually managed to make a passable job of it and that helped me to make arrows. I could fletch as well as any. I also learned skills from Megs. She liked to talk to me for I did not scowl as her husband did and she sometimes used me in the kitchen. It was from her that I learned rudimentary cooking skills and how to fillet meat. She was a little surprised when I produced my own filleting knife, courtesy of the fish boys, but I explained that away by saying I had found it on the road to London. She taught me tricks to make food tastier and even how to make bread. My time in London was not a complete waste of time but it changed me. I think I was like a caterpillar turning into a butterfly and my time in London was when I was a cocoon. I learned to sew, to cook, to become an archer and, thanks to my little gang, how to lead. I could not possibly know that my life would be that of a warrior and most of it would be spent outside England. I was starting out on my path and like all of us, once we step on to that path the only certainty of where it will lead is that at the end, we will die!

Chapter 1

Philip of Lincoln told us, in the early spring, that he would be leaving us and appointed Ralph the Mercer as the new captain of the London archers. The rest seemed unconcerned about that, but I was both curious and saddened for I had learned much from him. At the end of the session, I asked him why he was leaving.

"It is the Scots. Last year they defeated the northern lords twice and King Edward is sending Henry Plantagenet, Earl of Derby, to put them in their place. I march to the muster in Derby." I got on well with the archer and he leaned in and said, "I believe that when that campaign is ended then we shall go to Flanders! Keep up your practice, tailor, for who knows what the future holds for you! You are the best of these archers. King Edward asked me to make them into archers, but they do not have the heart, save you and Ralph. If England depended upon these then we would be lost."

"I would come with you!"

He laughed, "What, and fall foul of the law? You are an apprentice now, John Hawkwood, and if you broke your contract there would be retribution. I do not think it is what you were destined for and I see a warrior in you. I know that you are handy with your fists and others follow you, but I serve the King and cannot condone lawbreaking."

I did not know it then, but the seeds of dissatisfaction were sown that day. Until then I had been content with my lot in life. I will not say happy for that would not be true and I have never lied to myself. I know what I am like and content with the clay which God and the world have moulded. After he left, I wanted something different. When I went back to Needlers Lane I found fault with everything and I let my tongue run so that when Stephen the Tailor began to spit forth food as we ate the Sunday meal, the best evening meal of the week, I did not keep silent nor did I simply duck beneath the gobbets of meat which flew in my direction, I erupted, "You eat like an animal except an animal would not talk and eat at the same time!"

I stunned him into silence. I am not sure how my life would have turned out had not Megs agreed with me, albeit in a gentler fashion, "He is right, husband, and it is a most disagreeable trait!" Her tone was mild, but it had the effect of fuelling his fire.

He stood, "Who is Master here? I am a tailor and a member of the guild and I will not be spoken to thus by an apprentice, a piece of gutter rubbish who would have died but for my kindness. I have spared the strap but now I shall beat some obedience into you."

I stood and Stephen the Tailor suddenly realised that in the many months I had been with him, I had grown. When I had first come, I had been the same height as the tiny tailor, but I had grown and was now more than a head taller. And as if that was not enough, I was much broader. The archery and the hauling of bolts of cloth had given me arms like oaks and a broad chest. I said nothing nor did I even clench my fists, but he reacted.

"So, you threaten me! I will call the watch and have you thrown in gaol!"

The red mist descended for I knew what would be the result, and I just reacted. I pulled back my fist and punched him on the jaw. All of my anger and frustration was in that single punch. I took him by surprise and he simply collapsed, knocking over his chair in the process.

Megs shook her head and said, sadly, "I will miss you, John. He is a mean-hearted soul and he will prosecute you to the limit of the law. Get your gear and run." I stood stunned. "Hurry afore he wakes! I will get some food for you. You must leave London and you cannot go home for you will be sought there!" I had made the mistake of telling them where my home was.

I went to gather my belongings. They had grown. I even had a pair of buskins now made by Robert's master and stolen for me by my first London friend. By the time I had everything in the canvas bag I had sewn for myself, Megs had put some bread, ham, a hunk of cheese and a few apples in a hessian sack. I slung my canvas bag over my shoulder, and she hugged me and kissed me on the cheek, "I hoped you would be the son I never had. Now go, he stirs!" She held my hand and pressed five coins into it. "Go with God!"

I hurried from the door. My first task was to get out of the city for the watch had been set and both Aldersgate and Cripplegate would be barred and guarded. I knew the Chepe as well as the back of my hand and I knew I could get over the wall by the church of St Margaret on the Lotabury. Even back then I was able to break down a problem and solve it piece by piece. All else went from my mind and I ran through the streets. I chose St Margaret's because it was a quiet part of the Chepe. Robert and the others would be waiting for me by the Place of the Folkmoot in Farringdon. I kept to the narrow alleys and smaller streets until I came to the small church and graveyard. Unlike many, I was never afraid of the dead. It was the living who scared me. I slung my gear over my back and began to climb the city wall. None had fought on the fighting platform for many years and the top was covered in dead leaves and rubbish left by animals. I looked over the parapet and saw that the ditch, at this part of the wall, was also overgrown. I lowered myself down and landed in a bramble bush. The thorns went through the thin soles of my shoes. I would have to change into my buskins, but I would not do so until I was well clear of London. I scrambled up the bank on the other side of the ditch. I knew that there were houses there and I had to avoid them. Living so close to the wall the occupants would happily tell the City Watch of the young man they had seen scurrying from the ditch. My nightly forays helped me, and I skirted the houses until I was a mile north of the city. I stopped to rearrange my gear and to help me to think.

There was no point in simply running with no thought to the destination. Where could I go? Sible Hedingham was not an option nor was a return south. That left the north and I suddenly remembered the conversation, just a few hours earlier, with Philip of Lincoln. He was heading north to Derby for the muster. There would be other archers. It was not much of a plan but if I headed there, I might lose myself amongst the other archers who were being mustered. So long as I kept clear of Philip then I might be safe. I knew that the old Roman Road which led north was not far away and I headed for it. Even as I trudged north, I realised that there would be few men on the road at night and those that were upon it would be like me, outside the law. I had three knives and I knew how to use them. I set my foot on the road built more than a thousand years ago and started my new life.

The fact that I had run the first part of my journey meant that I managed to cover more than twenty miles that first night and into the next day. I knew this because of the mile markers left by the Romans. I was tired, but I hoped that I had outrun any pursuit. The road, both north and south, had been filled with travellers. Merchants had their sumpters and sometimes wagons. Lords rode horses and we scurried out of their way when they approached but the majority were like me, on foot. Travellers were going to London, hopeful of finding a fortune or, in some cases, fleeing the plagues and pestilence which still struck. Fewer people were heading north but all had one thing in common, we had to be out of London. I did not tarry long with any of the ones I passed walking north for I strode out and was, generally faster than they were. I did, however, talk to them for not to do so would have aroused suspicion. I had a vaguely honest story; I was going to the muster. That made some of the people I met smile for I had no beard. I did not mind the mockery for it allayed any suspicions that they might have had. I made sure that I ate when I was alone for I had little enough food as it was, and I did not wish to share. Had I not shared then that might have caused a problem.

As dusk descended, I saw, ahead, the town of St Albans, so I made plans to rest for the night. I was too close to London to risk an inn and so I looked for somewhere quiet, preferably with a roof. I had learned to find such places when I had travelled from Essex to London. When I came upon a farm, at the end of a track I nocked an arrow. I had not smelled woodsmoke and yet the farm looked to be whole. Even in summer farmers kept fires lit if only to cook. I saw that the farmhouse door was open, and I peered inside. The smell hit me immediately; there were dead people inside and I saw the rat chewed flesh of one of them. Another family, probably a couple of old people, had succumbed to one of the diseases which spread so quickly along this road. I left the house and looked for a barn. The animals who had been inside the barn had managed to escape and it was empty. I climbed up to the hayloft and after making a rough bed, ate. I was not even aware of finishing my food, I just fell asleep.

When I woke, I found that I had been undisturbed by mice, rats and the like. There were easier pickings inside the farm. I washed, ate and then left to join the road. I used one of the coins which Megs had given to me to buy some fresh bread in St Albans and filled up my waterskin from the well. As much as I wanted the healthier beer, I needed to husband my coins. It was as I headed up the road that I caught up with a small group of men. They were clearly archers for they had their bows in leather cases and there were four of them. I recognised the long hide jacket which Philip of Lincoln had worn and the hat they each wore which kept spare bowstrings dry. Coming up from behind I saw them before they realised that I was there, and I had a decision to make. They had to have spent the night in St Albans and heading north were obviously making for the muster. Did I risk making their acquaintance? What if they had heard of the apprentice with a bow who had fled London? It was still not yet noon and I was not tired. I decided to join them and if there was suspicion then I would take to my legs and flee.

I did not wish to startle them and so I deliberately made noise as I drew close. I began to hum a May Day tune. They turned as one and I saw hands go to the daggers in their belts. I smiled, "Well met, sirs!"

One smiled with his face but not his eyes. "Well met to you young fellow. What is your name and purpose this day?"

I had decided to keep my own name as it would be too confusing to change it. "John Hawkwood, from Essex and I am heading to Derby for I heard they need archers!"

Three of them burst out laughing. The man who had spoken held up his hand, "Forgive me, boy, but you have yet to shave."

I nodded, "And yet Philip of Lincoln told me that I would be a good archer one day and perhaps, if I join the muster, that day will come sooner."

That silenced them and their hands went from their daggers, "You know Philip of Lincoln?"

"I trained with him in London. When I heard that he had left to join the Earl of Derby at Derby then I decided to try my luck." I shrugged, "The worst they can do is say no for I know I am young, but I am guessing that archers need youths to help them and I am a willing worker. I can carry arrows and plant stakes."

"Aye, that shows spirit and I am sorry we laughed at you. I am Robert of Nantwich; this is Dai the Taff and Harry Red

Fletch. The one who did not laugh is Silent Simon. God did not grant him a tongue nor the ability to either laugh or cry but he is the best archer amongst us. Come, walk with us for we go to the muster and over the next days we shall get to know you."

The journey changed for the better when I took up with the small company of archers and I learned much from them on the road; they added to the knowledge already gleaned from Captain Philip. The four of them had been part of a larger company the last time that they had served King Edward and his northern lords. They had fought at Halidon Hill where their arrows had helped to destroy a Scottish schiltron. Once the peace came, they had gone their separate ways, but Robert was hopeful of joining up with former members of the company. This time I shared my food with them, and, in return, I was rewarded by ale and some of their food. When we had need of a bed, we negotiated a price for the five of us. True, I had to eat into my paltry pool of coins, but it was not by much. I discovered that Silent Simon could communicate; when it was not with his hands then it was with his eyes, his head and even his mouth. With guidance from the others, I soon learned to communicate with him. Of course, they had to know if I had spoken the truth and if I had skill. Not long before Derby we stopped to eat and to drink some ale. There was an empty field, empty that is, save for a single bale of hay which had, for some reason I could not divine, been left there. It was the size of a man and a hundred and fifty paces from us.

"You say that Philip of Lincoln thought that you had the potential to be a good archer; prove it. "Get as close to the bale as you can with a single arrow!"

I began to move forward but Harry Red Fletch grinned and said, "From here if you please."

They watched me as I strung my bow and then chose my arrow. I licked my finger to ascertain the wind speed and then I nocked the arrow. I was a better archer for having trained with Philip and I remembered his advice. I drew back and the wind dropped. I did not release but loosened my pull and then when I felt the wind once more raised my bow, pulled back and in one motion, released. I held my breath as the range was as far as I had loosed before and I did not wish to lose my new-found friends. The arrow did not fall short but neither did it hit the target. It landed a handspan from it. I turned to look at the four of them.

"Not bad and Philip of Lincoln was correct, you may make a good archer. You need a longer bow and more strength." He looked at the others and they nodded, "We have spoken together, and we are happy for you to be our apprentice." I gave him a sharp look. He misunderstood my look, "There will be no papers of indenture, you understand, but you will not stand with us in the front rank. Until you can loose as far as us then you fetch arrows and ale when we fight. You help to cook for us, and, in return, you can have a tenth of our pay!"

"How much are you paid?"

"As we are foot archers that is tuppence a day while we are in Scotland. We will pay you five pennies a week."

It seemed a reasonable offer and I nodded. "Aye, I will join your company!" We headed into Derby and the muster. I discovered that mounted archers were paid much more, and I asked them about that.

"Horses cost money but if you see any on the battlefield then grab them no matter what the condition. If you can find horses, then we will get you paid as an archer!" It was an incentive and I grasped it with both greedy hands.

There were fewer men at the muster than I had expected, and the disappointment must have shown. Dai the Taff, said, in his sing song way, "The men at arms and knights will be in the north, at Berwick, do you see? We will travel north with the baggage and the arrows and meet them there."

Robert added, "And besides, there will be more men coming but we will be accorded better accommodation. Harry, go and find the harbingers and get the best you can. I will tell Captain Philip that our company are all here." The harbingers, I had learned, where the men who found accommodation for archers.

I was relieved for it meant I could delay meeting with Captain Philip. I had learned that Captain Philip's actual title was centenar, or captain of a hundred, but such terms were ignored, and he would be our captain. Robert of Nantwich hoped that he would be appointed a vintenar or one who commanded twenty men. As the others and he were men of Flintshire and Cheshire they were considered the best of archers and frequently earned higher pay because of it. We found that we had a stable and that suited me although the others seemed less than pleased. They were good archers and expected a roof and the semblance of a bed. Our pay began as soon as we reached the stable and so the others were unworried about how long we might have to stay there. Food would be provided and although only a stable we had a roof and did not have to endure either a tent or a hovel. While we waited, they turned me into an archer. The first thing they did was to cut my hair so close that you could see my skull.

"It keeps away nits and lice, besides which the last thing an archer needs is hair in his eyes."

I noticed then that none of them had a beard. Their knives were kept razor sharp so that they could draw them over their chins and cheeks each morning. Once a week they drew them across their scalps. Then they gave me an old archer's cap. It had belonged to one of their men who had died at Halidon.

"You have no spare strings yet but when you get them then keep them here." Robert stood back and nodded, "Not quite an archer, but you are getting there."

In the end, we only waited two days and then began the long march to Hartlepool where we would board ships which would take us to Scotland. The ships were already ferrying the knights and men at arms and we had less than five days to march the one hundred and forty miles to the port.

Inevitably, as we moved north, I was seen by Philip of Lincoln. He now rode a horse and as we began our march, he rode down the line to inspect us. I tried to avert my eyes from his but without success. He turned his horse so that he could ride next to me. "You ignored my advice, John Hawkwood, apprentice tailor!"

I shook my head, "My master took against me, Captain, and I could not stay. My mistress gave me money and food! I went with her blessing." Even then I was being a little loose with the truth.

I am not sure that he believed me, but he nodded, "You were never cut out to be a tailor but this does not sit well with me. If you were not with four of my best archers, then I might send you hence, but Robert of Nantwich may be able to finish what I began. We shall see. Know this, John Hawkwood, my eyes are upon you and one slip shall see you dismissed from this host."

Harry laughed as our captain continued his mounted inspection, "I see that you have chosen which truths to tell us. You know the captain but what made you flee London?"

I sighed and told them a version of the truth, "I was an apprentice tailor but when I spoke out my master threatened me. I hit him and I fled. I did not lie about my mistress giving me money. She did."

Robert nodded, "No lies for we are now your brothers in arms. This is your company now and, as such, is closer than family."

That was easy to accept. I hated my brother and my father and already I felt more affection for this band of brothers. I think the march to Hartlepool made my mind up for me. I wanted to be a soldier. I found an affinity with all of my fellow archers. There were some I did not like and who did not like me; that is life, but the conversations and the banter were something I had only enjoyed with my Uncle John. My father had ended that and I decided to stay with this company as long as I could. Boarding the ship was an interesting experience for we were crowded together like cattle at a cattle market. I think that helped me because I could barely move and I was able to endure the day of sailing up the coast.

We landed at Berwick which was the mightiest castle I had seen thus far. We landed north of the Tweed for there was still in place a treaty which said English soldiers could not cross the river. It seemed to me to be splitting hairs, but we landed on the beach north of the river and the treaty was not broken by us! Sir Henry Plantagenet was only waiting for us, his archers, and then he could begin his march north. I now knew the purpose of our campaign. The Northern Lords and their Scottish allies led by Edward Balliol, the token Scotsman placed on the Scottish throne by King Edward of England, had lost the battle of Boroughmuir and the Battle of Culblean the previous year. King Edward was using one of his better commanders to remedy the situation. Lord Henry was highly rated, and I never served under a better. We had landed on the north side of the Tweed and so began my first campaign on foreign soil. We had mounted archers and they were with the vanguard. We tramped along at the rear with the baggage. I had long ago changed from my shoes to the buskins Robert the Cordwainer had stolen for me but I realised I would soon need more as the marching on the cobbled roads was wearing them out. We were also reduced to living in hovels. Scotland being Scotland meant that we had more rain than usual, and I thanked my Uncle John for helping me to oil my cloak. I was drier than some.

By the time we reached most of the towns they had been pillaged already for the horse archers rode ahead of us as scouts and they had the pick of the booty. We managed to grab some food and ale in most places, but the coins and the real booty had been taken by the knights and the mounted archers. I was disappointed but Dai pointed out that the places we passed through were small and inconsequential. He was looking forward to Perth and Aberdeen which both promised fuller purses. "Besides, we have already made a profit from this. We have each earned more than sixty pennies and you, young Hawkwood, have more money than you have ever seen. Am I right?" He was right but Henry had already warned me that pay could sometimes be in serious arrears!

We were at Pitlochry when the Scots finally attacked. It was our turn to be the sentries and I was with my tent mates. We had had no tents, but they seemed to like the term. We were guarding the horses of the knights. At night bows were of little use and the other four had short swords while I had my dagger and my two filleting knives. I do not think they thought they would be needed, and I was there largely for my young eyes and ears. We had spread ourselves out and were squatting. Silent Simon was the closest to me, but I knew that he had good ears which seemed to make up for his lack of voice and that gave me comfort. The insects were biting, and it was hard not to smack them but, if we had, then we would have alerted any Scots who were closing with us and so we sat in the dark and endured the almost invisible insects which seemed to be eating us alive. To help me I put them from my mind and tried to hear Simon breathing. When I had done that, I listened for the sound of animals in the woods which were just a hundred paces from the horse lines. At first, I could not hear them and then I did, there were deer grazing in the woods. No more sounds came to me and so I sniffed. I smelled the horses; they were easy and then I detected Simon. It was not an unpleasant smell, but he smelled of sweat and the linseed he had used to oil his bow before we came on duty. That pleased me. I then tried the deer. I knew that there were deer there, I could smell them. I was pleased with myself when I scented their musky odour and then I heard them move and move quickly.

I stiffened. The only predators for deer were men and so I sniffed again. I smelled sweat, but it was not Simon's sweat and then I smelled, not linseed oil, but sheep and cattle. I slipped my dagger from my sheath and began to crawl towards Harry. I knew that any words would alert the men who were approaching. It was the sheep which gave it away. We had not been near sheep in any shape or form and that meant that these were the Scots. I tapped Harry and was pleased when I surprised him. I pointed to the horse lines and my nose. I mimed sniffing. He sniffed and shrugged. I held up my dagger and he nodded. Drawing his sword, he moved towards Dai. I went back to Simon, but he had smelled them too and his sword was drawn already.

I now used my eyes to look into the forest and I saw them; they were shadows but shadows which moved and they were not moving like animals. They walked on two legs. I turned to Simon who just nodded. He had seen them too. I drew a second filleting knife. I rarely used my left hand, but I needed another weapon. Suddenly, from the other side of the camp, I heard a cry. There had been other warriors and they must have found sentries who were less alert than we.

Robert shouted, "Stand to!"

The nearest help to the five of us were the knights and men at arms and they would either have to rush to our aid without armour or we would have to delay whoever came to attack us. Before we had begun our watch, Captain Philip had said that the Scots might try to take the horses which we were to guard. A horse raid would mean just a few men. The shadows who ran at us were more than a few men. This was an attack and not simply a raid. With the need for silence gone the wild Scots screamed and cursed at us; at least I assumed they were curses for I was cursing these savages in my head but I could not understand their foreign cries. I knew that I could fight but fistfights with other boys were not the same as fighting with a man who had a sword and was trying to butcher you. The other four could not help me and I would have to help myself. To my right, I heard a cry as Silent Simon slashed his sword at an attacker. I saw a huge shadow racing towards me, and I chose a course of action which came from I know not where. I dropped to one knee and I waited for the man to come close. As he raced towards me, I saw that his eyes were looking horizontally and not at the open ground. I was just a shadow which he ignored. It cost him his life for as he neared me, I launched myself up at him with my two weapons. My stronger arm drove my dagger towards his throat while my weaker, slower left found his groin. Both razor-sharp blades drove deep into unprotected flesh and such was the power of my drive that he died without making a sound.

I heard cries behind me as Captain Philip led archers to come to our aid, and to my left and right I heard steel on steel as men fought. The dead man before me slid to the ground and I saw another running at me with a hand axe raised to end my life. This time I ran at the man and, as he brought the axe head down, I threw myself to the ground and caught his legs. I hit the ground hard and I felt something crack but the man tripped over me and his axe embedded itself in the corpse of his countryman. Despite the pain in my side I jumped to my feet and, straddling his back, drew my filleting knife across his throat. This time I took the axe and put my filleting knife in my buskin. I ran back to my first position and was almost hacked in two by a half-naked man at arms who swung his sword at me. The man had barely had time to pull on his breeks or perhaps he had slept in them.

My reflexes enabled me to pull back and I shouted, "I am an English archer! I am a sentry!"

He looked down at the two bodies and grinned, "Then you are like David who slew Goliath! Get behind me, David, and protect my back!"

Grateful to have someone before me who appeared to know what he was doing, I obeyed. I knew enough about fighting, from my conversations with my tent mates, that it was the man at arms left side which was his weakness and I stood there. A Scottish spearman ran at him and his long spear thrust towards the man at arms' left side. I clumsily brought up the axe and connected with the spear which rose in the air. The man at arms took advantage and he brought his sword around to smash into the spearman's shield. I stepped forward and stabbed the Scot in the side. As he reeled, the man at arms brought over his sword to smash into the neck and shoulder of the Scot.

I saw the first lightening of the sky as dawn approached and, as two mailed knights and their squires joined us, the Scots began to fall back. I knew neither of the knights for I had only seen their standards and surcoats in the distance. The two who were next to me had on their mail and held a shield and a sword.

One took charge. He turned to the half-naked man at arms, "Ralph of Malton, thank you for your service. Are the sentries here dead or fled?"

He said, "Neither my lord. Here is one that slew two and helped me defeat another."

He turned and looked at me, "This is an archer? But he is a boy!"

"Nonetheless my lord, it is true."

"What is your name, boy?"

"John Hawkwood, my lord!"

"Then while we scour the woods for more of these Scots you may take from your dead. You have earned whatever they have." He turned to Ralph of Malton, "And you had better stay here too, for you were lucky not to have been hurt! Fighting with a sword and pair of breeks!"

As they went off Ralph of Malton said, to no-one in particular, "Aye, well if I had stopped to put on my mail as you did, Sir Robert Fitzwalter, then this archer would be dead and the Scots would have been in the camp." He stuck his sword in the ground and said to me, "Well, John Hawkwood, I take it this is your first action?" I nodded. "Then you have acquitted yourself well. You have killed two and I believe that you might have taken this spearman. Let us see what they have. Scots are generally piss poor which is why we are paid less for fighting them but who knows. The axe you have is useful." He knelt next to the spearman and picked up various items. "The helmet is not even worth cooking in. Take that for your company can melt it down and make arrows." He tossed it behind me. "His dagger is a good one. I will have that and his spear." He found his purse. "Little enough in here and not enough to share. The helmet shall have to be your spoil." I saw that the man was barefoot and had no boots to take and the leather belt was old and worn. We left them on the corpse. The shield had been cracked by Ralph's blow. "Let us see your other two men." The first man had no helmet and no shield, but he did have a small dagger. Ralph said, "A dirk. A handy little weapon." He gave it to me. The man's short sword lay some way from his body. Ralph removed the scabbard from the dead man's waist and, sheathing the sword, handed it to me. "Archers need short swords." The purse had even less in it than the spearman. The axeman I had killed had neither helmet, sword nor dirk but he had enough coins in his purse for us to divide.

We had finished as the sun rose and Captain Philip approached along with my comrades, Robert, Harry and Dai. They all grinned when they saw me. Captain Philip said, "We thought to find a corpse!"

Ralph laughed, as he gathered his loot, "He killed two, Captain. This one is a warrior! He clasped my arm, "Farewell John Hawkwood. I will remember you."

Robert said, "I am happy that you survived." Suddenly he looked around, "Where is Silent Simon?"

I dropped my treasures which no longer seemed as precious. "I have not seen him since we began the fight."

I ran to the place I had left him. I looked down and saw him. His head was bloody and there was a dead Scot close by him. Dai raced to his side and shook his head, "Poor Simon! He could not call out for help." Then he put his ear to his mouth. "He lives! Let us take him to a healer!" Captain Philip turned to me, "Take your booty and that of Simon's foe to the camp. We four will tend to Simon. I am pleased you joined us, John Hawkwood."

As they left I felt like a giant. I had been accepted and was one of the company. More than that I had killed my first men and I had not hesitated. I had wondered could I kill. I now knew that I could, and it had been easy.

Chapter 2

My standing went up that day, not only amongst the archers but, as a knight who was close to Henry Plantagenet had witnessed it, in the whole army and I found men speaking to me as we marched north. Silent Simon was hurt but not seriously. The healers had him carried in a wagon for the next few days as we drove the remnants of the Scottish raid north. The mounted archers harried and chased them. We saw the bodies of the ones they had caught by the side of the road. There was no attempt to bury them as they were all local and this would act as a warning to the rest of the populace, rebel against England at your peril. It was a savage lesson I learned but I saw, in King Edward's penultimate Scottish campaign, that it worked. The purpose of the raid was clear; they wished to hurt our ability to move quickly and that was a lesson learned. We invested Perth and this time. although we did not burn it we did take tribute from them and ate well. Perhaps the Scots thought we had given up on the chase; we had not!

The Scots finally stopped running and faced us at Aberdeen. They had a wooden wall around the town and a wooden tower in the castle which they had built to replace the stone one destroyed by Robert Bruce during the war of independence. The Scots lined the walls and Lord Henry ordered the town to be surrounded. The captains and leaders were summoned to a council of war and we were reunited with Silent Simon. The blow to his head had needed to be stitched and our silent friend would have a savage scar across his skull. Robert was philosophical about the wound for, as he said, Simon had been lucky.

"When we attack, John, you shall fetch our arrows and you will need to carry many for an attack on walls requires hundreds if not thousands of arrows." He saw the disappointment on my face. "Do not worry. You have shown that you can fight and soon you shall be given the opportunity to use your bow. For now, be content with this task. Your purse is full, and you have yet to spend a penny."

I nodded, as I knew he was right. I had as much money now as my Uncle John had earned in three months of hard work. I would never be a farmer for the work was too hard and the rewards too few. I now knew my future lay with a weapon in my hand. We did not attack straight away for Lord Henry had us make pavise. These were man-sized shields which could be propped up so that an archer could shelter behind, nock an arrow and step out to expose himself to the Scottish archers for as short a time as possible and then be protected while he prepared his next arrow. While they were being built Simon and I made a mould for arrows. We used the river clay from the Dee, and we melted the poor helmet of the Scottish warrior as well as a couple of poor swords we had taken in the raid. Once a sword had been bent or buckled then it was useless as a weapon. We would be able to make thirty arrowheads. All of my arrowheads were hunting arrows and they were not good enough to penetrate mail. Although he was silent, Simon was able to teach me much about making arrows. I had no words to listen to and so I observed all that he did. The bodkin arrowheads we made were needle-pointed and that meant that they could pierce mail and, if close enough, plate armour. I learned later how they did this. The narrow end was small enough to enter a mail ring and then the force of an arrow, sent by a longbow, would expand and break the mail. Unlike a war arrow or a hunting arrow, the bodkin would drive deep into flesh. When they came from the mould, I put them in a hessian sack filled with sand and I spent a day smoothing off the edges. As a reward for my work, I was given two of the bodkin arrows when they had been finished. I chose my best two arrows and fitted the new heads to them. The hunting arrowheads I kept.

By the time that was done the assault was almost ready to begin. Lord Henry asked for the town to surrender. No one was surprised when the Scots refused. No matter what they said the town would be sacked, pillaged and burned! This was a formality of war for the lords on both sides like to have some semblance of order and such rules gave them that illusion. I was able to watch the gathered archers as they began to rain arrows on the walls. Each archer had fifty arrows in two war bags and they all loosed at a single command from Lord Henry. Over two hundred arrows descended upon the walls and the gates of the town. I was behind the pavise of Silent Simon and I heard the thud of Scottish arrows as they smacked into the pavise. Peering around the side I saw men plucked from the walls and I knew that anyone who was sheltering behind the walls would also be in danger from the falling arrows. It would not matter to the arrow if it struck a soldier or a civilian! I was amazed that ten flights were sent in such a short time. At the butts on Sundays, it had been a more leisurely affair and men had commented on an arrow which struck the target and laughed at one which fell short. Here men were nocking, drawing and releasing as though they were a machine. Simon patted me on the head and pointed to the arrows; they needed more. I nodded and ran to the wagons. Someone on the walls must have seen me running and an arrow hit the ground just a foot from my right leg. It was a lesson and I began to weave from side to side as I ran. There were others collecting bundles of arrows, but most were just boys who could use a sling. I was far stronger, and I was able to carry eight bundles at a time although, I confess, that was my limit. I wanted to endure the arrows from the walls as little as possible. I jinked my way back but, even so, one arrow hit one of the bundles. I heard a cry from my right and risked a glance. One of the boys had been hit in the leg. I dropped my bundles next to Simon and then ran to the boy. The archers in the tower had few targets except for those fetching arrows and I had barely managed to pick him up when arrows came at me.

Captain Philip's voice echoed across the battlefield, "Clear the tower!"

I knew that the boy I carried was probably the son of an archer. Every archer would take special care and try to kill the archers in the tower. I dropped the boy at the healers. He said simply, "Thank you!" and promptly passed out. My tunic was covered in his blood. I grabbed another four bundles and ran back. The arrows I had taken were no longer needed for the walls and tower had been cleared.

Henry Plantagenet raised his sword and shouted, "For God, King Edward, and England!" The knights and the men at arms ran towards the walls.

Captain Philip shouted, "Keep the walls clear!"

The men at arms had the ladders and it was they who placed them against the walls and swarmed up the crudely made escalade. I saw swords and axes raised and men fell. Some were Scottish but the men at arms did not have it all their own way. Then the gates opened, and the knights ran in.

Captain Philip shouted, "Right boys! Now it is our turn!"

Dropping their bows and drawing their short swords the archers ran to follow the knights. What followed would be the sacking of Aberdeen and it would be a harsh lesson for the Scots. It was the richest town we had found, thus far, and whatever they had we would take. I stuck close to Silent Simon and Harry Red Fletch. On the way north they had told me that sometimes, after a town was taken, it was more dangerous than actually fighting to take the town. As we charged through the gates I saw the effect of our arrows; bodies hung from the fighting platform while others were huddled at the base where plunging arrows had found nothing to resist them and not only warriors had died but also priests, women and even children. Already those who were the first inside the town, the men at arms, were plundering the houses and shops close to the door.

Harry said, "The best stuff will be close to the centre and the hall. If you know where to look then you can become rich quickly."

I heard screams and saw women, old and young being mounted by the first into the walls. I suppose they felt they had taken the risks and they should reap the reward. As I learned when I was older and more experienced, winning a battle made a man feel invincible and wish to spill his seed! That morning I just felt disgusted. I would witness far worse before I was much older. Some of the first archers who had gained access to the town had found a warehouse and were pillaging the boxes and sacks which it contained.

The expert in such matters, Harry, said, "Sometimes you can be lucky and find something worth stealing but they look like pots and cooking vessels! Not worth the effort. We are looking for gold, jewels, anything which is small, valuable and easy to carry. I saw Dai waving to us, and we headed to a large house just off the market area. Although we were all part of the company of archers, now we were five tent mates who looked out for themselves and Harry pushed away two other archers who looked like they might be heading for the same house. Part of the house had been ransacked already but Harry led us into the kitchen. The hall was a large one and necessitated a large kitchen. This one had a stone floor.

"John, grab a corner of the table." I knew not what we were doing but I obeyed, and we moved the heavy table out of the way. As soon as we had done that and created a space Robert stared intently at the stone slabs. Suddenly he pounced like a cat on one of the stones and I saw that he was using his knife to find an edge to the slab. He ran his rondel dagger along it.

"What are we doing, Harry?"

He grinned and lifted down a ham which was hanging above the fire. He sniffed it and sliced a piece off with his knife as he spoke. "We have been in these big halls before. The people fear being robbed either by the likes of us or their neighbours. It is a wild world north of the Roman Wall. They use this trick to keep their valuables safe."

"Simon, Dai, your knives!"

I looked down and saw that Robert had levered up a stone. I now saw markings on the stone. At first, I had taken them to be the marks of a careless mason but now I saw a pattern to them. Harry handed me a slice of meat and I watched the other three lift the stone to reveal a small chamber and a chest. Robert reverently lifted it out and opened it. There were documents on the top which he tossed to one side. Then he began to lift leather bags out, there were three of them and they contained coins, I heard them jingle as he lifted them. He laughed, "A good haul! You bring us luck John Hawkwood. You and Harry collect the food and we will see what else there is upstairs."

The hall must have belonged to a wealthy Scotsman for he had some fine clothes. We ignored women's apparel. My reward, because my feet were the right size, were a pair of buskins. When my present ones wore out, I would have replacements. I also acquired a pair of decent breeks. With the food and the coins we had found we had done well. As we left the hall, we saw more scenes of depredation. Harry said, when he saw my shocked face, "You must get used to such things. Not all men are as civilised as we."

A voice shouted, "Now we burn the town!"

Robert said, "Simon and John, take our haul back to the camp. We will help here."

It was as we shouldered our way out that we saw the Aberdonians who had survived taking what they could and fleeing. There were few men and the women and children had little enough in their arms. I could smell smoke and knew that fires had been started. The wind was from the north-west and Lord Henry had had the fires started there to help them spread all the quicker. By the time we reached our camp the smoke was rising in the sky and the flames were licking the top of the wooden tower where the last defence had been. The last of our men sprinted from the town which was becoming an inferno. Dai, Harry and Robert had sooty faces and clothes when they joined us, but they had managed to get more food, a haunch of venison which we put on to cook.

The fires in the town were dying in the darkness when Captain Philip joined us. "You five behaved better than most today and you are to be rewarded for it. You are to leave, tomorrow, with Sir Richard Elfingham and join the garrison at Carlisle. You have employment for the winter. Robert of Nantwich you are appointed vintenar for there will just be twenty archers."

"Thank you, Captain, but you will not be with us?"

"Not until Spring. The King will come north and will end this Scottish rebellion and I must help him muster the army." He looked at me as the others congratulated Robert. "When I return to London, if I hear that an apprentice tailor is sought, I will say that I saw one who might have been him perish in the attack on Aberdeen."

"Thank you, Captain!"

"I will do this because you saved the life of the son of Peter of Conwy and you have behaved well. God has given you this chance, John Hawkwood, seize it!" Captain Philip had been disappointed when I had fled London, but it seemed I had gone some way to receiving his absolution. I was desperate to please him.

We all marched south to Berwick and there the bulk of the archers were paid off and the men at arms and knights took ship to London. There were just fifty of us who were heading for Carlisle to reinforce the garrison there. The unemployed archers marched with us. Harry explained the reason. "They are no longer paid but we are. Sir Richard will have food for us on the way south until we head to Carlisle. We will share our food with the unemployed. Some will find employment in the castles and the rest will head south, even as far as Chester; the Marcher Lords always need archers to fight the Welsh."

I had noticed eight had stayed with the garrison at Berwick. More joined the King's Constable at Bamburgh. We left more at Dunstanburgh, Warkworth and Morpeth before we headed south and west towards the military road which ran south of the Roman Wall. The fifty or so archers who remained would go first to Newcastle and then the Palatinate and the great castles of Yorkshire. Garrison work in winter did not pay as much as a campaign but they would be fed and when King Edward came north and needed men then they would be employed once more.

It took us six weeks to march from Aberdeen to Carlisle. They had had the pestilence in the castle and the garrison had been down to just fifteen men. The Governor, John de Glanton, was pleased to see us. The first thing that Robert and Ralph of Malton did when we arrived was to light a fire in the barracks and put on damp material to fill the barracks with acrid smoke. With the door closed the smoke filled the sleeping quarters we would use. That first night we slept in the inner bailey.

Harry said, "The smoke will kill the pestilence and the fleas and nits. Better a soaking out here than we die of disease or are eaten alive."

And so began our five months in the castle. I worked out that I had been away from my home for more than a year and I had changed beyond all recognition. It was not just my cropped hair or the stubble that would have been a beard if I did not scrape a dagger across it each morning. It was the fact that I was bigger and growing taller each day. I had become a man and although I still had some growing in me, I was almost the finished product of God and the archers who had trained me. We ate well. As archers, we hunted across the river each day for the garrison. It was Scottish deer we were eating, and the Governor was happy for us to do so. We were also encouraged to take from the Scots who lived there, and we took the odd sheep and cow when we could. Sometimes we encountered Scotsmen who objected to our behaviour and, once or twice, I was called upon to use my bow against men. I managed to wound at least one Scotsman. When we were not hunting then we were watching on the walls. Any other time we had was spent in making arrows and practising.

I now had a new bow for I had had a growth spurt and was almost as tall as Harry and could use a man-sized longbow. I also had four spare strings and I had eight bodkin heads for my arrows. It was important that I practise with the bodkin heads for they flew differently from the barbed hunting or war arrow. Accuracy was all. I had a bracer for my arm, and I had made two war bags for the arrows I would carry. I also learned to use a sword. My friendship with the captain of the men at arms, Ralph of Malton, helped me for he took a special interest in me and gave me tuition. He had me at the pel, the wooden block where I could use the blunt heavy practice sword and I also practised with him. He taught me what he called the tricks of the trade. He practised every day and I was happy to be a sparring partner. The others, when they were off duty, liked to gamble, drink or simply sleep! I became a better swordsman than Robert or any of the others. I could never outdo them when it came to archery!

It was Spring when Sir Richard took us on a chevauchée north of the border. The English garrison in Stirling Castle had been attacked by the Scots and a message sent south to the King. We had left a garrison there when we had headed south the previous autumn. Our chevauchée was to try to draw Scots further south. The pestilence had taken men but the horses in the castle had been unharmed and we were mounted. I had never ridden before and that month of riding was my education. I was just pleased that I did not fall off but the pain from bouncing up and down was unbearable and I begged to be allowed to run next to the horse. Sir Richard laughed and told me to endure it.

The pain in my rear soon became immaterial as we started to raid. Robert of Nantwich explained what we were doing, "We cause as much mischief as we can. We raid farms and undefended towns, avoiding castles like Dumfries and Caerlaverock. If we can draw out men against us, then so much the better otherwise we have the licence to steal and to rob." He grinned, "Even churches!"

The first place we raided was Lockerbie which was just twenty miles north of Carlisle. I now saw the benefit of riding because we reached it by noon and swept through the land like carrion. The people fled and as we were on horses, they could not take their animals with them. We looted the houses and farms and gathered all of their animals. Our aim was not only to draw out soldiers to fight us but also to deny the Scots food. We slaughtered every animal we found. We ate well that first night and used all the salt we could find to preserve the meat. The next day we packed the meat in a wagon and headed north towards the next village. It took three days for the Scots to react and we had headed towards the coast before they did so. We had not had to string our bows nor even dismount such was the effect of our men at arms led by Sir Richard. We were heading for the port of Ayr. I was told that we had occupied it until some twenty years ago but with the castle destroyed by Robert the Bruce, there was little to stop us.

Perhaps the local lord, the laird of the Clan Maxwell, had had enough of us or perhaps they had been waiting for us to get too far from Carlisle and leave ourselves exposed. Whatever the reason they were waiting for us twelve miles from Ayr at a place called Cumnock. We still had the wagon and so we tied the horses to it leaving the squires and pages to defend it. I had feared that I would be relegated too but I was included in the archers who took our bags of arrows and strung our bows. That told me I was now an archer! Surprisingly, the knights and men at arms we had with us also dismounted. I had thought they would have used horses, but Harry pointed out that the Scots were using the long ten or sometimes twelve-foot spear. Horses could not get close to them and so we formed up behind the men at arms and knights. Our four knights formed the centre and we made the third line behind them. Robert was in command of the twenty archers and he walked down the line checking that we each had a war arrow nocked and ready. I stared at the Scots as they prepared to attack us. They had what looked like twenty knights and mounted men at arms but more than two hundred spearmen. The spearmen stood in a large block each of them holding his long spear above their heads to protect those in front. The front rank held their spears pointed upwards so that there was a solid wall of spears; it was like a human hedgehog. I saw that most had a helmet of some description and some had a small platter shaped shield on the left arm. They looked formidable and there were just twenty of us to stop them!

Dai shook his head, "This is foolishness. We should have had twice as many archers and half as many men at arms."

One of the men at arms standing before us said, somewhat grumpily, "You archers all think that you are the only ones who can defeat the long spear! Today, we will show you!"

Harry was always one for a wager. He had already doubled his purse gambling in the castle, "I will wager one gold piece that we stop them before you can even get close to them!"

"You are on!"

Ralph of Malton laughed, "Jack of Southwark, you are a fool and the archer is right! I for one also wish we had twice their number!"

Robert took his place between Dai and Harry; it was as though he had not heard a word of the conversation, but I knew he had. He took his position as vintenar very seriously. "Draw!"

This would be the first time I had drawn my bow in anger, and I had chosen my best arrow for the occasion. I pulled back to my ear. I now had a bracer and I felt and looked like a real archer. Until that moment I had thought that I was a fraud. The Scots all cheered and began to march, quite quickly in my opinion but then I was a novice, towards us. I learned later that they went as quickly as they could to avoid the arrows. It was a race between their feet and our arms!

"Release!"

I let the arrow fly and was already pulling a second from my arrow bag as Robert shouted, "Draw!"

I pulled back and heard him shout, "Release!"

I had no time to see the fall of flights I just kept nocking and releasing as I was ordered. Dai suddenly said, without missing a beat, "Pull all the way back, John!"

I was aware that my arms were burning, and I had not drawn the last arrows back to my ear. I pulled back and it hurt! It was a relief when Robert shouted, "Choose your targets!"

I saw why, immediately. The first of the long spears were already coming towards Sir Richard and the dismounted men at arms. I watched Harry's distinctively fletched arrow smack into the forehead of the spearman trying to skewer Sir Richard. I aimed at a man two spears back and the reason I did so was that I had a clear sight of him. I gained great satisfaction when my arrow was driven deep into the side of his head. The knights all wore mail and did not wear helmets but used a simple coif. Against spears, it was all the protection they would need. Their long swords were able to hack through the wooden shafts of the long spears and that rendered them useless. The men at arms' long kite-shaped shields afforded protection for most of their body. Only our front rank had been engaged and when the schiltron was hacked and savaged by sword and arrow the Scots broke.

Sir Richard shouted, "Archers, pursue them. The rest mount and pursue!"

We had been outnumbered when the skirmish had started but now, we were almost evenly matched. As we saw backs turned towards us, we sent as many arrows into them as we could. The long spears had obscured the men but now there was nothing to stop the barbed war arrows from driving deeply into flesh.

Dai said, "Drop your bow and arrow bag. This is time for your sword!"

I did as I was told and ran. I was the youngest and, it turned out, the fastest. This would be a test of my newly learned skill. Ralph of Malton had drilled into me that every blow I took should be one intended to kill. "A half-hearted blow will come back to bite you on the arse. Each time you swing then expect to kill or, at the very least, to maim for believe me your opponent will be doing the same!"

I was the first archer to catch up with the Scots and the wounded spearman had but a moment to look behind him and see my swinging sword before I hacked so hard into his neck that I half severed his head. I heard, behind me, the hooves of the knights and men at arms as they began to gallop to support us.

The Scots who ran before us began to hurl down their cumbersome spears, but it was of little use for we were catching them. The effort of carrying the long spear and attacking had sapped their energy and I learned that day that defeat disheartened a man and made him easier to catch and kill. As I hacked across the spine of another Scot, I saw Harry and Simon each slash across the backs of two more Scots. The Scottish horsemen could have intervened but the sight of our knights and men at arms racing forwards had made them think twice and they joined the flight west.

Once our horsemen overtook us Dai said, "We can do no more. Let us see what treasures we can garner from these apologies for soldiers."

We turned and walked back through the men we had slain. The weapons were poor ones, but they and the poor helmets could be melted down to make arrows. There was a weaponsmith at Carlisle and proper moulds. We would have many bodkins! Some of the Scots had coins and metal crosses. We took all that they had. So many had been slain that the few coins we took from each Scot began to add up and as there were just twenty of us who had the whole of the battlefield to loot without sharing, we all did well. It was dark by the time our horsemen returned and by then we had fires burning and food was being cooked.

When they reached us, I saw Harry seek out Jack of Southwark. He stood there grinning and held out his hand. I wondered if there would be trouble and then Ralph of Malton decided the matter, "We all heard you, Jack of Southwark; do not embarrass the rest of us who were too wise to let our mouths impoverish us."

The coin was handed over and, as we had found some of the distilled liquor the Scots like to make and drink, we slept well that night!

The next day we rode the last few miles to Ayr. Most people had fled for they knew we were coming and there was little for us to take. That was a mistake for we took it out on the small port and burned it and its quays to the ground. The boats we found were also wrecked and burned and the fishing nets we found were piled on to the fire. I was learning lessons which would stand me in good stead when I became a leader of men. We headed south and east and made our way back to Carlisle. When we reached it, we were all richer and the land for thirty miles north of the border had been ravaged. The last animals we took we did not slaughter but drove them, instead, back to the castle. We had also been lucky enough to capture ten horses and as our vintenar, it was left to Robert to decide who would have them. The five of us became mounted archers and our pay doubled in that instant. Life was good!

There was good news when we arrived. King Edward was heading north and our time in the garrison was almost over.

Chapter 3

It was summer when the King arrived, and we rode north to relieve Stirling Castle. By the time we left, I had not only learned to ride better but also Ralph's lessons meant I was a good swordsman and I was better than any of our company. Ralph of Malton thought that I had a natural ability and, if I chose, I could be a man at arms. The seed was planted and began to grow. At the time I only knew that when I fought with a sword, I did not expect to be beaten, the arrogance of youth.

Captain Philip returned and the King was accompanied by his household knights and bodyguards as well as the northern lords. We now rode with the mounted archers and so had a new Captain, Geoffrey of Nottingham. Perhaps the King thought the same as Dai for we had a thousand archers with us. Only one hundred were mounted but the sheer numbers made me confident that we could hurt the Scots.

We had horses and were paid more. In addition, we were the advance guard, the scouts. As we rode at the head of the column, snaking its way along the same roads we had raided in the spring, I asked Harry about sieges, "I know we can defeat their spearmen for they have no armour but those behind walls have the protection of stone and wood. Aberdeen was just wood. What if we find Scots behind stone walls?"

"When the King's grandfather, Longshanks, came north and hammered the Scots, he was careful to take over their castles and to build new ones. Until we reach Stirling there will just be wood before us. We can use fire arrows if needs be."

"Fire arrows?"

He nodded, "Aye, we do not like to use them as they can be dangerous to an archer as well as being difficult to use but with a thousand archers we can burn any town we find to the ground with little risk to ourselves."

The success of our earlier raid was clear to see for no one opposed us and we reached the River Clyde and the bridge at

Glasgow without incident. It was there that the men of Glasgow made the mistake of opposing us. They manned their wooden walls and King Edward ordered his archers forward. With the small town surrounded by horsemen, we began to send flights into the town. A thousand arrows make a sound like the wind and when flight after flight are sent into the air then the sky darkens. It was a sobering sight. We sent ten flights and then the order was given to cease. Silence descended and then we heard the moans and cries from within the walls. The gates opened and Glasgow surrendered without the loss of a single man such was the power of the longbow. None of us entered, just the King, his bodyguards and the senior lords and nobles entered to accept the surrender, but we heard later, from the men who were sent to recover the undamaged arrows and arrowheads, that almost every man on the wall and within thirty paces of it had been killed or seriously wounded. As we continued to head to Stirling the King sent us all a silver sixpence in thanks. It was a day's pay in addition to the pay we had already earned! My purse was now bulging, and I could not wait to spend some of it. I knew not what I wished to buy but it was burning!

The Scots had a choice, leave the siege and disperse, effectively handing over Scotland to King Edward, or fight us. The leader of the Scots was Sir Andrew Murray, the guardian of Scotland. King David was a child and he and his child bride were in France. Sir Andrew must have decided to make a stand for when we arrived at the castle, he had his army arrayed before it and it looked as though he would give battle. He had greater numbers than we did but his spearmen were outclassed by our archers. The King placed us before the men at arms, such was his confidence and the knights formed two blocks on our flanks. I did not know so at the time for I was too busy trying to be an archer, but I was learning about strategy and battles. I found it all interesting and while my fellow archers diced and gambled as we waited, I watched the dispositions. I realised that with mounted archers at his disposal King Edward could have mounted us and used our mobility to threaten the Scottish flank. He did not do so.

Sir Andrew Murray was a clever man, and no sooner had we arrayed for battle than he sent a herald to ask for a truce so that we could talk. The King and his advisers, as well as the bishops, rode forward and talked. I watched the sun begin to sink behind us and King Edward and his men rode back with the news that an agreement could not be reached, and we would fight on the morrow. We camped where we were stationed. The Scots did the same four hundred paces from us. Captain Philip who was in overall command of the archers was mindful of the time our camp had been attacked and so we had a strong line of sentries. Our band of archers was called upon to take the last watch of the night and I was woken for our watch by Robert of Nantwich.

I now had a sword and I would not be as helpless if attacked but, as I stood my watch and saw the flickering Scottish fires, I suddenly realised that I could not see any Scottish sentries moving around. I saw shadows by the fires but not sentries. I went to Robert, "Vintenar, there are no sentries."

"What?"

"See! I can see a couple of men by the fires but where are their sentries?"

He peered into the dark and then said, "You are right! Stand to and I will fetch the Captain!"

Captain Philip must have been already awake for he reached us in a few heartbeats. Robert pointed and the Captain nodded, "You have good instincts, Hawkwood. Vintenar, bring your men and we will investigate. We shall be silent and if we are wrong and they have hidden sentries then be prepared to fall back!" We nodded. "Draw your weapons."

With swords in hand, the six of us headed across the dead ground between the camps. Their sentries should have been as ours were, one hundred paces from their camp but we found nothing save the signs that they had pissed and shat. They had left men, but they were just there to tend the fires and give the illusion that their army remained. They had fled!

Captain Philip's voice roared out, "Stand to! Archers with me!"

While he shouted, we ran towards the men for there were horses and they were good ones. Once again, my speed and my youth came to my aid and I ate up the ground as I ran to the horse lines. There were ten men and animals and the Scots ran to mount their saddled horses. Silent Simon was also fast and the two of us reached the tardiest of the Scots first. One had missed his stirrup and was trying to haul himself into his saddle when Simon's sword hacked into his back. The rider I caught had managed to mount but his horse was facing the wrong way and, as he turned, I slashed with my sword. I bit into his leg and felt my sword grate across his thigh bone. I was still new to fighting but I learned that day, that the leg is very vulnerable for there are veins and arteries there which can empty a man's body of blood as fast as a strike to the heart. The blood fountained as the Scot fell from the horse. I think he was dead before he hit the ground. His good leg was in the stirrup still and I was able to grab the reins of the horse. Harry and Robert managed to capture a third man, but the rest escaped.

I calmed the horse and walked it, dragging the body, back to the horse lines. I tied it to the lines and then removed the body. The boots were good ones and I took them. The man had a better sword than mine for it was longer and had a good scabbard. I took that too. He also wore a good leather jerkin. Along with his dirk and his purse, I had done well but the horse was the greatest treasure for it was a palfrey and better than my own sumpter which I had from Carlisle. That had been borrowed. This new animal was mine!

There was little else to be had from the Scottish camp and I could not help but admire the way they had escaped. As I led my new horse, which I named Megs after the tailor's wife, back to our camp I passed King Edward and his senior lords. He was not happy for we would have to chase the Scots all over Scotland to try to bring them to battle. The month we spent chasing Murray's men was frustrating. The Scots headed north and east threatening the English garrisons. It soon became obvious that the army was too slow to catch them and so we were attached to Sir Richard once more and he led our two hundred horse archers and one hundred men at arms to keep the Scots from causing mischief. He and his ten knights were relentless in their pursuit and I learned a great deal about how to anticipate a clever and cunning enemy. We took it in turns to be horse holders. I never enjoyed that duty, but I recognised its value. Twenty-five of us each held four horses while the rest used their bows against the Scots. The men at arms would form up before us and the knights would remain mounted to charge down any attempt to attack us.

We almost caught up with them at Lochindorb where the English garrison held the small castle. The main army was fifteen miles behind them and we were greatly outnumbered. Sir Richard Elfingham did not panic, and we dismounted and strung our bows before the Scots could react to our sudden appearance. Ralph of Malton and the men at arms had their spears and shields before us even as we nocked our first arrows. The Scots saw a relative handful of men and they just launched themselves at us. Sir Andrew did not have control over his men that he needed. Our one hundred and seventy-five arrows plunged down like a snowstorm in winter and sliced into flesh. The Scots were brave, and they kept coming but we were able to release arrow after arrow and their wild charge was too uncoordinated. When their knights, who again outnumbered our knights, charged then I feared for Sir Richard and the lords he led.

Robert shouted, "Switch to bodkins and go for their knights."

I had only practised with bodkins and never used them in anger. The Scottish knights were just twenty paces from Sir Richard when our four bodkins struck. Some of the other archers were using war arrows and I saw horses hit but I also saw my bodkin drive into the thigh of a knight. Robert's arrow was even more successful, and his arrow drove into the skull of the leading knight. The result was that Sir Richard and his knights drove through the Scottish knights who had lost all order and cohesion. The Scots fell back, and we watched them. We had not enough men to attack and so we waited for King Edward and his army.

This time it was the men at arms who reaped the reward of our arrows. They scurried forward and stripped the dead of all that they possessed. It enraged the Scots who had retreated but we were still ready with our bows and the half a dozen men who ran to challenge the men at arms did not get within forty paces of them. Captain Philip sent three archers to butcher the dead horse which lay on the battlefield; we would eat well. When darkness fell, we dug a ditch and hewed stakes while we cooked the horse. There was enough for us all although I saw that the knights and their squires did not partake. We heard the Scots leave and even knew which direction they had taken; they were heading south and east! We did not chase them until dawn for they were largely on foot. The result was that King Edward and his army were able to close with us and were just five miles behind us as we caught up with them again. By the time we had crossed the Forth their army was disintegrating. We skirmished a little more although I was a horse holder on two of the occasions and we found ourselves at Dunbar when the Scottish army dissolved. It was a frustrating end to the campaign.

I say it was frustrating but that was only to the King. For us, it was a victory. We had full purses and better horses. We were now mounted archers and held in high esteem by our captains and the knights alongside whom we had fought. Even the King had noticed us and, as he took ship from Berwick, addressed us.

"Know you all that I am well pleased with the way you have behaved in this campaign and that I have authorised your payment to be continued for I shall need you if I am to take back France. I have written to King Philip, the pretender to the French throne and I have demanded the French crown." He was a relatively young king, but he sounded very confident. "No doubt he will refuse, and I shall have to take it back. You should all know that I have the support of the Holy Roman Emperor, Louis and the Pope. God is on our side. I am gathering an army to take back my land. It will meet at the Cinque Ports where we will embark. There you shall all be paid!"

Everyone cheered as his ships, filled with his knights, set sail. Harry was the exception, "He might be young, but the King is crafty!"

I was confused for I thought his words had sounded honest, "How so, Harry?"

"We have four hundred miles to travel and we shall have to spend our own coins to do so. Many will not make it to the Cinque Ports and the King will not have to pay them." He shrugged, "We have done well out of this and I shall travel south if only to collect my money. Who knows, I may buy an inn!"

I was surprised that he should wish to leave our company, but Dai explained on the long journey south, that Harry was always talking about becoming an innkeeper, but it rarely lasted. He enjoyed fighting too much. We crossed the Tweed in August and reached Dover in the middle of September. I enjoyed the ride south for Megs was a good horse and much easier to ride than the nag I had learned on. I was also accepted as a warrior and as

I had to scrape my face each day was considered a man. Indeed, I was almost fully grown, and I was as tall as Dai, the biggest of our companions. I managed, on the journey south, to drink too much and have to be put to bed after puking my guts out. The others were sympathetic and told me that it was something they had all experienced, but I should not repeat it. It was a warning and I heeded it. I was never drunk again! To be fair we were close to Burton on the Trent and they brewed good ale there and it was its strength which had caught me out. We reached the camp which lay close to Dover, the largest of the Cinque Ports, and Robert, as our vintenar, went to collect our pay. We had enough copper and silver coins to change some of them for gold. They were easier to carry and, while we waited for the orders to sail, I made a canvas belt which I wore beneath my tunic. The training I had with Stephen the Tailor meant that I made a good job of it and the others asked me to make one for each of them. I accepted the commission but declined the payment for I felt I owed them more than the effort it took for me to make them. I also bought some cloth and made myself a tunic with a hood. The most useful thing I made, from canvas, was a gardyvyan or haversack to carry my spare bracers, arrowheads, glue, candles, flint and everything else I would need on campaign. I had all the accoutrements now of an archer!

While we waited for our orders we practised. Some of the others gambled but I prepared myself for war abroad. Dai and Harry were the ones who would wager on anything and Robert of Nantwich did so now and again, but Silent Simon and I did not. I did not know what Simon's reasons were but for myself, I did not wish to be poor and so I intended to earn and to keep as much of my earnings as I could. I also shortened the hand axe for it was too cumbersome to carry in my belt and if I had to use it to fight then it would be as a close weapon. My sword would serve me in combat. Our gambesons with the red cross of St George arrived as did our pot helmets. On the advice of the others, I made a liner for it and I padded it to make it more comfortable. We would still wear our archer's caps but beneath the helmet. I watched Dai drill two holes in the side and asked him why. He told me that it could be hung that way and used as a cooking pot! September passed and October arrived. The weather became cooler and damper and the camp became a more unpleasant place in which to live.

Sir Walter Manny was appointed by the King to be our leader and he arrived in the camp on the second of October. He summoned the captains. Ralph of Malton and Philip of Lincoln were still with us. When they returned from the meeting our small band discovered that, along with another one hundred and ninety-five archers, we were to be retained and had a six-month contract. I did not know what that meant but Robert and the others seemed delighted.

Harry laughed at my face, "John, you have brought us great luck for we are now retained by the King and we are paid sixpence a day wherever we campaign. We will have our own helmet, gambeson and hose. Our horses will be stabled at Dover Castle and looked after at the King's expense."

"But will we not need them?" I was loath to lose Megs.

Robert shook his head, "Were you not listening? Our first campaign is in Flanders and we will not need our horses. The land there is marshy and would harm our horses. When we go to France then we shall need them. At Dover, they will have grass and cereal. We will return to horses with glossy coats and fat bellies! Life is good, John Hawkwood."

We left at the start of November when the icy wind from the east found every gap in our clothing. As Harry said, "It is a lazy wind, it does not go around you but straight through you."

We headed for the Flemish island of Cadzand. Flanders was part of France and the port of Sluys was on a nearby island. Sir Walter was known as a sailor as well as a soldier. He had captured the famous pirate, John Crabbe and King Edward hoped that our presence on the island would provoke a response as the French would not wish their rich port to be threatened. We learned this from Captain Philip. He was as close to the King as any commoner and seemed happy to tell us interesting snippets. I do not think he told us anything that was not common knowledge at court but that was so many degrees from where we were that it came as complete news to us. The King had told us he had the support of other kings and princes but what he had not told us was that he had had to support them financially. The three and a half thousand men whom Sir Walter led represented the only army which King Edward could afford. He would need five times that number, at least, if he was to regain France!

The seas, to me, seemed mountainous but the others just called them choppy. The almost black water rose and fell revealing crests and troughs which threatened to bring up my last meal. The ship appeared to be too small to contain the number of men it did, but the crew seemed content and went about their business cheerfully. I had been told that we would not have to sleep aboard the cog and for that I was grateful. I believe that staring out to the horizon helped me a little and I avoided the indignity of vomiting all the way across. When I saw the islands of Flanders approaching, I almost sang with joy. The crew said we were heading for a small island called Cadzand and, as far as I could tell, the only reason to go there was to annoy the French. I didn't care so long as my feet were on dry land!

I wanted to be the first one off the boat, but it was the knights and men at arms who swarmed ashore to the marshy little island. It was a wet landing as we had to drop from the side into the black and muddy waters. My bowstrings were safe under my hat and helmet, but the water came over the top of my buskins and I endured wet feet! There was a village on the island, and it was quite a large one for the folk on the island were fishermen and self-sufficient. Other ships had landed first and by the time we scrambled ashore with our gardyvyans, arrows and bows the looting and pillaging had begun. I did not know it then but the island and port I could see just across the channel was Sluys and as such a jewel in the kingdom. It was high tide and all I saw, as night fell, was the black sea. We had little to do that first night. The men on the island had been slain by the men at arms. All that could be taken was taken and so we made ourselves as comfortable as we could on the exposed and marshy island. Already the campaign had lost most of its appeal. I was not hungry, and I found it hard to sleep; partly because of the wind and rain but mainly from the screams as men enjoyed themselves. Sir Walter had planned it this way. The cries carried across the narrow channel to Sluys and the French garrison there would hear them.

When dawn broke and I went to the shore to make water I saw that the tide had gone out and whilst Sluys was a good two miles away, the channel to the mainland was just a few hundred paces wide. I saw armed men gathering there and I hurried to the camp to tell the others. Captain Philip was pleased, "The sooner they decide to come here then the sooner we can be rid of this insect ridden, pestilential hole!" I saw that his face was already covered in the red bite marks of the almost invisible flying insects.

"But Captain, why should they come? There is nothing here worth dying for!"

"No, but our presence here threatens their port and the fact that we have hurt their people may stir them. Let us hope so!"

I was now hungry, and I ate the fish which had been taken from the islanders and then we waited. Our leader, Sir Walter, visited all of us and spoke in turn to each company of men. Neither King Edward nor the Earl of Derby had bothered to do so and it impressed me. Sir Walter seemed to know what he was doing and, indeed, seemed genuinely interested in us. It was when I stood a watch later that night that I divined the reason for this. He had made us all feel that he was our friend rather than our leader and I could see how that would make us all fight harder for him. It had cost him nothing save a little shoe leather and he had bought the loyalty of three and a half thousand men.

The French garrison did not come the next day but the one after. We saw them boarding their boats on the other side of the channel for the short journey. They would all be afoot and as soon as Sir Walter saw them then he made his dispositions. I thought he would have had us shower arrows on them as they tried to leave the boats, but he was a clever man and he had grander plans than that. He drew us up before the village just beyond where the mud and marshes began. The ground on which we drew up our men was higher and drier than the rest of the island and the archers were behind the men at arms and knights. We had a clear line of sight to the landing area and it was well within range.

Robert of Nantwich nodded his approval, "I like this captain, he knows his business. He intends to pack them together with nowhere left to retreat and then we will rain death upon them." He looked at my arrow bag. "Put your bodkins on one side of the bag. When we are done here, I would suggest you dye the flights of your bodkins a different colour so that you know which to draw. There will be few mailed men this day, but you should save your bodkins for them!"

As the boats approached, it became clear that they would outnumber us. Whoever led them intended to make a statement; he intended to warn the English to stay away from his land! I saw the tide was going out as the first of the flat-bottomed boats approached. If they were surprised that we would allow them to land it did not make them cautious. They formed their battles as soon as their feet squelched on the mud. They seemed not to notice the shifting ground but just spread their lines out. Our men at arms and knights had their spears planted haft first in the more solid ground, with their longer kite-shaped shields also embedded in the ground; it was as though we had a mobile fort before us. We archers each had an arrow nocked but not drawn and we waited. My new helmet made my head itch for this was the first time I had worn the helmet, liner and hat. My head was hot! Over the years I became used to them but that first day, along with the irritation of insects, they were an annoyance.

Once the ships had disgorged their men, they presented their spears and shields and began to march towards us. I saw that they had a few crossbows, but no bows and the crossbows were useless as they needed a flat trajectory to be able to hit us and we were above them and their own men. They began to march, shouting and jeering as they came. Remarkably we were silent, and I think that showed the confidence of our men. I saw Sir Walter raise his sword and Captain Philip shouted, "Draw!"

A thousand bows creaked as our oaken arms pulled back our strings beyond our ears. I found it easy now. I had a full-sized bow, but I had practised each and every day. I knew which man I was aiming at. I knew my range and I was confident about getting close to him. He was a man at arms, and I had a bodkin nocked. There had been closer targets who could have been hit by a war arrow but I wished to test myself.

"Release!"

The sound of a thousand arrows is unlike any other noise you have ever heard but I had no time to admire the beauty as the sky before us darkened. I drew a war arrow and nocked it.

"Draw!"

I lowered my aim slightly for I saw an axeman who had a helmet but no mail.

"Release!"

Even as I released and then drew another war arrow, I saw that my first arrow had hit the mailed man at arms in the shoulder.

"Release!"

It seemed that we had no limit to the number of times we could draw and release. I just used my war arrows and sent them into the mass of men who flooded ashore like a spring tide.

"Choose your targets!"

Captain Philip command told me that the back of the enemy was broken and now we had to destroy their knights and mailed men at arms. I picked a bodkin and licked the top flight. I drew back and aimed at a knight who was flailing his double-handed axe like some Viking berserker. The arrow flew straight and true for he was just eighty paces from me and about to decapitate a man at arms. The bodkin, which I had made myself, struck his mail and I watched as the needle point arrowhead drove into a mail link and tore it apart as though it was made of cloth. Then it penetrated his gambeson, through his flesh and muscle and into his heart. The axe dropped at the feet of the surprised man at arms who thrust his spear at the next man. I was able to loose the last arrows of this battle with leisure. I had the time to take my arrow and ensure that the feathers were smooth. I could aim, not only at the man, but also the place on the man I wished to hit. In those days I was merciful, and I gave them all the swiftest death I could: the eye, the head, the heart.

Soon I heard the horns of the French sound retreat and Captain Philip shouted, "Drop bows and use your swords! We have won!"

Such a command was wise for the last thing we needed was for men at arms to race to finish off a Frenchman and have an arrow slam into their back. I drew my sword and my hand axe and raced forward. Up until now, I had been fighting for Sir Walter and King Edward; now I was fighting for me! I raced towards the French who were trying to get aboard the ships which were starting to leave. Others were risking the channel and discarding their mail. A mailed man at arms must have sensed me coming for he began to turn and to swing his sword at me. I raised my hand axe to block it and swung my sword at his shield. It was not a kite shield and he had to lower it. I was now very strong, and the blow hit his shield and knocked him into the shallow water. As he fell backwards, I raised my hand axe and split his skull in two. As I stood, the sea lapping around my buskins, I saw that barely a hundred men had made the ships and the sea was taking the rest. Looking back there were few English red crosses lying on the bank. We had won.

    The man at arms was a rich prize. He had mail, a sword and a purse filled with Flemish and French coins. He wore no helmet, but I had done well. I could sell the mail and the sword for I was happy with mine and the coins showed that he was either a saver or one who had gambled and won from his comrades. I was content and I walked back to our camp feeling satisfied.

Chapter 4

We sailed back to Dover just three days later. I never served under Sir Walter Manny again for he became an admiral and ruled the seas for King Edward, but I would have done so for he was a good leader and knew how to fight. Back in Dover many of the army took their coins and left. At that time there was little prospect of further fighting in France or Flanders as King Edward needed money. My four comrades decided that this was the time to enjoy their money and they left Dover. It was a sad parting for I had enjoyed their company. They each went their separate ways and although we all believed we would fight together once more, the battle of Cadzand was the last time the five of us were a company. I knew nothing of their lives, but I guessed that some would become bored with a life of peace and seek a war somewhere while others might actually make a successful transition. I suspect that a couple may have been in the army which King Edward led to France and in which I served but my life and position had changed by then.

After they left, I felt deserted and abandoned. Most of the other archers who had been hired by King Edward left. If they had stayed, then they would have been paid but we had all made more in one battle that we would have earned in a year as archers. My problem was that I had nowhere to go. I could not and would not go home and London was not for me. It was Captain Philip who saved me. He approached me one cold December day.

"John Hawkwood, I have been appointed to command the archers of Portsmouth. I need a good archer, would you come with me?"

"Without a moment's hesitation, Captain!"

It was a prayer answered and I left for Portsmouth, happy that someone else had made a decision for me. Captain Philip took just ten of us with him and, as most of the others had fought together many times I rode with the Captain. "I am honoured that you chose me, Captain, but I do not know why. I am still young and there are better archers than I."

He smiled without turning and nodded, "Aye, you are right but there are two reasons. One is that I feel responsible for you. I know that one of the reasons you are an archer is because you met me. Had you not heard my stories then you might not have run away from Needlers Lane." I shifted uncomfortably in my saddle as he seemed to know more than he was saying. "The second reason is more practical. We will be garrison troops when we are in Portsmouth and you are right, other archers have more skill than you, but Robert of Nantwich told me of your skill with other weapons. He also said of your hunger and desire to win at all costs. You are not afraid to take on someone whom you think has greater skill. Dark times may be ahead of us and your sword, dagger and axe may be needed."

"Dark times, Captain?"

"King Edward wants the French crown, but King Philip has the young King David at his court and the French and Scots have ever been allies. Until we can land soldiers in France and threaten the French then we are in danger from King Philip as well as the Scots. Sir Walter is, even now, gathering a fleet to counter the French threat but Portsmouth will need to be defended. The castle there is not as strong as Dover and we need to protect the anchorage."

And so I began my service in Portsmouth Castle. It proved to be a most eventful time. There were no stone fortifications and the wooden walls looked remarkably flimsy to me. Even then I had a critical eye for such matters. I had fought in Scotland and seen the advantage of stone-built structures and, as an archer, I knew the vulnerability of wood. The castle lay outside the town but guarded the entrance to the harbour. We had wooden towers dotted along it and it was in those that the archers were housed. Our arrival doubled the garrison archers and I was honoured to be with Captain Philip and five other archers in the one which lay closest to the harbour and the ships.

We were shown around the walls by an old archer, Paul of Portsmouth. Until the arrival of Captain Philip, he had commanded the archers and I think he was relieved to have that duty taken from him. In the short time I knew him, Paul of

Portsmouth did not seem a well man, but I never discovered his ailment. Paul told us of an attack two years earlier on the Isle of Wight. Portsmouth had not been directly threatened but the constable and the King had begun to add the towers. Our arrival meant that the garrison now had forty men to defend its walls. Besides the garrison, the men of Portsmouth could be called upon to fight from the walls of the town. Our duties were simple, the other five and I had the responsibility of the harbour tower. During the day four of us would be on duty while at night two of us would watch all night. The night duty was rotated.

    We were fed and we were paid but the pay was only half that of a mounted horseman. I had husbanded my money and that did not worry me. I had a roof and I was fed, more importantly, I was learning. I now knew that I wished to be a warrior and I was ambitious enough to want to be Captain Philip. I spent every moment I could with him and tried to emulate him. When we had the daytime duty, we saw him as he walked the fighting platform and the towers. His eyes were everywhere seeking imperfections. It was easy enough to maintain our standards and any archer who suffered his wrath deserved it. The ones who were found wanting were the original archers of the garrison and they learned to dread the heavy step of Captain Philip as he stomped the wooden walls. At night it was Paul of Portsmouth who was in charge and I found that I liked him, but he was no warrior. He was a fair archer, but he had spent his whole life in Portsmouth and had yet to draw a bow in anger. He was three times as old as I was and yet I had fought in more battles and killed many more men than either Paul or any of his men. I saw now why King Edward had sent his Captain of Archers to Portsmouth.

    I had been at Portsmouth for some time and was a comfortable member of the garrison when the French fleet arrived. I was on the day shift and, after breakfast, I had just arrived on the walls when I saw Captain Philip staring out to sea. I joined him but said nothing for all that I could see was the sails of a couple of ships coming up from the Isle of Wight. He turned and said, "John, sound the alarm, I believe I see French ships approaching. I will find the Constable! Prepare for war!"

I ran to the bell which was in our tower and I began to toll it. A few moments later it was answered by the town's parish church. Men would grab their weapons and race to the walls. Once the church bell tolled, I stopped hauling on the rope and ran into the tower to get my bow and arrow bag. My sword hung from my belt and my hand axe was jammed in it. I was not used to my helmet but after donning it and the arming cap, I was ready. I took my place on the fighting platform at the top of the tower. The men at arms would guard the walls but we archers would use the elevation of the tower to stop an enemy further from the walls. Our fort was guarded on two sides by water. One side was the harbour while on the other was the estuary. I glanced into the harbour. It was too late for the ships there to escape and so the captains were binding their ships together to make a floating fort. I now saw that what I had taken to be a couple of ships was a veritable fleet. I had been too inexperienced to recognise the number.

The fighting platform shook as the men at arms ran up to take their places. It was as I looked around that I saw we had too few men to man the walls effectively. When I had seen Aberdeen, the walls had been a sea of steel. Here we were dotted around. As far as I could see our only hope lay in the levy who would be summoned from the countryside but by the time they reached Portsmouth it might be too late. King Edward had not sent enough men. I looked around at the others; I was the youngest, but they knew I had experience. Three of them, Rafe, Jack and Will had been at Cadzand while John and Matty had spent their whole lives watching Portsmouth's walls. As there was another John and he had been here first I was Hawkwood. I had resented it at first for it reminded me of my father, but I was now used to it.

Captain Philip climbed up the ladder inside the tower and, when he reached the top, he strung his bow. He shook his head and gave us all a rueful smile. "If we had a stone castle then we could have fire here and those ships would not be a threat. As it is, we are the ones in danger from fire. Let us look on the bright side, we have arrows aplenty and we are all good archers. We will make each one count."

The French fleet was now closer, and I counted at least thirty-five ships. They could carry more than a thousand men and all of them would be fighting men. I chose a war arrow as I could not see any mailed men yet. Their plan became clear. The wall of the wooden castle was so close to the estuary that they would not be able to land close enough to it and so they were heading for the harbour and quays.

Captain Philip realised that the only tower whose arrows could reach the ships if they attacked the quays was ours and so he shouted, "Every archer who is not in the harbour tower man the harbour wall!"

Archers scurried down their ladders and raced to obey the command. In our tower, we turned to mirror the movements of the ships although they were out of range. There were fishermen on the mole, and they ran for the safety of the town walls. The crossbows on the ships cut them down to a man and then the weapon invented by the devil began to loose bolts at the crews of the ships. We were just too far away to do any good and we watched helplessly as the French crews poured over the sides of their ships and boarded the floating fort. We could see the one-sided fighting. The French had protection in the form of helmets and metal studded jerkins, and they had better weapons. The sailors were hard men and they fought well but when we saw them hurling themselves over the side to swim to the shore then we knew it was over. Not long after the last living sailor had left the ships, we saw flames licking the ship in the centre and the French ships left to land men on our side of the harbour. The English ships would soon become hulks, and the French would attack us and the town of Portsmouth!

As soon as the ships tied up and the men began to land Captain Philip shouted, "Loose!"

I sent an arrow at the seaman tying the ship up to the bollard. Captain Philip had seen me as he sent a bodkin into a knight leading men towards our walls, "Forget the sailors! Kill the soldiers!"

I drew a bodkin and aimed at a man at arms who ran with a burning brand, obviously taken from the inferno that was the flaming fort, towards our wooden walls. As he raised his arm to throw it at our palisade my bodkin tipped arrow slammed into his chest and threw him and the brand into the harbour.

"Better!"

Our twenty-one bows each managed to send an arrow into a Frenchman every time we drew our longbows back but there were not enough of us. Rafe pointed to the town side of the harbour, "Look!" There were even fewer archers on the town walls or archers who had bodkin arrows at any rate, and already the walls had been scaled. I saw flames licking the wooden parapets and it became obvious that this was no invasion but just a way to hurt us by burning one of our most important ports to the ground. I determined to kill as many as I could. I drew and released until my stock of arrows was gone and I raced into the tower to grab another sheaf. When I came out, I saw the French had managed to set fire to the wooden wall behind which we fought. Our men at arms were busy trying to douse the fire but it was a losing battle. The walls were old and dried.

"Keep fighting for help is on the way!" Captain Philip knew that all around Portsmouth the men of Hampshire would be roused to come to our aid. However, that relief would not be swift!

The six of us had a better view of the battle than any and we had a clearer sight of all the targets. The French leader, we later learned his name was Nicolas Béhuchet, ordered his crossbows to concentrate on us. Matty was the first to die and a bolt struck him squarely in the centre of his forehead. I sent a war arrow into his killer and the death of one of our friends incensed us and we slew all the crossbowmen. It was a mistake for while we were doing that other Frenchmen were setting fire to other sections of our walls and the men at arms were losing the battle. The Constable had already fallen, and it was left to Captain Philip to give the order, "Men at arms, save yourselves for the citadel is lost. We will cover you as long as we can!"

Portsmouth was ablaze and I hoped that the populace had escaped. I had no idea how we would get out of our predicament, but I trusted in the Captain. The one advantage of crossbows is that, unlike a longbow, you need very little training to be able to use them. Other men had picked up the crossbows and although most of the bolts missed us, John was hit in the shoulder and he would not be able to use his bow.

"John leave us and try to save yourself!"

"Aye, Captain! Good luck, lads!"

Another archer plunged from the walls and I saw that we could not escape through the main gate. We were trapped as the fighting platform was burning fiercely. It was clear that the other archers, the ones on the walls, could not last and so Captain Philip, coughing through the smoke shouted, "Archers on the walls, save yourselves! May God be with you!"

There were just five of us left in the harbour tower and our escape would be through the sally port which led to the estuary and the main channel.

"Rafe, you and Will make sure that the sally port is safe. We will cover you."

As they descended the ladder they would be exposed and the three of us who remained kept up a withering rate of arrows. I confess that I thought I would die in that tower, but I was proud that I had slain so many of England's enemies. When flames began to lick our tower the Captain shouted, "Time for us to go. Hawkwood, you lead!"

I slung my bow over my back, aware that I only had six arrows left in any case. As I hurried down the ladder, thankful that the billowing, choking smoke hid me, I almost lost a finger as a crossbow bolt slammed into the ladder. I did not hesitate when I reached the bottom of the first ladder and I began to descend the second ladder. This one was hot to the touch and if not alight already then it soon would be.

"Captain! Hurry! The ladder is almost afire!"

When I reached the bottom, after slinging my bow, I drew my sword and my axe. As far as I knew the French were on the other side of the blazing inferno. Jack dropped to the ground just as the ladder burst into flames and we both stepped away as Captain Philip crashed to the ground, landing badly on his ankle. He took his bow and used it as a staff. "Hawkwood, you are handy, watch our backs and we will try the sally port."

"Aye, Captain." I took the order as an honour. I walked backwards towards the sally port. The estuary wall was the furthest from the fire although what we would do when we reached the other side, I had no idea. The tide was on its way in!

I had almost reached the gate, which, when I glanced over my shoulder I saw was open, when I heard the clash of steel on steel. As soon as I stepped outside, I was in a battle. Will lay dead and Rafe was trying to hold in his guts but he still held his sword in his left hand. The Captain was flailing with his bow and Jack was using his dagger and short sword. There were six Frenchmen and two of them were mailed. I knew then that I was going to die but that thought gave me the confidence to do what I did. I screamed and threw myself at one of the two mailed men. My shout was so loud that everyone looked around and that allowed me to take three steps and to bring my sword down to split the coif and head of the mailed man. My speed had taken me next to another Frenchman and I just reacted, almost blindly, and hacked sideways. The hand axe was very sharp and the head was heavy. It drove through the skull and almost sliced off the top of the Frenchman's head. The two deaths almost evened up our numbers and when Rafe launched himself at the other mailed man Jack and the Captain also attacked.

When Rafe paid the price for his courage and the mailed Frenchman took his head I saw red and I ran at the Frenchman's back. My sword scraped off the mailed man's armour, but the speed of my charge and my weight drove us into the water. I swallowed a mouthful of seawater but held on to my axe and sword. I was on top of the Frenchman and as I raised my head to cough out the water he tried to rise. I brought down the axe but a combination of the sea, his coif and the short swing meant that the blow was not decisive. However, I managed to drive his head back down and I put my hands and our weapons together and leaned on his mouth. I felt him struggling to move me, but I was heavy, and I was strong. He tried to bite me but only succeeded in taking a mouthful of axe haft and the struggling stopped.

I stood and saw that Jack was down and the Captain was fighting two men. He could not move very well and was using his sword and his bow stave. I hurled the axe and it struck one man in the back of the head. As he fell, he knocked over the Captain but the last man standing saw me as the threat and he lunged at me with his sword. I was wet and bedraggled, and I was struggling to keep my feet. The result was that I was slow to block the strike and the tip hit my waist. He drove the sword at me, and I expected to feel the edge tear into me, but I just felt pain. The man looked at me in surprise and I backhanded him with my sword. I caught him under the chin and sliced off half his face. He might have screamed had he a mouth to do so and I drove my sword into him. The Frenchman who had knocked over the Captain was struggling to his feet and I put my sword into his back and just leaned. The sword drove through him.

Looking around I saw that I was the only man left on his feet. The Captain was alive, and he put out his hand for me to help him to his feet. "You should be dead!"

I nodded and put my hand to the tear in my gambeson and then I smiled. "My money belt, with the gold within has saved my life!"

He smiled, "Fortune favours you, now let us go! Head down the estuary towards Southsea. The fire here will soon consume the wall!"

I had to help him as we struggled to cover the half a mile or more to the open ground at Southsea. The heat from the burning wall made us use the shallows of the estuary. By then help must have come for we saw the French fleet as, ship by ship, they left the harbour and headed out to sea. I had suffered my first defeat and lost most of my comrades. It was a hard lesson to learn! The Captain was a tough man, but his ankle had swollen to twice its normal size by the time we reached Southsea. I looked back and all that I could see of Portsmouth was black smoke and flames rising into the sky. Just the hospital and the parish church looked to have survived and they would be soot coated and blackened shells when the fire had finished. It looked like my time in the garrison would be a short one. People were rushing past us and heading for safety. I shouted, "Have you any ale? This soldier is hurt!"

I saw a man laugh as he ran holding a jug. If he had not laughed, I would have done nothing, but he laughed and I jumped to my feet, ran after him and, grabbing him pulled his around. I grabbed the jug.

"Hey, that is mine!"

I smiled, "It was yours and now it is mine!"

He made the mistake of swinging at me and holding the jug in my left hand I swung out of the way and hit him so hard in his face that he fell to the ground as though struck by an anvil. I walked back to the Captain who was shaking his head but smiling, "You have a way with words, Hawkwood."

"Here, Captain, drink deeply. We may be here for some time." I pointed to the estuary where the long line of French ships was edging out to sea. "I cannot see that they will stop raiding so easily. We did not hurt them. There were too few of us."

"And yet we acquitted ourselves well."

"Do you see any more archers, Captain? They are all dead! The only way out of that fire trap was through the sally port and the wall burned soon after we left. They are all gone."

He drank deeply and then handed it to me. I drank too. I had drunk better but, right at that moment, it tasted like the nectar of the gods.

Not everyone fled. When they saw the two of us, with our bows and the cross of St. George many refugees stopped and gathered around us. Perhaps they thought that we could protect them. The youth who had laughed had disappeared. I do not think he relished another smack. Some of the monks from the hospital arrived with patients who would otherwise have died for the stone of the hospital could not save them from the smoke which killed as easily as fire. It was they who saw to the Captain. By the time darkness fell, there were fifty of us or more and two men at arms, one badly wounded, limped into the camp. The four of us were the only ones left alive from the garrison. Paul of Portsmouth had only fought in one action and it had killed him!

I lit a fire, it was more to attract attention than anything and, sure enough, the High Sherriff of Hampshire, Robert Daundelin, with his knights and men at arms arrived. He recognised our livery and, I think, he knew the Captain. The Sherriff wisely took him to one side to speak with him. They were away for some time. The Sherriff spoke to myself and the two men at arms when he returned. "Portsmouth owes you four a debt and it shall be paid. Give your names to my squire so that they may be recorded, and I can send payment when the time is right."

"Thank you, my lord."

Financial reward seemed to be the last thing on my mind. When they had gone, I said, "Captain, I will go and do something with the bodies of our archers, if they are still there."

He smiled, "And help yourself to the purses of the dead Frenchmen." I shrugged. "You deserve it for you saved my life and almost those of the others. You were not at fault."

I unsheathed my sword as I headed back to the water. The tide was on the way in and I would be lucky to find anything. I followed the glow from the burning embers of the wall. In the town fires still burned but the wind from the sea had accelerated the work of the fire. I was about two hundred paces from the place I hoped to find the bodies when I sensed a movement from my right. I whirled and held my sword before me, "One step closer and you die!" In answer, Megs whinnied and was answered by three other horses which had escaped from the fire. I sheathed my sword and, grabbing a hunk of mane, held her close. "I thought I had lost you! This makes up a little for some of the losses which we endured."

Megs appeared to be the leader for when I took her reins and led her, they followed. I saw that the tide had taken some of the bodies. Rafe and Jack were there, and I lifted their bodies on to the backs of two of the horses. There were two Frenchmen left. One was mailed and I found that he had a good sword and a fat purse. The other had a dagger and a paltry purse. It was not too bad. I jumped on Meg's back and led the other horses back to the camp. More people had arrived, and the food was being prepared.

I dismounted and with the two men at arms and Captain Philip, took the two bodies from the horses. The monks from the hospital said a few words and we buried them on the salt-washed turf. There was no marker but then none of the others who had died would have a marker. At least their bodies were in the ground and we knew where they were. The Captain and I spoke long into the night. I had no sleep that night for I watched my captain.

The next day I rode with the Captain and the two men at arms, bareback and we headed for London. Captain Philip needed to report to the King, and we hoped he would be there. I had spent less time in Portsmouth than I had expected but my time there had been an education. As Captain Philip said, "That which does not kill you, makes you stronger."

As we rode north to London, he told me that he hoped I would continue to serve the King. "You showed me once again, John Hawkwood, that you have unique talents and those talents ought to be used by the King. I know that your purse is full, and I would not blame you if you sought another life, but I beg you to come with me."

"I will think on your words, Captain Philip."

And I did. It took us two days to reach London and I had made my mind up long before reaching the Thames. I would continue to fight for England.

Chapter 5

We found the King at Eltham Palace along with his son. Edward, Duke of Cornwall. The young Prince was to be important in my life but that day was the first time I had met him. He was just ten years of age but seemed a very serious young man who was most interested in our report. Also, there was Henry, Earl of Derby, who had led King Edward's army in Scotland. Captain Philip had me with him, not least because he was able to use me as a human crutch. He still could not walk well. I saw that day how kings treat their people. The Captain was not offered a chair because no one sat in the presence of the King! The other reason was to confirm the disaster of Portsmouth. As two of the few to have survived from the garrison our testimony would be important.

Captain Philip gave an honest account of the events and he did not try to garner himself in glory.

The King nodded thoughtfully when he had finished and said, "I know, Captain, that you will answer me truthfully. Could aught have been done to save the ships and the town?"

He shook his head, "With the numbers of men we had, the wooden walls and the lack of a fleet then no. Had Sir Walter Manny been close, with the fleet, then we could have defeated the French but otherwise, we were doomed to lose."

He looked at Lord Henry, "It is as I feared! We need to make our defences of stone and build a fleet."

"And that takes money, my lord, and if we spent money on those then we could not afford the men. Now that we have the support of Europe then we just need money."

The King sat back in his chair, "Then I need to go to the moneylenders once more. How many men can you muster, Earl?"

Lord Henry rubbed his beard, "We have, perhaps, five hundred men at arms and I could muster six hundred archers."

"Not a great army but one which will have to do. Sail for Dunkerque and join with the Count of Flanders and the Count of Hainault. Try to draw the French towards you. I will secure the loan and follow you there. I will have Salisbury and Suffolk join me." They all nodded. He seemed to see me for the first time, "Is this the young archer both of you mentioned to me?" I was shocked and surprised that either of them had spoken to the King about me.

"He is, King Edward, and he helped to save not only me but four other archers. Sadly, they later died but that was not Hawkwood's fault."

The King nodded, "And will you serve your king, Hawkwood?"

"It would be my honour."

"Then take him, Lord Henry. Captain Philip will command the archers and he shall be a gentleman and paid accordingly."

"Thank you, King Edward."

"You will earn the extra pay, Captain, for our archers will be the difference between success and failure. I am afraid that we may have to empty the gaols to fill the ranks of archers. If we cannot afford to pay them then let us offer them freedom if they please us."

And so we rode, once more, to Dover. There were still some men there who had fought at Cadzand and the Earl of Derby's men were also there. We learned that the Duke of Lancaster, Lord Henry's father, who was one of the richest men in England, had settled a large sum on his eldest son and Lord Henry was using that to help his cousin, the King. While Captain Philip rode with his lordship I was relegated to the baggage but I did not mind. The King knew my name. I wished that my father could know about this and my mother. She would be proud, and he would be apoplectic with rage! Both outcomes would please me!

When we reached the camp, I found I knew some of the archers but none of them were my tent mates and I was saddened. I got on well enough with the other archers but the four with whom I had first served had a special bond with me and from the moment we set foot in France I felt different and a little alone. I was not distant with my fellow archers, indeed I got on well with them all but none were close to me. I did not confide in them as I had with Harry and Silent Simon. All my fears and hopes were kept inside, just for me! I was helped by the fact that I no longer looked like a new archer. I had a gambeson and helmet and the gambeson, with the red cross, showed wear and tear. The others knew I had fought. The story of my rescue of Captain Philip at Portsmouth was also widely known and as I had not sought aggrandisement, others thought well of me. That and the nods I received from lords like Lord Henry, Sir Robert Fitzwalter and Sir Richard also told them that I was an archer of repute. Although there were archers who had been with us at Cadzand there were others, the men who had come from Lancashire and Derby with his lordship, for whom this would be a new experience. In addition, there were the men who had been released from gaols with the promise of freedom. All I met asked me about the ships and the crossing. I was honest with them for that was one part of the campaign that I would not enjoy. This would not, however, be a raid like Cadzand. We would be landing at Dunkerque and riding forth into enemy land. We would neither know the land nor the language. When we had been on Cadzand I had vaguely recognised a couple of the Flemish words but other than that it was like the language Dai the Taff had spoken to fellow Welshmen; incomprehensible.

Once more I was to be paid as a mounted archer and I would be with the van. It was a place of honour. It also meant I would take Megs with me. I found myself confiding in Megs in the same way I had confided in my tent mates. I am not sure if any of my words made sense to her, but she sometimes nodded and just the speaking of the words to her gave me comfort. The other person I spoke to each day was Captain Philip who used me as a sort of servant while he was recovering. The healers told him to keep off the injured foot for at least a week and so he gave his commands from his tent. I often summoned his centenars and vintenars and that also enhanced my position. The men who gave commands on the battlefield chatted easily with me. I think that also made it harder for the other archers to become close to me. Soldiers like clear divisions between those who give the orders and those who follow them. Robert of Nantwich had been close to the four of us but not the others. We knew what he was like, but they feared his wrath. I was neither fish nor fowl and men distrust that which they do not know.

It was the same fleet which had taken us to Cadzand which gathered off Dover and Sir Walter Manny commanded. This time I had the confidence to speak with the sailors. They liked

Sir Walter and told me that once we had been landed then they were going back to Sluys to entice the French into battle. I had had an inkling of this as I had caught some of the conversation between Lord Henry, the King and Captain Philip. The coast of England had too many places where the French could attack and cause mischief and the only way to guarantee that they could not hurt us, as they had at Southampton and Portsmouth, was to destroy or, at the very least, damage the fleet. I was just worried that we might lose and then we would be stranded on the island of Englishmen in France that was Dunkerque!

This time we had a flatter crossing, for it was shorter, and a dry landing for there was a stone quay. We were also welcomed by Englishmen and there were so many of us that it was English which was spoken in most of the taverns and inns. By the time we landed Captain Philip was almost fully recovered and the day after, he led the mounted archers to scout out the Flemish and French defences. The Flemish had tired of their French overlords for King Philip had had many Flemish executed after Cadzand, blaming them for the attack. Sir Walter Manny and his fleet, off Sluys, would encourage them to rise in revolt against King Philip. We were sent to find weaknesses.

The land south of Cambrai was known as Cambresis and even I, a relative novice, saw that it was an area which was ripe for the plucking. The land was flat and suited mounted men. All that we had to do was to take Cambrai. The walls were stone walls and it looked to be well defended. As our band of two hundred archers drew up outside the town walls, Captain Philip spoke to his officers. We were a good six hundred paces from the walls and beyond the range of crossbows. As he was speaking, I saw the gates open and men at arms and crossbowmen raced out aggressively. Our time in Dover had not been wasted and Captain Philip roared out, "Horse holders! String bows!"

I was now more than a competent rider and I put that down to Megs being such a good horse. I let her reins drop knowing that Jacob, the designated horse holder, would have no trouble with her. I was in position before anyone and that included the vintenar. I could string my full-sized bow easily and I had dyed my fletch so that I knew which arrow to draw. The crossbows were the danger and I drew a war arrow which would tear through the padded jackets of the crossbowmen. We all hated crossbows and the men who used them. Any fool who could pull back a string could use one, but it took years and God's touch to make an archer. I had an arrow nocked even as Jack of Tarporley, our vintenar, shouted, "Nock!"

I had never faced so many crossbows before. Hitherto I had seen them used from walls and the decks of ships. Here I saw that the men who used them had to kneel and to use their knee for support when they released them. A crossbow is not a thing of beauty, it is ugly and front heavy. A longbow is a craftsman made object and a joy to use. While we could send volleys, they had to send their bolts almost individually. The fact that we had to dismount and, in some cases, string bows, meant that they were in position and sending their bolts at us first. They drew first blood and some of our men were hit. I smiled when I saw some bolts fall short.

"Draw!"

I pulled back and heard the reassuring creak of the bow.

"Release!"

Even as the arrows flew, we all took a second arrow from our war bags. The crossbowmen had to stand and put their foot in the stirrup to draw back the string using the spanning hooks attached to their belts. In the time it took to do that we had sent three arrows each. The French managed one more ragged flutter of bolts before the horn sounded and the French pulled back. They left the ground littered with bodies. We cheered until Captain Philip shouted, "Silence! Mount your horses and tend to the wounded." As we did so he added, "John Hawkwood, find me a wounded man to question!"

I had slung my bow and mounted Megs before the words had stopped echoing. I knew time was not on my side. The crossbowmen would be on their walls as soon as they could and if they had forty crossbows aimed at me then one would hit! I saw that we had killed at least thirty crossbowmen and one man at arms. The wounded who could, were hurrying back into the town. I saw one crossbowman whose leg was pinned to the ground. The arrow had struck his shin and he looked in agony.

I stopped Megs and leapt from her back. With the reins on the ground, she would graze. The French soldier had a helmet and a leather brigandine. When he saw me, he tried to reach his sword. From the walls, I heard shouts and a couple of bolts came in my direction. They were half-heartedly released as they did not wish to harm their own man. I took my hand axe and, reversing it, hit him on the back of the head to stun him. He fell back and I jammed my axe back into my belt. I snapped off the arrow and picked him up. I threw his body over Megs' neck and then mounted her. More bolts flew at me and one clanged off my helmet making my ears ring. I had outstayed my welcome. The other archers cheered as I rode back, and I saw that Captain Philip was grinning.

"I hope you have not killed him!"

"Just a gentle tap, Captain."

"Bring forth the spare horse and tie him to it. Let us return to the army! We have enough now to tell Lord Henry."

My standing rose even higher that day but the proud smile from my Captain was all that I needed. Of course, I had also taken the purse from the Frenchman as I had ridden back and so I was in profit. I also took his bascinet helmet which was a good one.

When we camped for the night the prisoner answered every question. He was encouraged by the fact that Captain Philip would not allow our healer to tend to his wound until he did. The commander of the garrison was Étienne de la Baume who was the grandmaster of the French crossbows. It explained the aggressive nature of their defence. There were three hundred of them in the town and men at arms too. That posed a problem for while crossbows were not a real problem on the battlefield when used from inside a town or a castle, they could be effective. You could kill the operator, and another could use the devil's machine.

Three days after we returned to Dunkerque, King Edward and his eldest son arrived with more men. We were ready to go to war and the whole army headed back to Cambrai. The King surrounded the town and the entire cohort of archers ringed it. King Edward demanded the surrender of the town and, of course, de la Baume refused. We advanced behind a line of men at arms and sent wave after wave of arrows at the walls. Crossbow bolts slammed into the shields of the men at arms. Some fell and some of the bolts hit archers. When we had exhausted our supply, we withdrew and King Edward, Lord Henry, the earls of Salisbury and Suffolk retired to come up with a plan. This was not Aberdeen. The wall was made of stone and they had stone towers. The stronghold would require a good plan for us to reduce it.

A day later and we were ready to go again. Ladders were made although I did not envy the men who would use them. These were not knights but men at arms who hoped for a reward from the King. It was as we were lining up that the French unleashed a new weapon and one I had never seen before. From their walls, a metal tube disgorged flame and such a crack as to make us all think that a thunderstorm was overhead. There was a whistling sound, and something flew towards one of the tents, tearing a hole in it and setting it alight. Some men cowered but I stood and watched, fascinated. This happened ten times along the wall. Whatever weapon it was they had ten of them. The missiles they sent appeared to do little damage save setting alight two tents and killing an unfortunate horse. They did, however, dishearten the men. The French prisoner we had taken was still with us and King Edward himself questioned him. The prisoner was quite happy to tell us that they were a metal tube called a *cannone*, he said it was an Italian word, and that they used a black powder and flame to send a rock at an enemy. I learned this later on. I watched the men on the wall beavering away. They must have been reloading. The cannone fired a second time. We saw the tongue of fire, like a dragon, spew forth and there was a smell of sulphur in the air. This time all ten weapons were used at once and a black cloud filled the ground before the walls.

I turned to Captain Philip, "Captain, I am guessing that these weapons take as long to reload as a crossbow and that while they are reloading, they are both vulnerable and blind."

He gave me a shrewd look, "They do not frighten you?"

"Two burned tents and a dead horse? I think not."

"Let us see if you are right."

The King and his advisers, with men carrying shields before them, advanced so that they could observe these *cannone* in action. I learned the word for I was close by Captain Philip when

Lord Henry told him. "They are metal tubes which throw rocks at us. The flames cannot hurt us. We know that trebuchet and mangonels are only useful against walls."

"Aye, Lord Henry. Hawkwood here seems to think that they take a long time to load and while they do so the smoke and the fact that they appear to have to lean out to load them makes them vulnerable."

The Earl nodded, "Then the next time they belch forth, take some of your men and see if they can hit the men operating these machines!"

It took a long time for the *cannone* to be ready and Captain Philip had, by then, gathered his chosen men and told us what he intended. "Mark where these weapons are and when they loose their rocks we run forward, hidden from the walls by the smoke and loose three arrows in swift succession to see if we can rid the walls of the men."

As soon as the *cannone* cracked we ran, knowing that we were hidden. We needed no order and I had marked the place already where I would stop. I nocked a war arrow, drew back and loosed. I heard a cry for others were loosing their arrows too. I heard shouts and the crossbows cracked. The difference was that we knew where the parapet was to be found but we were hidden. After my third arrow, I ran back. As the smoke cleared so we saw the effect. Two archers had been hit and lay on the ground but there were five of the French lying before the walls. For the next seven days, we duelled with the French until they decided that the *cannone* were not worth the effort. The men who operated them were highly skilled. It allowed King Edward to assault the walls.

The archers had an easier time when we began our next attack for we were more than one hundred and fifty paces from the walls. Our task was to keep the enemy from pushing away the ladders or using their crossbows. We did not always succeed, and some men fell to their deaths. Once they made the walls then we had to stop and, in that interval, the men at arms were driven back. We spent five fruitless weeks attacking. We lost men and so did the French, but no gains were made and then we had a message that the French were sending an army to relieve Cambrai. The message said it was a large army and so we headed back to Dunkerque. It was a disappointment to all of us for although we had been paid there had been no booty!

The plain of Cambresis was a rich one and we plundered and pillaged our way back to the toe hold which England retained in France. Sir Richard Elfingham was left with a strong garrison at the castle of Thun-l'Eveque which was not far from Cambrai while the rest of us advanced to La Capelle where there was a ridge backed by a wood and we proceeded to make a defensive position. We hewed down saplings, sharpened them and placed them before and around the archers. The horsemen were dismounted and formed a block between the two sets of archers, and we waited. We did not go hungry for we had taken a great deal from the farms on the plains of Cambresis and we emptied the forests of game!

When the French did arrive, it was a huge army but, as we were to find out six years later, size did not always matter. It was an allied army with no one in real command. King Edward impressed me with his defensive strategy. The French and their allies could attack but it would be uphill and with fifteen hundred arrows raining down on them. Here their crossbows would be of little use as we were on the heights and could outrange them. What we, the ordinary archers, could not possibly know was that King Edward had persuaded the Flemish to change sides so that when their contingent left the French army and their cities threw out the French soldiers, King Philip was isolated and he fell back to Paris. The battle never took place and we did not have to draw a bow, but we won the war.

We retired, not to Dunkerque but to Brussels where King Edward ordered a tournament to celebrate what had been, in effect, a bloodless victory. The levy went back to England and that would save the King enough money to provide prizes for his knights. It was an excuse for most archers and the poorer men at arms to become drunk while the knights tried to show their prowess at the tourney. I confess that the few bouts I watched were a little more dangerous than I had expected, and I saw a couple of lords who were seriously hurt. As Captain Philip said, when we discussed it over a jug of Brussels Black Ale, "At least this way the fact that they were not good enough will not lose us a battle and the ones who won will be stronger!"

Lord Henry left us to join Sir Walter Manny with the fleet and King Edward took his son and most of the army back to England. Many of the archers, myself included, stayed in the Low Countries along with five hundred men at arms. We were under the command of Sir Richard Elfingham who had shown his worth in the Scottish campaign and in the fighting around Cambrai. I liked him and I was happy. I knew it not then, but my future was now in Europe. I spent most of my time as a soldier in France, Gascony and the Low countries and I think that shaped my life. I learned from the French, Flemish, Bretons, Gascons and Poitevin. I either fought with them or against them and I learned all the time.

I used some of my back pay to rent accommodation in Brussels. It had a stable so that Megs was looked after and I was able to enjoy better food than at the camp with the other archers. Archers were well paid, but many had vices: women, gambling and the love of too much ale. I liked women but I would not pay for a whore and I was young enough to be able to bed comely young women. I did not gamble, and I always stopped drinking before I began to fall over. My first experience of drunkenness had been enough for me! I had a thirst, instead, for knowledge and I liked nothing better than to speak with other warriors. All were older than I was and came from many different nationalities. During that time, I began to learn languages. Most men could speak French and that was always a starting point, but I tried to learn from all those I met. Sometimes Captain Philip would be with me for we enjoyed each other's company, but, after we had been there for a few days, he discovered a woman he liked, and he spent an increasing amount of time with her. I did not mind, and most men were happy to talk with me. I found it easy to be pleasant. Occasionally I was told to clear off, but I did not take it personally.

It was in a small inn just off the main square that I met an Italian youth. He was the same age as me. but he was the squire of a mercenary who was fighting with the Count of Hainault. The Italian city-states, Venice excluded, were generally small and had many wars amongst each other. The knight whom Giovanni d'Azzo degli Ubaldini served had managed to upset factions on both sides of the Paduan, Florentine conflict. He had taken service in Flanders until it was safe for him to return. Lord Bartolomeo, like Captain Philip, had found a Flemish woman and he spent most nights with her. Giovanni kept watch from the inn and if his master stayed the night then Giovanni slept in the stable with the horses. We got on immediately when we met.

In the month that we spent in each other's company, I learned to speak some Italian and he learned English well. We both benefitted from the skill and while I learned about Italy, I was able to tell him of the politics of France, Scotland and England. We had much in common. Even though I was an archer and he would be a man at arms or, if he was a lucky a knight, we both appreciated that being paid to fight was far better than any noble or chivalrous quest. As luck would have it, we both ended up fighting on the same side. Not long after Sir Walter destroyed the French fleet at the Battle of Sluys the Flemish went to war with the French and Sir Richard took the one thousand men of the English contingent to fight alongside them. Giovanni and I did not march together but, when we camped, we made sure that we found time to talk to each other.

The Flemish army headed for the French border. The French had been hurt by Sir Walter and I think that the Counts of Flanders and Hainault saw their chance to garner some of their own glory. What I saw was the same problem which had beset the French and their allies. The only way to win a battle was to have one man in command and all of the men knowing not only their place in battle but the mind of their leader. Sir Richard was a good leader, but it was the Count of Flanders who led the army and he was not a good general. We had marched towards Saint Quentin where the French and their allies awaited us. The English contingent was placed on the right flank and Sir Richard had us use stakes to protect ourselves. He had mounted men at arms to our right and we had dismounted men at arms behind us. More mounted men at arms and the knights were to our left. The Men of Hainault had the left flank and it was the Count of Flanders who had his men take the middle ground. We were the only archers and the men of Flanders relied on their crossbows.

The crossbows and archers were ordered to advance. This did not sit well with us for we preferred our enemies to come to us, but we obeyed. Captain Philip still had a slight limp, but he marched forward well enough. The problem as I saw it was that we would be isolated and not able to get fresh supplies of arrows. I had just thirty! The French and their allies seemed to mirror our moves. I looked around and knew that English archers would die and there was no need! We halted when the Flemish did, and I nocked an arrow. The men of Flanders and Hainault began to send their bolts piecemeal and I heard Captain Philip curse.

"Draw!"

We pulled back and I saw two archers hit by Genoese bolts! "Release!"

Our arrows rose in the sky and we all nocked a second and were ready when the order came, "Release at will!"

The faster men, such as me would empty our war bags sooner and the French and their allies would die quicker! The French were using their Genoese allies and I had heard that they were good men. They were not facing us but the Flemish in the centre. Our arrow storm was so withering that the crossbows who were opposite us had no answer and the first couple of archers who were struck were our only losses. The French we faced were decimated and they turned and fled. Their flight availed them little as we continued to kill and wound them as they ran.

Captain Philip was mindful that a sudden movement of our men to the rear might be interpreted as some sort of retreat, "Fall back slowly but face the enemy at all times." I think he was aware that the crossbows to our left were weakening for even before we had taken a step backwards the Flemish crossbows in the centre simply disintegrated and fled. All of us still had a couple of arrows in our arrow bags and we each nocked them. The men of Hainault saw their fellows run and then began a hurried retreat. It was only the English longbowmen who maintained a steady pace.

The French King ordered his men to charge. The whole of the enemy front erupted, and I smiled. I was a novice at this but talking with others and having witnessed some war I knew that mounted men succeeded only when they kept a steady pace and a solid line. Quite simply the French did not. Those on our flank had to negotiate their fleeing crossbowmen and that put them behind the others. Although even they had to navigate around

Genoese and French crossbowmen. The result was a series of knights who had managed to clear their fellows and with lances ready charged towards us. The last four arrows in my bag were all bodkins, I had not needed them against the crossbowmen. I had not been ordered to, but I stopped and nocked my bow. I saw some of the more experienced archers doing the same. It was always better if you could manage it, to face your enemy and avoid the wooden lance in the back!

    I pulled back and tried to gauge when the knight on the courser would reach me. I had time to take in that he had an open bascinet and a long kite shield. I watched the end of his lance wave up and down as his horse galloped. When I had watched the tournament the speed at which the knights had approached each other was slower than this and they seemed to have time to steady and aim their lances. Perhaps the ones I had seen had been the best. I was confident enough to know that I could stop the horseman before he reached me, and I hoped that when I had been told that a horse will not willingly ride a man down it had been the truth. I waited until the rider was just fifty paces from me. I watched him pull back his arm in preparation for a lunge with his lance and I released my bodkin and drew another. The arrow slammed into his chest and buried itself up to the fletch. He fell to the right and his horse struggled to keep its feet. The animal was dragged to the ground and the next horseman, who tried to clear the fallen horse and rider, was also struck in the middle by another English archer. By now we had all stopped and were spread out over a large area, but we all had arrows left. My second arrow struck a man at arms in the right shoulder. I saw his lance fall to the ground and I drew another bodkin. I had two left. I had no idea how the rest of the battle was going but we were winning. Had they been in one solid line it may have been a different story, but we had time to choose our targets and know that if we hit the nearest one we would have time to nock and aim at another. When I had sent my last arrow, I simply slung my bow, turned and took to my heels drawing my sword when I had the opportunity. I was not the first to use all of his arrows and as I passed two, they slung their bows and followed me.

It was when I heard hooves thundering a little closer to me that I drew my sword and handy little axe. I saw Captain Philip sling his bow, draw his sword and he shouted, "Hawkwood! Turn!"

I trusted the archer I had now known the longest and, even as I turned, I was swinging my sword and drawing my hand axe. The man at arms with the lance thought that he had me for he was pulling back his arm ready to strike. I was on his right and without a shield had no means of defending myself. I whipped up my sword as the wavering lance aimed first at my leg and then my head. I caught it when it was aimed at my shoulder and the lance went up in the air. I stepped closer and hacked at the rump of his horse as it passed with my hand axe. The effect was remarkable. The head bit deeply in and the horse almost screamed and then arched its back. The man at arms had his feet in his stirrups but he could not keep his saddle and he was thrown to the ground. As the wounded horse raced off, I ran to him and brought down my hand axe across the bridge of his nose. He died before I could pull it out.

From the corner of my eye I saw another horseman, it was a knight, coming at me. This time I waited until he was committed to an attack and then danced to the left side of the rider and swung my sword at his leg. He wore mail cuisse covering his legs but I drew blood and he veered away from me. I saw no horseman closer than sixty paces and so I turned and took the sword from the man at arms and reached into his mail to take his purse. I ran back to the men at arms who opened their ranks to allow us through.

Captain Philip shouted, "Archers, mount!"

It was as I slung my leg over Megs that I saw why. The English contingent was the only component of the army which was unbroken. The French and their allies were driving the Flemish from the field.

Sir Richard shouted, in English, "Fall back in good order!"

Over the next three days, we worked our way back to Dunkerque. We were pursued all the way, but Sir Richard knew his business and we frequently stopped, dismounted nocked and released our arrows driving hence our pursuers each time they came too close. We lost not a man. The battle had been lost, but not by us!

I also observed, after the battle when we were recovering in Dunkerque, the rewards for courage and bravery in action. John Chandos had been a man at arms fighting for Sir Richard. He fought well, but no better than I had done, and the result was that he was knighted. If I wished to be a knight then I needed to be a man at arms but I still enjoyed, at that time, the life of an archer.

Chapter 6

As is the nature of such things some men chose to go home. However, in our case, one of these was King Edward. We fought his enemies abroad but, at home, he had to deal with those who sought to undermine him. As men went home then the ones who remained became more important. I was learning that my status as a retained archer was a good one for it meant I was paid and fed. Of course, I could leave the King's service but what fool would? If I was not a soldier, then it might be an option, but I had chosen a martial path. Surprisingly, some men bored of the life we led and left for England. The result was that I stayed in Dunkerque with Captain Philip and now became a vintenar. When I had first become an archer that had seemed a lofty ambition, and now I commanded twenty men. There were just one hundred of us and that made me privy to far more privileged information. As soon as Captain Philip was informed of intelligence which might be useful, he told his vintenars and so I learned more.

Over the next couple of years, we were involved in fights and battles, but none were decisive. We would ride with Sir Richard's men at arms to support the Count of Flanders. He rarely defeated the French but the reason he was never destroyed was because of Sir Richard and Captain Philip. The French and Genoese crossbowmen came to learn not only to respect English archers but to fear them. It was not just our skill with the bow that made them unwilling to fight us, it was our tenacity when we put down our bows. Those forays were a monthly occurrence and each time we rode I learned more about myself and leading men. The booty was not as good as it could have been but that was because we rarely held the field. Had we been in an army led by Lord Henry then we would have been for he commanded Englishmen and we were just part of the Flemish army. I began to tire of serving under Flemish lords. I was not only one of Captain Philip's vintenars, but I also helped to train men with a sword. My work with Ralph of Malton and some natural skill which came from I know not where, helped to make me a good swordsman. I enjoyed the times I spent training men to use a sword and a dagger.

It was not long before our service in the Low Countries came to an end that Captain Philip sought me out. It was not a rare occurrence for he seemed to like me, but this time was different. "John," the use of my first name was unusual and he had my attention, "you know that there is a lady in Brussels and, well, that I am fond of her?" We all knew that he often took himself off to Brussels, ostensibly to meet with our Flemish masters or to be with Sir Richard when he discussed strategy but more often than not it was during a quiet time and we all knew that he was meeting his lady. As we sometimes went with him, as an escort or to collect supplies, I learned her identity. She was not a young woman, she had seen twenty-four summers, and her name was Mathilde. Over those months that he visited with her, I learned that her father had been a Flemish lord and her mother a Norman lady. He had been killed serving the Emperor and when her mother had died the Lady Mathilde had been left with a house in Brussels and the income from a small village which now lay in France. The Captain had been helping to support her financially.

I hid the smile, "Aye, Captain!"

"I left her too soon and I would return to Brussels to speak with her, about…, it matters not but I would have you come with me. I fear no man but the roads in Flanders have many bandits and brigands. I am aware that I have a responsibility here. I have spoken with Sir Richard and he is content to let me have a sennight to ride to Brussels and settle my affairs. Would you come and be as a squire for me?"

I was flattered and responded without even thinking, "Aye, Captain!" When he had travelled before he had not worried about brigands and I wondered why he had sought permission to take a week off. Then I realised that the other occasions had been times when he had a legitimate reason to be in Brussels so that this would be personal.

The distance was not great but, as the Captain had said, the uncertain nature of the war and the deserters who had left every army meant that the road was not protected as well as it might have been. The journey would take us three days and we would have one day in Brussels before we had to return home. We did not take our bows for that would mark us as archers and we knew that if there was danger on the road then our bows would be of little use. Instead, we took our swords. I now had a spare and my first sword was in a scabbard on Meg's saddle. The sword in my new scabbard was the one I had taken from the French man at arms. Neither did we wear our helmets nor our archer's hats, instead we were hooded. We stayed at inns and the Captain paid. I slept in the stable and I did not mind. When we ate, I carefully studied, everyone that I saw or we met. I could not help my nature which, thanks to my brother and my father, was suspicious. I viewed everyone as a potential enemy until proved otherwise. I saw smiling men who smiled only with their eyes and I saw men look at us from under hooded eyes. They were the dangerous men and I marked them. My fears appeared to be groundless for we reached Brussels without incident and even arrived slightly earlier than we had expected, the journey having only taken two days thanks to sparse traffic on the road and clement weather. This time I had a room and the Captain disappeared to meet with his lady, leaving me to explore the town.

Thus it was that I reunited with Giovanni. It was not totally unexpected for I sought out the bar I had frequented when we had been in Brussels. He was sat in the usual place and greeted me warmly. I discovered that fate had intervened for his master had also returned to meet with his lady.

We spoke in Italian for I was keen to become skilled in other languages; I could already speak a little Flemish. He always addressed me as Giovanni for that was my name in Italian, "It is good that we are met for I have something to tell you. You see, Giovanni, that I fear we may be on opposite sides in this conflict and I wish you to know that if we have to fight then I will give you a swift death."

I was a little taken aback but I smiled and nodded, "And I will try to do the same for you. Why will we have to fight each other?"

He shrugged, "The French pay more than the English and the Flemish do not pay at all! My knight intends to marry this woman and then we will go to Normandy for we have accepted a commission to fight for a Norman lord on the border of Brittany."

"And the pay is worth changing sides?"

"The pay is everything." He leaned forward. "Soon I will have enough money to leave his service and when I do then I shall become a man at arms. I can return to Italy for I upset no one. As much as I enjoy taking English and French coins, I know the lands of Northern Italy better than this land." He smiled, "And both the food and the wine are better."

We ate together and we shared the bill. As we parted I told him that I hoped we would not have to fight against one another for I enjoyed his company and he said the same. We were both mercenaries and as such, we fought whomsoever our paymaster determined. A man did not fight to wound, he fought to kill.

The Captain was in our room when I returned, and he looked happy. "John, I am to be wed. We return tomorrow with Mathilde who has agreed to be my wife. I shall return with her to England to become a gentleman. Since the King raised me the thought has been on my mind that I could leave this itinerant life and, perhaps, even have a family. You are young and when I was your age, I enjoyed this life. I am older now and the wound I had sustained at Portsmouth was a warning that I am no longer able to shrug off such injuries as easily as I once did."

I was both pleased and devastated. I was happy for him, but I was losing not only a friend but the soldier who had helped to make me what I was. I smiled as I had learned to put on the face that men expected of me, "Congratulations, Captain."

"The journey back will be a little slower than the one here, John, for the lady has a maid and some furniture which she wishes to take." He smiled, "She is leaving this life here and the furniture and pots are reminders of her parents."

The carter we hired looked to be a capable man and as he was local, he would know the speediest route. It turned out to be a familiar one for we had travelled it many times when travelling between Dunkerque and Brussels. Captain Philip and Mathilde seemed engrossed in each other's company and that allowed me to study the road as though there was an ambush around the corner. The lady and her maid were seated in the middle of the wagon on what looked like a sack of bedding. It would have been a comfortable ride. The captain rode next to the wagon on the lady's side which meant that I was forced to either speak with the maid or with the carter. The carter did not seem disposed to conversation and so I spoke with Joan, the maid. She was of an age with her mistress, that is to say just a year or so older than me. Some men might have called her comely, but my loins were not stirred despite her obvious attempts to flirt with me. I used it as an opportunity to improve my French as although her mistress was Flemish, she was Norman. The conversation was pleasant enough, but I learned something about women that day, when they try their wiles on a man he should pretend to be engaged. I was too honest, and, on the second day, she gave up and tried the same with the carter with an equal level of failure.

I confess that I became bored on the journey back from Brussels and my vigilance had relaxed when we were on the final stretch. I learned much from Captain Philip who, despite his attention to his lady, still had more of his wits about him than I did! It was when we were a few miles from Poperinge, just forty miles from Dunkerque, that he said, "Carter, stop here for I have a stone in my horse's shoe. John fetch your knife."

My suspicions were aroused for the Captain was a good horseman and had a suitable knife himself. I tied Megs to the wagon and walked around the other side. Using the horse to shield us from both the wagon and the road ahead he picked up his horse's right leg and said, so quietly that I had to lean in to hear him, "There is an ambush ahead."

As much as I wanted to ask him how he knew or where exactly it was, I resisted and asked a more obvious question, "How many men?"

"I think just five. When we stayed in the last town I noticed five unsavoury characters. They left the inn before we did, and I have been watching for a site where they may ambush us. I saw it just ahead and studied it as we rode. There is a small copse up ahead and opposite is a ruined home. There are two who wait in the one near to the ruined home. When I give the command then ride and take them out! I will deal with the other three."

I nodded and headed back to my horse. I saw the carter give me a curious look; he must have known that there was nothing wrong with the horse's hoof. I saw him pick an axe from close to his feet and put it on the seat next to him. The women were looking back down the road and saw nothing. I mounted Megs and surreptitiously slipped my sword in and out of the scabbard; I did not want it sticking. I looked ahead and while trying to appear casual, studied the ambush site. Had not Captain Philip spotted it then I would not have seen it but knowing that there were men there made me look for clues. I saw that there were no birds yet a flock of them pecked at the harvested wheat field which lay closer to us. In the copse I saw what looked like shadows, but they could have been men and then I caught the glint of light on a weapon close to the ruined hut. Later, I would ask Captain Philip what had prompted his interest but for now, we had five men to fight! It was a tall order for two of us to take on five men, but we were still warriors. These were, at best, former warriors. Most importantly we knew they were there and that might give us the edge as we would initiate our own attack and they would not be prepared for that eventuality.

    I had my heels ready to kick into Megs' ribs. We were just sixty paces from the ambush site and the two men hiding there were more obvious although they still thought they were hidden and unseen; one had a horse and I saw its tail switch. I wondered if Captain Philip had left it too late when he suddenly shouted, "Ambush! Now!" The first part was for the carter who raised his whip to make his team move.

    I kicked hard and drew my sword, leaning over the neck of Megs to make a smaller target in case they had bows or crossbows. It was the latter and a bolt whipped over my head as I ducked. A horse can cover many paces and the crossbowman had to drop his now-useless weapon and draw a sword. I saw the two of them as they left their place of concealment to try to get me and hit me with clear strikes. The crossbowman was behind his fellow and, having dropped his crossbow, he was trying to draw a short sword. The other had an axe and ran at my right side. As he was ahead of the crossbowman, he would be my prime target. I had never fought from the back of a horse, but I had fought horsemen. I made a move to my right and the road and as the axeman made a slight adjustment in his feet to counter the move and to begin his swing I jinked Megs to the left, jerking her head hard with the reins. I leaned out as the axe swung to where

Megs' head would have been had I not moved, and I slashed at his head. I connected with his cheek and his nose. The sword was not only sharp and well-made it was also heavy, and bones were broken. I continued my turn and the luckless crossbowman was just turning to come to his friend's assistance when Megs' foreleg smashed into his knee. He fell screaming and writhing to the ground. I then heard the sound of steel on steel. Captain Philip was fighting two men while a third lay trying to hold in his guts. The wagon was a hundred paces down the road and the ladies were safe. One of the bandits was holding on to the Captain's horse's reins and trying to skewer the Captain on his left side. The Captain was using his leather gauntlet to hold him off. He was my target and I did not hesitate as I galloped across the road and swung my sword at the middle of his back. He was wearing a leather brigandine but that made little difference as my sword broke his back and the blade tore into his flesh. His feral scream made his fellow turn and that was all that Captain Philip needed. He split his skull in two.

I saw that the Captain's hand was cut, and I said, "I will tend to that!"

Shaking his head, he said, "No! Get the horse and take their weapons if they are of any value and if not then bend them. Any coins are yours for I owe you my life. I would have us leave here as soon as we can. If there are five such bandits who knows if there are more?"

I nodded, "There is one, perhaps two, left alive."

"If they can walk then kill them. If not let them die. That is all that their kind deserves."

I nodded and he rode off down the road to catch up with the wagon. Two of the swords I found were of poor quality and that was confirmed when I bent them easily. The third was not as good as mine but would fetch a coin or two and I took it. I took their daggers. They were always saleable. Their purses yielded ten florins; it was more than I expected. With a drawn sword I walked across the road to the other two. The man whose face I had slashed had managed to stagger towards the horse and then died as he bled out. The other was trying to crawl away trailing his leg behind him. He was no threat.

"Take me to a healer!" He was English!

I ignored him and picked up the crossbow. I smashed it so hard that the infernal machine disintegrated. I took the axe and hung it from the horse and, after lifting his purse and dagger, walked over to the lamed man. I picked up his sword and saw that it was both notched and bent already. I put it between two stones in the ruined hut and broke it. I threw the man on his back and he screamed. "Have you no mercy?"

"For the likes of you, no!" I searched him and took his purse to add to the others. I turned my back on him and walked to Megs. As I left leading the bandits' horse, I heard him sobbing. Men made choices in their lives. I had made one when I left my home and sought a new life. You lived by your decisions and with the results! He would not die but if he did not find a healer soon then he would be a cripple for the rest of his life. One thing was sure; he would ambush no other travellers.

I caught up with the wagon in Poperinge. The two ladies were shocked and shaken but the carter was grinning, "I will stand you an ale, young archer, for that was as neat a piece of riding and swordplay as I have seen in many a year." For some reason that made me feel inordinately proud.

When we were in the inn in Poperinge Captain Philip sought out the captain of the watch and told him what had happened. The shamefaced look told us all that we needed to know. They knew of the bandits and all of the village were complicit. When we did not have to pay for our food, ale and accommodation I knew that we had done them a favour and it was another lesson learned.

The Captain's hand was hurt and, after it had been tended to and the ladies retired, he turned to me as we finished off the jug of ale, "I will retire to England, John. I have grown old doing this and with the money I have accrued and my new wife I would like to enjoy life as a gentleman. This wound will heal but when I hold the bow, I will always fear that it will weaken and that is not good for an archer."

"Where will you go?"

"There is a farm I bought some years ago. My cousin was lord of the manor, but he died long since in the Holy Land. His steward takes care of it for me and now I can return it to its former glory. The farm is in the Palatinate and is in the manor of

Hartburn which is not far from Norton. I thought to give myself the chance to farm! He patted his leg, "My leg aches and I fear that I would not give a good account of myself if we had to fight again."

I nodded but I could not hide my feelings, "I shall miss you, Captain, for you have been my rock and I know how much you have done for me."

"Fear not, before I leave for England I shall tell Sir Richard what I wish. You know how to lead and until a new captain is appointed you should lead the archers here and be paid accordingly."

The Captain was generous. I kept the horse, the saddle, the weapons and the purses from the bandits. I sold the weapons and kept the horse with Megs. It was not a riding horse but would make a good sumpter to carry arrows for the company. He and his bride to be left a few days later and Sir Richard showed that he was a gentleman by placing me in command of the seventy archers who remained from the original force sent to help the Flemish. The appointment was not universally accepted. There were two other vintenars in the company: Ned and Ralf. Ned the Wanderer was an older man, he had seen almost thirty-five summers and he was also close to Captain Philip. He accepted my command readily but Ralf who was but a year or two older than I was, did not and he challenged my authority immediately. The man was a fool for he did so while Sir Richard was still present and even as Ralf asked what right I had to command Sir Richard turned on him.

"Every right, Ralf of Rotherham, for it is at the request of the best archer I have ever known, Philip of Lincoln and I concur wholeheartedly with it. You have, by this challenge to my authority, lost your post as vintenar. I am the King's representative and any further questioning of my authority will result in your dismissal!"

That ended any open hostility, but I knew that this was not over, and I would have to sleep with a dagger in my hand. However, my first task was to appoint a vintenar to replace Ralf and that was easy. Jack of Crewe was not only a good archer but a friend. He had not replaced Robert and the others, but he came the closest and we got on. I know that it fuelled further resentment from Ralf as he saw it as a sort of nepotism. I cared not for it was the right choice and he proved to be an able vintenar. Indeed, he became a great Captain of Archers, but that story had yet to be written then.

I knew that Ralf had not forgotten the slight even though more than a month went by and he had yet to show his teeth. He was in Ned's company and obeyed all orders. In truth, Ralf had little opportunity for mischief as we were kept busy patrolling the road between Dunkerque and Poperinge. The attack on the Captain had made the Constable of Dunkerque realise that order had to be kept and he used the archers to do so. It was neither practical nor wise to use all of our archers and so the three of us, Ned, Jack and I took a third of the archers in rotation. My promotion had also brought me accommodation in the castle of Dunkerque and so I was safe from a knife in the night. I frequently dined with the Constable and Sir Richard.

Ralph Earl of Stafford arrived in the early spring. He brought news and my elevation meant that I was privy to his meeting with his captains. "The King has decided on a three-pronged attack on the French. Lord Henry Plantagenet will take a small force to Gascony of which I shall be a part. The Earl of Northampton will land a force in Brittany and the King himself will come here. Lord Henry will sail in May, the Earl of Northampton a month later and the King a month after that."

I had grown in confidence and spoke. A few years earlier I would have sat like a mouse and hoped not to be noticed. Perhaps Sir Richard's defence of me and the support I had received from Captain Philip had emboldened me. "So, my lord, the King hopes that, when we land in Gascony, France's eyes will be drawn south and, hopefully, his knights too."

Sir Ralph looked at me, "A sound sense of strategy from an archer. Aye, Master Hawkwood, that may well be the case, but we still have to make a nuisance of ourselves and achieve some sort of success. To that end Sir Richard and you will bring your companies with me at the end of the month and we will be the vanguard. I have orders for the lords of Gascony so that they may prepare. Constable, the men whom King Edward will use are already gathering in England. You will not be without English support for long." He leaned forward. "This is for your ears! Do not tell your men until they are lining up at the quay to embark. We do not wish the French to know of our departure!"

I confess that I was still young enough to be excited at the prospect of seeing somewhere new and while I could not tell my men that they were heading south I could, at least, encourage them to prepare for war. I did this through Ned and Jack, "I have the men's pay from Sir Richard and that means that there will be some action soon. When they are not riding forth on patrol, we can relax our rules and allow them some time in Dunkerque town. It will not hurt."

Ned nodded, "Ralf is still a problem, Captain John." Ned and a few others called me captain. I had not been appointed as such and so when men called me vintenar, I did not take it as an insult.

"He obeys orders?"

"Aye, but with ill grace."

"Then perhaps this potential action is a good thing for it is hard to hold a grudge when you are nocking and releasing as fast as you can."

"Perhaps but I would still watch your back." He smiled, "The other men all like you and call themselves Hawkwood's men." That was an honour for even Captain Philip had not been accorded that honour by the men he led.

Knowing that we would be heading south I made preparations myself. I went into Dunkerque to find a cordwainer. My time in London had not been wasted and I knew exactly what to ask for. I had more than enough coins to be profligate and I ordered two pairs of buskins. I did not waste my money on doxies and gambling and thanks to the attack at Poperinge I had more than enough money. I ordered them and was pleased to hear that they would be ready the day before we sailed. As luck would have it, that day I was on the Poperinge patrol and when we entered the castle, I handed Meg's reins to Will the Fletcher, one of my most trusted archers. I gave him a penny, "See to Megs, Will, for I have business in the town."

He gave me a lascivious leer, "Is it Betty Big Breasts?"

I laughed, "No for I waste no money there. You should know that I have ordered boots!"

He laughed, "Aye, Captain, boots!"

I slung my sword on the saddle and strode into Dunkerque. I was well known now. I had learned in London that a smile and a friendly welcome always bought you friends. Some would be out to get what they could from you but not all of them and I had learned to read men's faces. Folk smiled and nodded as I passed through the streets. The boots were fitted, and they were comfortable. By the time I left, having paid for them, it was getting on to dark. There was an alley we all took to get to the castle, and it was as I entered the dark place that Ralf of Rotherham stepped out and he held a bodkin dagger in his hand.

"Thought I had forgotten, eh, Hawkwood? I was just biding my time and as soon as I heard you would be out alone; I knew this was my opportunity."

Ralf was as strong as I was, and my rondel dagger was in my belt while my hands held my boots. I played for time as I worked out how to extricate myself from this predicament. "Do not be a fool, Ralf! Put the blade away and I will forget this." Ralf was just four feet from me. I calculated that I could drop the boots and distract him. That would allow me to grab my dagger. I would have to fend off the strike from his bodkin. I knew that he would ignore my words for I saw murder in his eyes.

"You might forget but I will not. You shall die!"

"And you will be hunted down and hanged for others know where I went and when you are gone they will search for you! This is not England and you cannot escape justice."

He laughed, "No one will find your body until the morrow and I will be long gone. There are lords who will value the service of such a fine archer!"

He was halfway through his words when I dropped the boots and reached around for my dagger. I held out my left hand, now wrapped in the cap I had taken from my head. He was also quick, every archer was, and he lunged at me. A bodkin dagger is a perfect weapon to sink into flesh, but it had no edge and the woollen hat deflected the blow. My rondel blade, however, was the one I used to shave my head and chin and I slashed across his middle. He also used his left hand, but it was unprotected, and the blade slashed across the back of it, grating off the bone.

"There is still time, Ralf, put down the blade!"

In answer, he lunged again but instead of using my left hand, I used my own dagger and sparks flew as the two blades rang together. We were close enough to the castle for it to be heard and a voice, one of the sentries, called out in the dark, "What ho?"

"They will come, Ralf!"

"And you will be dead." This time he lunged at my eye. It was the perfect place for a bodkin to strike. It was how we ended the lives of men at arms we fought. They might be armoured but a bodkin dagger in the eye would end a life almost instantly! I punched at his hand as the blade came at me and it slid over my shoulder. His movement meant that he ran into my blade which sliced into his left side. I heard cries coming from the castle and then the sound of feet.

Ralf heard them too and he suddenly punched at me with his wounded left hand and caught me unawares. I staggered back and he ran off into the dark. The Sergeant at arms and the sentry had torches and when they saw my face and the blood which covered it, they both thought the worse.

"Vintenar! You are hurt?"

I shook my head, "It is not my blood but that of Ralf the archer. He tried to murder me and fled."

"We will send men to look for him. Let us get you within the castle."

The delay meant that Ralf escaped. He had planned it all well for his gardyvyan and bows were gone. What he had not been able to take were his horse and saddle. It meant we had another horse to take to Bordeaux. I knew that I had been lucky. As with the attack on the wagon I had allowed my vigilance to drop and it had almost been my undoing. From that moment on I was always vigilant! The attack was viewed with anger by the other archers. Ralf had never been popular, but his resentment had driven away even those who had been his tentmates before. We put that behind us as we boarded the ships to sail to Gascony.

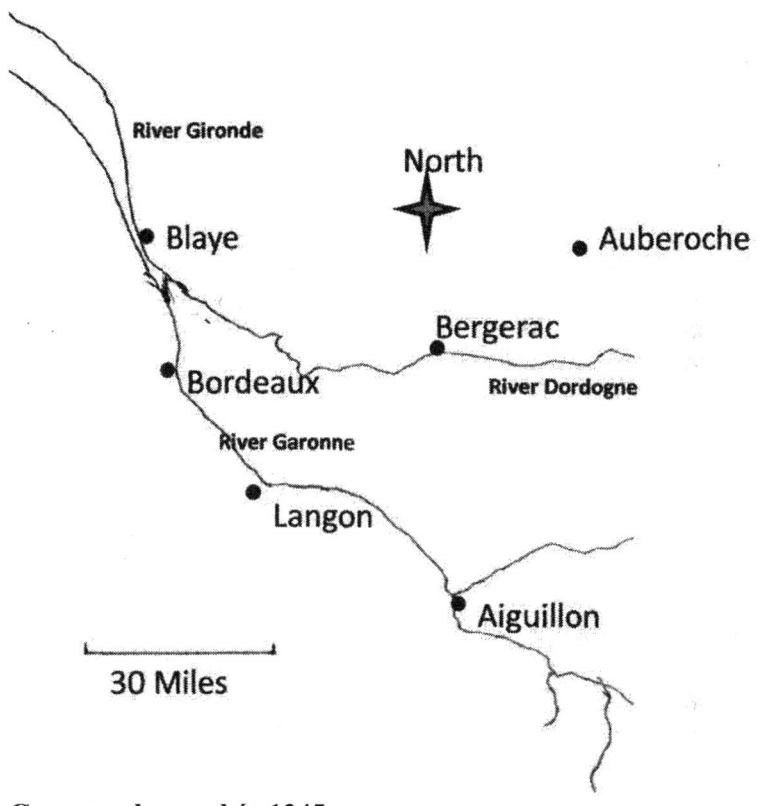

Gascony chevauchée 1345
Author's Map

Chapter 7

We sailed down to Bordeaux across a dark and threatening sea with black clouds as permanent company; it was a rough voyage, but I had learned to cope with the sea. I had my archers spend time with their horses as they were more affected than we were. When we arrived neither man nor beast was fit for anything and the Earl of Stafford ordered that we just rest. Indeed, there was no need for us to do much else as we were the ones who warned the lords of Gascony that they were going to war soon and they had to make preparations. Megs had not suffered as much as some of the other horses and the Earl took me with four other men as an escort and we scouted out places where Lord Henry Plantagenet could attack when he arrived. We rode with a local lord, Count Guillaume de le Porge and some of his men. I was the only archer, but the count took men who were lightly armoured and, like me, could move quickly. I was close enough to hear the words of the Earl and the Count as they rode. My French had improved dramatically, and I understood every word. The count was contemptuous of the local French lords and it oozed from his words.

"There is no border here, my lord, Gascon and Frenchmen are neighbours, and some owe allegiance to King Edward and King Philip. It is a chaotic situation for who is the lord of the land? I serve King Edward and my family always have."

We had crossed the Gironde and were heading along the north bank of the Dordogne towards Montravel, a castle whose lord was French and had allegiance to King Philip. As it was just under forty miles from Bordeaux it was a good place to start our campaign.

"Perhaps, Count, your judgement is coloured by the fact that your lands are to the west of Bordeaux and far from French influence. If I was a lord who held lands in two countries, then I might be more pragmatic. When King Edward has reconquered the land that King John lost then the chaos may disappear." He reined in. "Is that the castle of Montravel ahead?"

The Count said, "Yes my lord."

Sir Ralph turned to me, "Archer, string your bow and you and I will ride forth to scout out this castle. Two men may not alarm the garrison, but your bow will be security against a sudden attack."

"Aye, my lord." I dismounted to string my bow.

I saw the Gascons looking at me with interest for the longbow was an English weapon and not a Gascon one.

"Is this wise, Sir Ralph?" The Gascon lord did not wish to lose a senior English knight before the campaign had begun!

"If we ride close with all of these men then they will know that there is an army coming and will summon support. Two of us have more chance of escaping observation." I had strung my bow and remounted. I held the bow and an arrow in my left hand, and I nodded to Sir Ralph. He dug his spurs in the flanks of his courser and I followed. Megs was no courser, but she was game, and she kept up with his mount.

The wooden castle had been built upon a high piece of ground just above the small village and the river. The Dordogne protected one side of the castle which was a larger version of the castles which were dotted around England. As we neared the castle Sir Ralph slowed and stopped and then he stood in his stirrups to gain a better view. We were two hundred paces from the village and three hundred or so from the wooden walls. I spied the ditch and the two towers over the gatehouse. There was a keep and I saw movement there which told me that they kept a watch. I dismounted for the movement suggested that they had seen us. Two men might not alarm them but the prospect of capturing a knight and holding him for ransom might rouse their interest. Sir Ralph's spurs and fine horse marked him as a knight. He glanced down as I dismounted and nocked an arrow, but he said nothing.

Perhaps Sir Ralph was looking for things I had not seen for he kept studying the walls and the castle for so long that five riders left the castle and galloped towards us. He looked down, "Show them your skill archer and then we shall leave!"

I had nocked a bodkin and I saw that the man at arms who led them was mailed. I drew back and sent the arrow at him as he and his four companions passed through the village. Even as my arrow hit him in the chest and threw him from his saddle, I drew a war arrow and sent it into the shoulder of the warrior wearing a leather brigandine. I did not look to see if the other three had either slowed or stopped, Sir Ralph and I could deal with three warriors and I mounted Megs whilst still holding on to the bow. My demonstration had the desired effect and the three survivors decided to tend to the other two men. The mailed man at arms would be dead. Even if the arrow had not killed him instantly the fall and the wound would have made him bleed out. The other would survive.

Sir Ralph smiled as we headed back to the others. He nodded at me, "You are a cool one, Hawkwood is it not?" I nodded. "I can see that you and your fellows will be useful, but it is a pity that there are so few of you, Lord Henry has more than a thousand with him but they are still in Southampton."

"When do they leave, my lord?"

"May and they should be here by June, but you saw the weather we endured. Their departure could be delayed by as much as two or three months. We cannot afford to sit idly by. I will raise the local lords. With your archers and the men we brought we can make mischief here. If we can draw the French from Normandy and Picardy, then King Edward will have a much better chance of success. Paris is the jewel the King desires. If we have that then Gascony will be safe and both Normandy and Brittany will fall!"

When we reached Bordeaux, Gascon lords were summoned, and the levy was mustered. Unlike in England where there was often resentment, here the Gascons could not wait to go into battle against those that they thought had tried to steal their land. I organised my archers for I knew that we would be the deciding factor. They were my company now and although there were just forty of them they had already begun to call me Captain. We called ourselves Hawkwood for that meant I could order them all to obey my words in the heat of battle. I also told them the way that we would fight. They were my men and would reflect that. I managed to procure four more sumpters so that we had six horses to carry spare arrows. I also made sure that every archer carried a spare bundle of one hundred arrows on his horse. My short time with Sir Ralph had shown me that speed was vital in this war and we could not afford to wait for a wagon. There would be a wagon which accompanied the army but that would carry our spare bow staves and even more arrows as well as food. We could wait for those. All of our archers were experienced and so I approached the Earl and asked to hire men to hold our horses.

"We have few enough archers as it is, Lord Ralph, and if one in four holds horses then we will be a fifth of our men down before we draw an arrow!"

I liked the Earl of Stafford for he was decisive, and he paid for fifteen men to be horse holders and to act as servants and cooks while we were on campaign. The Gascons were more than happy to supply the men for we would be, hopefully, making their lives and their land safer. A small ship arrived at the beginning of June with bad news. Storms further north had driven Lord Henry's fleet of one hundred and fifty ships to take shelter in Falmouth. He would not now reach us in June and so we set off without him. We left Bordeaux with two thousand men at arms and five thousand infantry. Some of the Gascons had bows and others crossbows but their numbers were so small, and their effect would be so limited, that it was my archers who would be the best defence against the enemy. It was as we headed for Montravel that we begin a system which was new to all of us but became normal as years went on. Sir Richard and I formed one company, a vanguard of mounted archers and men at arms, and we were the potent strike force at the head of the column. Sir Ralph gave us the freedom to act as we saw fit. Our orders were the same ones which King Edward had given to Lord Henry, *"si guerre soit, et a faire le bien q'il poet"* (... if there is war, do the best you can ...). It showed the trust which existed amongst our leaders and it contrasted with the lack of trust and confusion on the other side.

As I had scouted with the Earl it was I who led and, as we neared the castle of Montravel I saw that our first encounter with them had not increased their vigilance. In fact, as we rode towards the village, I saw that the gates of the castle were still open. Sir Richard was next to me and I said, "We can take this castle without losing a man! I will ride and take the gates!"

There was mutual respect between us and he said, "Go!"

Drawing my sword, I shouted, "Archers! Ride!" I was in the lead and I knew what I intended so that I had a four-horse length lead before Ned could react. I would not have made the gates in time had not the villagers heard the hooves thundering and ran, screaming and shouting towards the open gates. The sentries tried, in vain, to close them but the press of people was too great. I could hear French voices ordering people away from the gates, but they feared us. If this was a chevauchée and we could achieve this effect again then we might bring hell with us! Megs was at full speed as we approached the people and I shouted, in French, "Get out of the way or you will be ridden down!"

The ones at the rear saw the great beast that was Megs and the shining sword held by the giant and those in the centre pushed to the side. People fell into the ditch and the press on the door diminished but by then Ned and Jack had caught up with me and it was not a solitary horseman who tried to push his way in but six archers. I had learned to make Megs rear. When I had first mounted a horse that had been an impossible dream, but I had improved, and her flailing hooves caught the gates just as they were about to close. Indeed, I think one of her hooves mashed a man's hand to a pulp and the wooden gates flew open. As Megs galloped through, I slashed down and split open the head of one sentry and Ned drove his sword into the throat of a second. We did not stop but rode towards the inner wall and the gate there. This time it was not civilians who were running for the safety of the keep and the inner bailey but the garrison. They had been racing to man the walls of the outer bailey and had now reversed their journey. Even though we were going uphill our horses were faster than the men on the walls and as they descended the ladders to make for the gates my archers spread out to charge them down. The French arms came up in surrender for Sir Richard and his men at arms were now flooding through the gates of the castle. Ned, Jack and I galloped through the second gate, trampling men as we did so. This time the gates were not defended and the men inside the inner bailey made the keep.

I reined in Megs as I saw crossbows peep over the top of the keep. I wheeled her around as a handful of bolts struck the ground where we had just stood. The infernal machines needed to be reloaded and I dismounted and grabbed my bow stave. I smacked Megs on the rump to make her go into the outer bailey and strung my bow. It says much about the difference between the two weapons that I managed to dismount, string my bow and nock an arrow before the crossbows had been reloaded. Ned and Edward were equally fast and as the crossbows appeared over the wooden parapet, three arrows were sent in their direction. I know not if we killed, wounded or just frightened them but only two bolts came our way and they were sent so hurriedly that they missed.

My archers had dismounted in the outer bailey and were flooding in, I shouted, "Hawkwood, two lines." The three of us were ready with our bows as the others strung and then nocked an arrow. When I saw crossbows begin to appear, I shouted, "Release."

Sixty arrows fell. The crossbowmen had to show themselves to use their weapons and that was their downfall. When the screams and shouts had subsided a French voice shouted, "We surrender! Cease! We give in!"

"Then open the gate to the keep and come out showing us your hands!"

Every one of my archers had an arrow nocked and as the eight men left the keep, I knew that there would be no attempt at treachery. We had taken our first castle without losing a man!

Sir Ralph was delighted and the only disappointing part of it all was that one rider had been sent to Monbreton, the castle which was just three miles away. We could not repeat my trick and we might have to fight to take that castle. My initiative was rewarded in a number of ways. I was invited to dine with the earl and the count, and I was richly rewarded. There was treasure in the keep and I was given a share. I ensured that my archers received some of the coins I was given but I knew that I would need to find some way to keep my increasing fortune safe!

"Monbreton will be harder to take as there is a ford across the river and they will defend it." Sir Ralph looked at me, "Can your horses swim the river upstream from the ford and out of sight of the castle?"

"Some can swim, my lord, but not all."

He looked at Sir Richard, "And your men?"

"Some can."

"Then, Hawkwood, you will lead the archers and the men at arms who can do so and swim the river. I want you to appear at their rear and distract them. Make them think there are more of you than there actually are. We will let you attack first, and we will begin our attack when we hear you."

"Then if we leave when it is dark, we can be in position by dawn." I gave the suggestion and not Sir Richard. My mind was always several steps ahead and when Sir Ralph had given me the problem then I was coming up with the solution.

The Count asked, "Is that not dangerous, swimming a river in the dark?"

"If we do it in daylight, my lord, then there may be men who see us, and we need to be invisible until we attack. Besides, my horse is a good swimmer and I can cross first with a rope to help any who fall into the water. If we tried that in daylight, then we would be seen."

This time I would be the one commanding not only archers but also men at arms. The swimmers all managed to nap for an hour or so before we took ropes from the castle and village and headed south towards the castle. The river helped us to find the castle and prevented us from getting lost. I did not rush into this. I rode Megs along the bank until I saw somewhere which was suitable for us to cross. The river appeared to be narrow and relatively shallow but, more importantly, there were a couple of trees we could use to secure the rope we would use. Tying one end of the rope to a tree I headed into the dark waters. We had had to tie a number of ropes together and that was the only weakness in my plan. If the knots gave way, then we would be in trouble. The current was strong and so I swam Megs upstream knowing that we would be driven downstream a little. We had just crossed halfway when Megs' legs found purchase on the bottom. It felt like rock beneath her hooves. Once I reached the other bank I stopped and listened. There were no noises which alarmed me, and I rode downstream until I found a suitable tree and I tied off the rope. I headed back upstream and reached the place I had left the water. Ned was waiting for my signal and he sent the others across. We were lucky. Only three men fell from their horses. The horses swam ashore and the riders were swept down to the safety rope. They hauled themselves ashore. When this was all over the three knew that they would be the butt of jokes. We did not ride our horses but walked them until we found ourselves within three hundred paces of the castle. We led our horses into the woods there and then returned to secrete ourselves just two hundred paces from the wooden wall.

This castle was sturdier than the one we had first taken, and the inner wall was, even in the dark, clearly made of stone. To me, it looked to be reused Roman stones which had been taken to build the stone keep and to modify the old Roman fort. I spread out the men at arms amongst my archers. We needed the enemy to think that they were being attacked by a force which was twice as big as it was. When I was satisfied with their positions then I headed to get closer to the wall. There were no sentries on this side of the wall or, if there were, then they were sleeping! I spied a sally port in the stone wall, and I risked, as there was no one on the wall, getting closer to it. The ditch had been recently dug but I lowered myself gently into it and saw that there were no obstacles in the bottom. It looked to rely upon a steep leading edge which would make it difficult to escape. When I climbed up the other side, I saw that the stonework around the sally port door was very poor and that they had filled in a much larger door, a Roman one. I put my fingers in the cracks between the newly and badly laid stones and found that I could pull out the mortar. An idea formed in my mind. I went back to the ditch, it was harder to get out, but I was strong, and I pulled myself up. Had there been men hurling stones and darts at me then I might have struggled. While I walked back, I realised that there was cover within one hundred and forty paces of the wall. As they had no sentries on this side then we could move closer. The closer we were the more effective would be our arrows and the more Frenchmen would die!

When I reached my men, I called over the Sergeant at Arms in charge of the men at arms. "Jamie, have you men with axes?"

"Aye Captain, why?"

"There is a sally port in the wall, and it has been made with poorly mortared stones. I believe that if your men were to use the flat side of their axes, they could break through. I would have you send them over the ditch while it is dark and wait close to the wall. Once they are at the gate and dawn breaks then my archers will keep them safe."

He nodded and I knew why he looked pleased. He and his men were keen to show us that they were our equals. Sir Ralph expected us to keep the French occupied. This way we might be the ones to break in! I spoke to the men on either side of me. "We will move forward, closer to the ditch. Tell the men to watch for my signals." I started to move as soon as I heard the whisper travel down my two sides, and I walked to the edge of the undergrowth. The natural defence was not made of trees, the barrier before us was a natural untidy growth of brambles and other shrubs which had spread over the years since the ditch had been dug. The garrison should have cleared them to allow them a greater area that they could control with their crossbows. When we reached it, I strung my bow and selected two arrows, one a bodkin and the other a war arrow. My choice would be determined by the target I selected. Then we waited. The first cock crowed and a short while later the second. I smelled the smoke from fires being lit for food and then heard the noises of men being roused; the castle was awaking. I saw that the five men at arms had reached the gate and were pressed against the wall. They would feel exposed, but they were invisible A sentry would have to lean over the wall to see them and in doing so would expose themselves to the finest archers in Europe.

The first sentries arrived on the wall as the first thin light appeared in the eastern sky. I heard the two of them talking and even made out a few of their words. They were not being careful for apart from a cursory glance towards the woods they continued their conversation. As the light improved a mailed warrior stood and I saw the light glinting from his coif. He barked something and the two sentries who had first emerged separated and another four men appeared. While the mailed men walked the wall, the new sentries spread themselves out but as soon as he disappeared, presumably to check on the other walls, they split into groups and I saw a wineskin being passed between two of them. I did not give an order, I merely nocked a war arrow. I knew the rest would do as I had done. I pulled back on the bow and the yew groaned. When the others did so one of the sentries, more alert than the rest, turned to stare into the woods. He, perhaps, was the only one who saw his death as it approached for I released and with a noise like a small flock of birds taking to the air our arrows soared towards the wall. Then the men at arms standing with us began to shout and beat their shields to distract the enemy from looking down and the axemen began to smash the stones around the door.

A horn sounded. We had no targets for all the sentries had been struck, some by five arrows and as yet had not been replaced! I switched to a bodkin and when the mailed man appeared with another three mailed men and four others, I led him with my bow, as he raced along the wall. He stood above the sally port and did as I had expected, he leaned over. My arrow pinned his head to the wall. The others all raised shields and I waited for the crossbows to release. They did not use the fighting platform but the arrow slits in the walls. The foliage and poor light meant that none of us was hurt and I saw daylight appear in the sally port.

"Sergeant Theakston, take your men and enter the sally port. The time is ripe!"

As the men at arms ran the crossbows switched target but the men at arms had shields and were protected. They were able to reach the wall unharmed.

I shouted, "Archers, when the gate is open, we join the men at arms!"

By now I could hear the sounds of battle on the river side of the castle. Sir Ralph had begun his attack. I watched as the first stones fell from around the doorway and then the rest of the men at arms clambered up the side of the ditch. Sergeant Theakston hurled his body at the gate, and it fell inwards. He and the others were showered with small stones, but they were inside. I slung my bow and shouted, "On!"

I knew the way and having done the journey in the dark it was far easier in the daylight. When I climbed up to the sally port, I saw that the men at arms had all joined the attack. Sergeant Jamie was having his head tended by one of his men and he gave me a rueful shrug as, with sword drawn, I entered the castle. I heard the sound of axes on the main gate and already men at arms were running to allow the rest of our men to enter. I led my men to the keep. Our attacks had sent most of the men to the walls and the keep door was invitingly open. I ran towards it and hoped that I had men following me. When I entered, I heard the sound of the horn from the top floor. I guessed it was the order to fall back to the keep but it was too late for the foxes were in the henhouse. It looked like the ground floor was being used as a dining hall. There was a table and chairs with the remains of what looked like breakfast. I ran up the wooden ladder to the first floor which I saw was a sort of guardroom but there were no warriors within. The floor above were the sleeping quarters of the lords and senior warriors. It too was empty.

It was as I climbed the last ladder that I heard a voice shout, "And make sure you have barred the door!"

As we burst into the light and the top of the fighting platform the French knight and ten men at arms and crossbowmen who were there had the most unpleasant of surprises. I dropped my sword and unslung my bow, drawing an arrow and nocking it before the French could react. One sergeant at arms was the first to react and he took two steps towards me. At a range of four paces not only was there no way I could miss, but the arrow also drove so deeply through his body that the fletch was all that I could see. I nocked another as my men emulated me. The knight and his men might have fought twice our numbers had we been knights or men at arms, but fifteen English archers were another matter! They surrendered and we had a second castle.

Chapter 8

Sir Ralph was ecstatic as not only had we had taken two castles we now controlled both the Dordogne and the Gironde; all had been achieved with minimal losses. Once more we all benefitted from the victory and the knights we had taken in both attacks would bring us great ransom. Both castles had a great store of weapons and armour, it was resolute men that they were lacking. Leaving garrisons of Gascons in both castles we headed north to the substantial castle of Blaye-et-Sainte-Luce which lay forty miles north-west of us on the Gironde. This was a major castle which stood on the river and could control shipping sailing to and from Bordeaux. It would require a siege, but our two victories had made the Earl confident that we could do anything. As we rode north, I discovered the town was important mainly because of its wine and the fact that it was downstream from Bordeaux meant that it could ship its wines easily and be reinforced. I learned much from Sir Ralph as he knew that by besieging the town, we would force the French king to act. He never lost sight of our prime objective. He was to draw the French on to us so that King Edward could raid northern France.

The town had a stone wall and a stone castle. We would not be able to enter the gate as it had a drawbridge on one side and the river on the other. While the archers kept the walls clear of defenders, ditches and ramparts were dug to surround the castle while men took the town and drove the inhabitants east. During the time we dug and built, we ate and drank well for the people had not had time to take everything from their homes. We slept in fine beds and the castle was starved of supplies. They had a well and the river, but their siege supplies would only last for three months or so. After a week we were all surprised when the Earl took five thousand of us, mainly the English with some Gascons and we retraced our steps south. There were still enough men for a good siege to be maintained but the bulk of our army was heading south of Bordeaux. Sir Ralph could use a relatively small number of Gascons to keep the French trapped and the town isolated. Sir Ralph was a bold knight and with a handful of men, he hoped to give Lord Henry complete control of the land around Bordeaux by the time he eventually arrived. What surprised me was that the French had not reacted for there was no news of an army coming to shift us. It came to me that they had known of the strategy and that meant a spy in the court of King Edward. That was not a surprise and I learned another lesson. Keep plans as secret as possible and trust no one!

Two days later we left and headed south. We rode another forty miles to Langon which lay south of Bordeaux. Once more the speed of Sir Ralph and his mounted column caught the French unawares. Word had spread that we were at Blaye-et-Sainte-Luce and the last thing they would have expected was to be attacked at Langon. When we reached the castle, my heart fell for it was not only a stone castle with a curtain wall, huge keep and towers at each side, but it also had a moat. It had been built in 1306 by Cardinal de la Mothe, the nephew of Pope Clement V. King Edward had permitted its erection and now we would have to take it. Once more we dug defences and, once again, cleared the town so that we could eat and drink well. This was a siege which needed no men to assault the walls; we could just starve them out. With the limited number of men at his disposal, Sir Ralph had done the best he could. We had taken two castles and trapped two garrisons. The French had also reacted and were besieging Gascon and English castles; Casseneuil in the Agenais; Monchamp near Condom; and Montcuq. Of these Montcuq was the strongest and lay south of Bergerac. Strategically it was of little importance, but the French had sent their largest army in Gascony under the command of Bertrand de l'isle

Jourdain from the most important town of Bergerac, to take it.

We waited at the siege works during a hot July. Each day Sir Ralph would walk around the siege works to speak with the men there and sometimes I accompanied him. "I am new to this type of war, my lord, do we really need to besiege these two towns? This one," I pointed to the tall towers, "looks to me to be a veritable fortress!"

He smiled, "The two fortresses are important for they are both close to Bordeaux. When the French come, they will need to use the two of them to launch an attack on Bordeaux and first they have to dislodge us. If they were here now then we would be in trouble but they are not. Lord Henry, the Earl of Derby, will be here soon and then we can use our mounted men to make a proper war."

I frowned, titles confused me, "The Earl of Derby, lord?"

"He has now inherited that title and when his father dies, for I hear he is ill, then he will become the Earl of Lancaster and his rank will be just below that of the King. You have fought alongside him and know of his skill."

I nodded, "Aye, my lord, in Scotland and the Low Countries. He is a good leader as are you." I was not flattering the Earl and he knew it.

"I will take that compliment from a warrior such as you, John Hawkwood. There are some men at arms and knights from whom such words would make me suspicious. As we are being honest with one another then I should tell you that you, too, are highly thought of. Captain Philip, before he left, made a strong case for you to become Captain. From what I have seen you are unique for not only can you use a bow and lead, but you can also use a sword and use it well. It would not take much to make you into a man at arms and then, who knows, a knight."

I laughed, in a self-conscious sort of way, "I am not sure that I need a title but I will give your words thought for if I am to continue to be a warrior then I have to think of the future."

The Earl of Derby finally arrived at the end of the first week of August and we left Gascon warriors to prosecute the siege of Langon. I was a little disappointed in the quality and the numbers of men that King Edward had sent. Including the men I led he had just five hundred mounted archers and a thousand foot archers. He had also brought with him five hundred men at arms but many of them were convicted felons who had been promised a pardon in return for their participation in the campaign. Lord Henry did not seem unhappy and we spent a few days to allow the men and horses to recover from the long and rough crossing of the seas. One of the men at arms who came was Ralph of Malton and now that we were of equal rank, I was able to talk to him better. I took him to a decent inn in Bordeaux and over a bottle of wine, he explained the facts of life to me.

"When we are assembled, John, we will just be a distraction and, as such, expendable. I think King Edward hopes we would make a nuisance of ourselves and make mischief here to draw greater armies from the north and to allow King Edward to take Paris. It does not really matter what we do here for our sole purpose is to draw the French here. The convicted felons were cheaper than hiring men at arms such as me. Do not worry about them for many are veterans of the Scottish and Welsh wars. They may be rough and inclined to wild behaviour, but they know how to fight." I nodded; it made sense now. "And you, what of your life? Is this the same stripling I met so many years ago?"

"It is true that I have changed much, and I do not think that the changes in me are yet complete." I told him of the campaign in Dunkerque and the attempt on my life by Ralf. I told him of the attacks on the castles here in Gascony and he was impressed. "Sir Ralph seems to think that I have a future as a warrior."

"That you have, and we have a good leader in Lord Henry. I was with him at the sea battle off Sluys and although the victory was Sir Walter Manny's, Lord Henry showed that he can fight at sea as well as on land. He will have a plan."

And he did. A week after his arrival, with the reinforcements rested and ready to ride, we were ordered to move east. Sir Ralph had told Lord Henry of my archers and we were accorded the honour of becoming his scouts. We raced the sixty miles towards Bergerac. This was unfamiliar territory for me, but I had begun to understand this land. I saw how the rivers shaped the land and the roads twisted and turned to match them. I had just eight archers who would ride with me while the rest, under the command of Ned and Jack would be two hundred paces behind us. I remembered how Sir Ralph and I had managed to get close to Montravel without being seen and I thought that a small number of archers could achieve the same effect. The Earl of Derby had the army heading slightly south of Bergerac towards Montcuq where Henri de Montigny, Seneschal of Périgord, had recently taken command. We were close to Montaul, a small village at an insignificant crossroads when we came across the mounted men at arms who must have been watering their horses in the village. They saw us and began to mount. My initial reaction was to turn and run back to the main column, but I saw that there were just ten of them.

"Dismount and string your bows!" The ten men at arms vacillated and that is always a dangerous thing to do. "Draw!" As we pulled back, they realised their mistake and turned their horses to flee. For three of them, it was too late, and three Frenchmen fell from their saddles. I did not want to risk hitting villagers and so I ordered my men to mount and we rode into the village. One of the Frenchmen was wounded in the shoulder and I had him tended to. I had two of my men put him on a horse and sent him back to Lord Henry. I waited for Ned and Jack to bring the rest of my archers. Once they arrived, I rode hard after the survivors from our attack. I saw one loose horse soon after leaving the village and knew that we were on the right track. We did not see the Frenchmen for another mile or so as the road twisted and turned, rose and fell along the contours of the heavily farmed land. When we did see them they were approaching the vanguard of a French army. I saw knights, men at arms, standards and marching foot soldiers. As soon as the Frenchmen reached their vanguard, I heard horns sound and when the rest of my archers joined us then I saw hands pointing in our direction.

"What do we do, Captain?"

I had to think quickly. The smallest of my archers was Robin Goodfellow and he was also the cleverest and best of my scouts. "Robin Goodfellow!"

He trotted up on his small horse, "Aye, Captain?"

"When the French come to see us off, we shall run. I want you to hide yourself and follow the main army. I think that they are heading down this road to Bergerac. If the main body leaves this road then find us and tell us. If not, then just keep following! Be careful!"

Grinning he said, "Aye, captain!" He turned his horse and headed down a shallow tree-lined valley and within a few moments had disappeared. His real name was Robin of Wakefield, but he was so adept at hiding that he had been given the nickname of Puck, Robin Goodfellow. He lived up to that name as he vanished from sight within thirty paces of our position. I could trust him to stay hidden.

I turned my attention to the French. They would not want a large body of archers so close to them as they appeared to have few crossbowmen to keep us at distance. After a short discussion, I saw a hundred light horsemen detach themselves from the main column and head towards us. I let them get to within four hundred paces and then gave the order to fall back to the main body of our army. As we rode north, I noticed side roads and tracks leaving the main one. A good scout missed nothing! After a mile or so the light horsemen gave up their chase and we rode to meet with the Earl of Derby. He and the Earl of Stafford were galloping to meet us with their household knights. They reined in, "Your archer said it was the French army?"

"Yes, my lord. I have a man watching them and they were heading for Bergerac. They were in line of march!"

I saw his face light up. That was crucial for it meant they did not expect to have to do battle. "Then we have them. Are there roads we can use to set up an ambush?"

I pointed to the north. "There is a small road there, my lord, although there will not be much cover for us."

He nodded, "Stafford, take the Gascon spearmen and I want them to be able to stop a retreat back to Montcuq. Some will try but you will stop them. I will go with the archers and we will use arrows to dismay them and then cold steel to slaughter them. Hawkwood, lead on! I can see that you bring luck to our battles!"

It was an improvised plan but clever for all that. The Gascon foot would take time to get in place but once they were astride the road then the Earl of Stafford could be an effective barrier to the fleeing French. Besides, he would probably be able to take their baggage train! He and his household knights rode with me. The one thousand foot archers would take some time to reach us but so long as our five hundred horse archers and the men at arms were in position then I hoped that all would be well! We pushed our animals and reached the road well before there were any signs of the French army. They were moving at the pace of the foot soldiers and they would be looking to the west for signs of us. The village of Issegeac suddenly emptied as we appeared, and the villagers fled east. We let them go.

"This is perfect, Hawkwood. You and the archers secrete yourselves in the village. The spearmen on foot will join you. I will take the men at arms four hundred paces down the road. I think that there is a convenient hollow we can use. As soon as the French are in range then rain death upon them and continue to keep doing so until we attack."

"Aye, my lord, and after?"

"Then mount and join us to chase them, we can take Bergerac!"

Ever decisive he turned and rode off. There was a Captain of Archers who had come with Lord Henry, Jack of Nottingham who was a good man but the fact that Lord Henry almost deferred to me meant that he looked at me and I said, "Let us put our horses somewhere safe and use the houses and their roofs to find protection."

He smiled, "Captain Philip said you were a good man. I will follow your lead until I know this land!"

The Welsh and English foot archers were out of breath when they ran into the village and, from my vantage point on the top of the roof of a small house, I could see the standards heading up the road. I waved at Captain Jack who shouted, "Nock an arrow and await my orders. When we begin to release I want your arrow bags emptied so quickly that the French will think that the sun has set!"

I would not have said that, and I learned from it for all of the archers cheered.

The vanguard was made up of the light horsemen who had chased us, and Captain Jack wisely allowed them to close to within a hundred paces of the village. There was no metal for the sun to catch and Captain Jack wanted the juicy prize that was the large body of knights and lords who followed. We let the light horse pass us and then listened for the order.

"Release!"

This time I was not in command and I was free to be an archer. I sent five arrows, all bodkins, at the mailed men and then risked looking to see if all of my archers had obeyed. They had and I emptied, as commanded, my war bag! Some of the foot archers took longer to empty their arrow bags but as soon as the arrows stopped and we could view the devastation we had caused, I heard a horn and Lord Henry led five hundred men at arms to charge into the shocked and disordered French knights and men at arms. My men all had a second war bag and I shouted, "Kill the horsemen!"

The light horsemen had, very largely, escaped injury and now that the initial shock was over, they would seek to hurt us. I took my time and selected good war arrows to hit, first the leaders and then the braver souls. As our arrows took their toll so the French fled. Some tried to make their way through the village but the foot archers who had used all of their arrows merely drew their swords and axes to hack both horses and men. The wiser men used the fields to the east and west of the village.

I shouted, "Hawkwood! Mount your horses! We ride to Bergerac!" I slung my bow and slithered down the roof to the ground. I knew that I was lucky with my horse for while others were skittish, reared and pranced, Megs just waited patiently. The result was that I was the first to mount and as French knights began to gallop through the village and the Welsh and English archers wisely took shelter, I was able to follow. I saw that Lord Henry and Sir Ralph were leading the chase. Their mail was spattered and smeared with blood. They had fought and they had killed; that was what good leaders did. This was a race to Bergerac, and it was a race we had to win.

I drew my sword for I had chased fleeing men before and you took your chances when they presented themselves. I saw a man at arms whose horse had a wound. From the look of it, the animal had been hit a glancing blow from a war arrow and it was bleeding. That meant it would slow. Added to that the man at arms wore mail. The fact that I did not, allowed me to close with the Frenchman and draw further ahead of Lord Henry and Sir Ralph. The man at arms knew what was coming and he kept glancing over his shoulder in fear. I was new to this but even I knew that was a mistake. I held my sword to the side and approached the left hindquarter of his horse. The man at arms had a shield but he was also holding the reins and it was hard to do both. I just had a sword. I urged Megs on. I knew that I was trying to impress Lord Henry for he was a good leader and I was desperate for his praise! When Megs' head was level with the tail of the French horse I stood in my stirrups and began to swing. I knew it was pure luck for I have never practised this, but my swing brought my sword across his shoulder and back. My sword had a good edge and I was strong. I sliced through mail links and the man at arms' gambeson and then through flesh as well as muscle until, finally, it ground on the man's spine. He may have been dead before I slid out my sword and he fell from the saddle!

Bergerac was just a couple of miles ahead. I tried to remember what I knew of it. There was a bridge and, so I had been told, a barbican at the end of the bridge. If that was closed to us, then we would have to besiege. I was aware that there were, perhaps, less than a hundred men before us but they were all important. That might be our way in. The attack at Montravel had shown me that a man should never give up and so I urged on Megs. The nearest Frenchman was now more than five lengths from me and so I risked glancing over my shoulder. To my great relief, Ned and Jack were closer than Lord Henry and Sir Ralph and that meant that they would watch my back. Behind them, I saw even more of my archers. I was truly proud of them.

It was when we neared the river that the French began to bunch up as they tried to cross the narrow bridge. They went from twenty men abreast to ten and then six. Some of the men at arms turned to fight us and that allowed our own knights and men at arms to bring their skills to bear. I was no fool. It was one thing to slash at a man's back but quite another to try to fight, on horseback, a mailed man at arms with a shield. I blocked the blow from the knight who tried to punch me with his shield. Sir Ralph galloped up and contemptuously hacked across the knight's back. He and Lord Henry and their household knights ploughed through the men trying to get through the barbican. It was like Montravel all over again. The sentries should have been ruthless and closed the gates, but they did not for it was Henri de Montigny, Seneschal of Périgord and Lord Bertrand who were trying to reach the safety of the castle. That decision doomed them!

I merely followed Sir Ralph and watched his back. I hacked down and slew two men who sought to slay him and then we were at the barbican on the bridge. It was different from Montravel because the knights had bigger horses and were mailed. Both of the leading knights wore greaves and cuisse. They were impervious to all that the sentries on the gates could do. As we passed under the wooden barbican and our horses' hooves clattered on the wooden bridge then I knew that the Earl of Derby had won a great victory. Men threw themselves into the river as the steel snake pushed them aside. More knights had joined the two earls and Ned, Jack and I had an easy time. The men we slew were the ones who had been ridden down by the knights and were just rising to their feet. As we galloped into the town, I could not resist a cheer. It was not like me, but this seemed to me to be a perfect victory. We now had Bergerac and we controlled all of the lands to the south of the Dordogne!

We not only captured the town and the bridge but had also slain six hundred men at arms and captured an even greater number. The Earl of Derby's share of the ransom was over thirty-four thousand pounds! It was an incredible amount! Thanks to my endeavours I received one hundred pounds! I was now a rich man! More importantly, all of my men benefitted from the victory and I was held in higher esteem than even Captain Philip. Men called me lucky. We enjoyed many days in Bergerac and then the Earl of Derby took us north, first to Mussidan, which was an Anglo Gascon stronghold and then Périgueux, to which the survivors from Bergerac had retreated. I wondered if we were going to endure another siege, but the Earl of Derby surprised me. Having left a strong garrison at Bergerac we headed back to Bordeaux for more men when a small force of French soldiers approached. Lord Henry was the best teacher I ever had for he knew that we did not have enough men, having left garrisons, to fight another battle and guarantee victory!

His senior sergeant at arms, Will, Tom's Son, rode next to me and explained what his lord was doing. "We have left strong garrisons in all of the castles and the French would have to build siege engines to reduce them. His lordship wants to do battle with the French and defeat them." He laughed. "He knows we have a weapon the French do not, the longbow! I cannot, for the life of me, understand why some of these other armies, the Italian, the Spanish, the Flemish, do not have longbows! The likes of me and the men I lead know your value and we are just simple soldiers. You would think that the lords and kings who lead these others would see what is as clear as the nose on your face."

I nodded and explained the realities of it to him, "The trouble is, Sergeant, that you need to begin preparing for such a force when boys are yet to become youths. My uncle started to train me when I had seen but seven summers and this chest and these arms are the results of much work. It needs planning and any king who began to create such a force would not see its benefit in their lifetime. I am just surprised that these kings do not simply hire English archers. We would not cost any more than a Genoese crossbowman and we can send more arrows than they can."

"Then when this is over, John Hawkwood, why do you not do so? Hire yourself out and you could be a rich man and a great lord within a very short time!"

I laughed but he had planted a seed there and I did not feel it growing inside me, but it did. Instead, I replied, "Let us do this task first and then I will think about it. I am still a young man and I have much to learn!"

When we reached Bordeaux, we prepared to return to Périgueux. We had good news and bad news in equal measure. King Edward had been forced, by inclement weather, to abandon his attack in the Low Countries but the Earl of Pembroke was on his way to support us. If the French thought that there would be no invasion which threatened Paris, then King Philip could turn his attention and his might to us! We could expect a much larger army.

A messenger arrived from the castle of Auberoche. The French army, led by Louis of Poitiers, was besieging the castle which lay close to Périgueux. The commander of the castle, Frank van Hallen, did not have enough men to hold off the huge French army. The messenger who had made it through the French lines told Lord Henry that there were at least seven thousand men besieging the castle. The Gascon joined us at our camp while Lord Henry and the Earl of Stafford considered their plans.

"Five of us set out but the other four must have been captured." The Gascon looked around our camp. "Where are the other camps?"

"What you see is all we have. The rest of the men we brought are now in garrisons in the castles and towns we recaptured. By my estimate we have a thousand archers, less than five hundred men at arms and knights and just over a thousand English and Gascon soldiers."

The Gascon's shoulders slumped, "Then my lord is lost, and my journey was a waste."

"Why?"

"The Earl will not attack against odds of almost three to one."

It was my turn to laugh, "Then you do not know Lord Henry Plantagenet. He believes he can defeat any French lord and, thus far, he has been proved to be right!" The Gascon was not convinced.

My estimate of the numbers and my estimation of the character of Lord Henry were both accurate. Two days later we returned to the east. Another two hundred horses had been found and we took eight hundred mounted archers. Four hundred men at arms would be our only mounted support and we had one thousand two hundred English and Gascon soldiers. Jack of Nottingham commanded the archers and he honoured me by having me ride with him.

"His lordship knows we are outnumbered, and we will use stealth and surprise as we did on the road to Bergerac. The messenger described the land around the castle well and the French are camped in a large meadow."

We camped close to the castle so that the messenger's information could be confirmed. We were camped less than a mile from the French encampment, but such was their confidence that they did not keep a good watch. Lord Henry and Jack of Nottingham went to spy out the French camp and when they returned, I saw that the news they brought was not good. I was invited to the meeting with Lord Henry.

He was an honest man and I liked that, "The French have reinforced their army with many thousands more men. I estimate that we will have to fight at odds of five to one. However, I lead better men and we have surprise on our side. There is a wood which lines the French camp and we will position the archers at the tree line. Some of the foot soldiers, led by Sir Raymond, will block off one end of the meadow while the rest will follow myself and the men at arms will lead a charge through their camp as they eat their evening meal."

I nodded, for the plan was pure genius. No one in any army ate a meal with their weapons to hand and most took off their mail. They would not be expecting an English army to return so soon, and their guard would be down. The French, especially, liked their food! The odds did not worry me. Each archer had more than fifty arrows with them and we had five times that number in the wagons which followed us. We could slay an army four times the size of this one and if we fought from the edge of the wood then we had the means to escape.

It was late in the afternoon that we parted from the main body of the army. We went with two hundred foot soldiers under the command of a Gascon knight, Sir Raymond de St. Emilion. When we reached the wood, we tethered our horses at the edge and then, after Sir Raymond and his men had left us, we made our way through the woods to the French camp. We could smell their fires and their food. We heard their laughter and the noise from the camp. It was as we stood on the edge that I became just a little daunted. Normally a camp would be spread out over a large area but here, the enormous meadow was so covered by men, fires and tents that I could not see how men could move around. The Earl and his men would not be able to get through the camp! There would be no path for them and I wondered if Lord Henry had miscalculated.

I had no time for speculation as Jack of Nottingham nodded for me to take my position at one end of the line of eight hundred archers. Other vintenars were spread out along the line. We did not speak, although we could have for the noise from the camp was loud enough to drown us out. Instead, as I walked down the line, I patted each of my archers on the shoulder, spoke to them and they nocked an arrow. When I reached the end of my company, I did the same with the rest of the men. I had told them all, while we rode, that we would be using war arrows. There was little point in wasting bodkins for the men in the camp would not be wearing mail. Jack of Nottingham would begin the attack. The archers around him, Lord Henry's men, would launch their arrows and a heartbeat later we would send ours. After that, the arrows would continue to be loosed until we saw the horsemen, hopefully, sweeping all before them. I used the half draw while I waited for I knew it would not be long before the harvesting of the French began. I heard the sound of the arrows and I pulled and released. My men did me proud and their arrows were sent at the same time as mine. I then began to nock, draw and release almost like a machine. The sounds of laughter in the camp ended and were replaced by screams and shouts of panic. It was not yet completely dark, but the French would have had no idea of where we were. I emptied one war bag of arrows and I replaced my string. I did so for two reasons: one to give my right arm some rest and to ensure that my arrows flew as hard as possible.

I had sent three arrows from my second bag when Jack of Nottingham shouted, "Cease! Draw swords and await my command!"

I slung my bow and as soon as the sounds of the arrows stopped, I heard from my right the cheers as Sir Raymond led his men from one end of the French camp and then the thunder of hooves as four hundred mailed men galloped from the opposite direction. Then Jack of Nottingham shouted, "Attack!" We were given the freedom to kill!

The French were being attacked on three sides and their only escape lay towards the castle. I had my sword and my hand axe as weapons, and we tore into the camp. The only ones who stood any chance of survival were the lords for they could surrender, and we would receive the ransom. The ordinary soldiers and crossbowmen would be slaughtered even if they did surrender for we knew that if they escaped we would have to fight them again. We recognised that if the positions were reversed then we would receive no mercy!

The hardest job was to negotiate the two thousand or so men we had slain with arrows already. The thought passed through my mind that when this was over, we had many arrows to recover! The French had tried to form lines but the charge of the men at arms had caught them out and we were faced with bands of tent mates who fought together. Most wore just tunics and breeks or hose. That made us equal except that my archers had arms like young oaken saplings, and we were not demoralised. Ned, Jack, and Robin Goodfellow were all close to me. Robin was a deceptive man for although short, he was strong, and he used that to his advantage. Quick as quicksilver I watched him race and duck beneath a scything sword and ram his dagger into the throat of a French man at arms. I blocked the swipe from a sergeant at arms' sword with my rondel dagger and sliced my sword deep between his ribs. I pushed him to the ground and hacked at the back of the French soldier who was trying to hew Robin's head from his shoulders.

Darkness had fallen but there were still fires and some tents had caught alight. The whole scene looked like a picture of hell. The gates of the castle had opened, and the garrison was pouring out to completely encircle the French army. The butchery began. Four French knights surrendered to my men and me, and eight men at arms promised us ransom. Even as we continued to fight our way through the seemingly endless French army, I left men to watch the prisoners. They were human gold! It was dawn by the time the fighting ended. Some had escaped, that much we knew for there were too few of us to be able to completely contain them, but Gascony was now English once more.

Chapter 9

The victory was so complete as to be almost unbelievable. Louis of Poitiers, who was the French leader, died of his wounds. He had been hit by two arrows as well as enduring cuts and blows from knights. There were over seven hundred French men at arms who died. The ransoms were so great that the Earl of Derby received fifty thousand pounds in ransom which was more income than King Edward earned from his lands in a year! Henry Plantagenet became the richest man in England. Thanks to our capture of the knights and men at arms I had a hundred pounds and my archers divided up a further two hundred pounds. The Earl of Derby also appreciated what the eight hundred archers had done, and he paid each of us twenty pounds! The army of thirty thousand men led by the Duke of Normandy abandoned their advance and went home. The Duke himself and his household knights retreated to Angouleme. For the next three months, we took castle after castle and often we did not even need to draw a bow. The sight of a thousand archers was enough to make every castellan concede defeat.

I often wonder what would have happened had I stayed with the army of Henry Plantagenet, but it was not meant to be. It was Christmas when we were in our winter quarters of Bordeaux. The majority of the army were in garrisons but the men who had first followed Sir Ralph remained and it was we who were chosen for the task of delivering the despatches to the King. Although we ruled the land many pirates used Brittany and Normandy as bases from which they could raid ships. The last two ships which had carried despatches home had been taken and the Earl of Derby was determined to remedy that situation. I was given forty archers to defend the ship, **'Maid of Harwich'**. We were to sail to Southampton, and I was to deliver the despatches personally to the King.

The Earl himself saw us off, "You have shown yourself, John Hawkwood, to be a most resourceful man and if any can see that these despatches get through then it is you. I suspect that King Edward will hang on to you and your archers for your names feature prominently in my message to the King but if he does not then you shall always be welcome to be part of my retinue."

"And I would be honoured, my lord. I will do all that I can to see that these messages reach England. Pirates I can fight, it is nature and the sea which are the problems!"

"Then fear not for God is on our side and he will watch over you!"

The only horse we were allowed to take was Megs for the archers who remained needed to be mounted. The ship we took was also filled with barrels of wine. Bordeaux shipped so much wine that the tax taken was more than the rest of the tax collected in the entire kingdom. There was also a crew of fifteen which seemed to me to be quite large but, as I discovered, it was not enough when the seas became rough. Before we boarded, I divided my archers into three watches. As I had been allowed to keep Ned and Jack, I had complete confidence in the way all of the watches would behave. The first day was a gentle day as we edged up the estuary towards the sea. It was only when we struck the open waters that the movement of the ship became more violent. The ship had a forecastle and a sterncastle. There were thirteen men in Ned and Jack's watches and fourteen in mine. It meant we could have six men in the bow castle and the rest in the stern. Not only could we fight, but we could also act as extra lookouts.

The voyage was not swift as the ship was laden. All of my archers had bought wine themselves which would reap a great dividend when we landed in England. The prices we had paid in Bordeaux were a tenth of what we could sell them for in England, even with the taxes! The Earl of Stafford had told me of a merchant in Southampton who could be trusted, and I intended to leave some of my gold with him. I had too much for the money belt and, also, I had a small chest which I kept in the sterncastle. It was a long and slow haul up the coast of France. There were savage rocks and vicious estuaries close to the land while further out to sea there were troughs and crests which threatened to engulf our ship. The captain knew his business, but this was unfamiliar territory for me and I liked the reassurance of a coastline to which we could flee. We made it to the Cherbourg Peninsula before we ran into trouble. The wind was from the north and east. The captain had already told us that we would have to head further west to negotiate Cherbourg which was a pirate haven and we were ready for the move. As soon as he put the helm over, we began to speed up and the sails billowed alarmingly. Of course, once we had cleared the coast we would have to turn north, and then we would slow. The two pirate ships were waiting for just such a move and one suddenly leapt out from the coast to position itself behind our stern.

It was one of the crew who spotted him and he gave the warning. I shouted to my men, "Stand to!" then took my bow from its case and the bowstring from beneath my hat. I could do all of this without looking and I studied, carefully, the pirate ship. It had a simple lateen sail and was rowed. The number of oars suggested a crew of either twenty or forty! As it was a pirate then the latter seemed more likely.

The captain shouted, "With their oars, they will catch us!"

"She is lower in the water than we are, captain, and my men are the best."

Just then there was a shout from Ned in the bow castle. His words were largely lost in the wind but I saw his pointed hand and a mile or so ahead, emerging from the gloom of the coast, was a second pirate ship. I could not make out all of the details but it seemed likely that they would also have a crew of at least forty. We were now seriously outnumbered and when a third ship came from our beam then I knew that they would catch up to us for they were ahead, behind and to the side of us.

The Captain looked nervous as though he had no answer to this. I was no sailor, but I was a soldier and I looked upon it as an exercise in strategy. If we continued our present course, then they would catch us. The one astern was less than ten ship's lengths from us. The one on our starboard beam was fifteen lengths from us but she had the wind and would close with us the fastest. The least danger to us was presented by the one ahead who would just wait to see what we did.

"Captain, if we turn and head south then we will travel faster for we will have the wind with us, is that not right?"

"Aye, but it will take us further from home."

I used my bow to point, "We cannot get home so long as there are three ships following us. The pirates cannot know that there are forty longbows aboard. When they are less than one hundred paces from us we can shower them with arrows. If we lead them on a chase, then we can take them one by one. The course we follow just draws us closer to them."

He nodded, "Prepare to come about!" The crew knew where to go and they ran to the sails, sheets and stays.

Cupping my hands, I bellowed, "Ned, fetch our men here!"

"Come about!"

The ship heeled sharply as we changed course and with the wind behind us and from our larboard quarter, the ungainly beast almost flew. As my men arrived, I shouted, "Line the stern rail. You will be able to protect the captain with your bodies. Do not release until I give the order and keep your bows hidden until the last moment."

Ned shouted, "The spray will not help our bows, Captain!"

"I know and that is why we will only release when they are less than a hundred paces from us. You will raise, draw and release on my command. I want as many rowers as we can hit to be killed."

Our turn had taken them by surprise, but the two closest ships were now within two lengths of each other and the closest to us was just eight lengths away. I could now see that there were helmets in the ships and that there were closer to fifty men on board rather than forty. It explained how they could move so fast as they had two men on every oar and three on the ones closest to the stern! With the wind behind them as well then both ships were not only keeping pace with us but closing. However, the advantage we had was that we were not rowing and they had to begin to tire soon. A pirate in a helmet wearing a leather brigandine stood at the prow of the nearest ship. He held on to the rope I had learned was called a forestay and he had a sword in his hand. He was a soldier and had been, perhaps, a man at arms at one time. I saw him urge his rowers on. They began to close and I deemed that they were close enough. Each of us had three bags of arrows with us and there were more in the hold.

I nocked an arrow and shouted, "Draw! Release!"

It came as a complete shock to the pirates that we had longbows. Loosing into the wind and with damp strings, we should have dropped short, but our arrows fell on the rowers. I was in the sterncastle and I sent my arrow into the chest of the former man at arms. He spun around and tumbled into the sea. As I nocked and drew my second arrow, I paused to look for another target. Our first arrows had hit at least ten of the pirates and she was now merely holding her own. Her consort, however, was racing towards us. I aimed at the man at the helm of the first ship. The wind and the movement of both ships did not help but I sent my second arrow at him. I was lucky and I pinned his left leg to the hull of the ship. It made him lose control of the ship, albeit briefly and when another five pirates were hit the pirate ship slewed around.

The second pirate was cleverly heading down our larboard side while the third one was heading for our starboard. I shouted, "I want the next arrows to make the second pirate awash with blood. Send as many arrows as you can!"

This time the pirate's position meant that the wind was coming from our larboard quarter and we did not have to fight it as much. We sent five arrows in such quick succession that none of us had the chance to see the effect. As my men continued to rain death, I looked at the pirate ship and saw that the oars were at different angles. Some men lay over the thwarts and I could only see a few men still rowing.

"Captain, you may turn if you wish and we will tackle the last pirate although I suspect they will turn!"

The captain actually smiled, "I will heed your advice, archer, for that was a smart piece of work. Prepare to come about!" The crew raced to adjust the sail, "Come about!"

The pirate ship suddenly found us heading for her. I shouted to my men, "Line the starboard side and if you have a target then loose your arrows." Once again, my men and I high in the sterncastle had an advantage as we were elevated and the seven of us sent a flurry of arrows. We hit men and the pirate turned to sail in the opposite direction. It was a mistake as they were now sailing into the wind and they slowed. All of my men now had targets and forty arrows slammed into the ship. I saw oars fall into the water and the sails flapped as they hit the wind and I realised that the helmsman was dead, and the pirate was no longer under man's control. My men used it for target practice until the range became too great. We had won and although there was neither treasure nor booty, we were all satisfied.

It took another ten days to reach Southampton. I was not concerned about my archers for after the victory over the pirates they were in good humour, but Megs was not happy at being cooped up for so long. When we saw the Isle of Wight, I breathed a sigh of relief. Megs could enjoy the open skies and pastures until we were needed again.

The Captain and his crew were immensely grateful to us, "It is a pity we could not have you sail with us all the time!"

I pointed to the shore, "There are many archers in England who seek a paymaster. They are a good investment. Even had we just had ten archers we could have easily dealt with one pirate ship."

"I will give thought to your words and if you ever need to have cargo brought to England, I will bring it for free!" He tapped his nose and I knew what he meant. He would not declare it to the King's tax collectors!

The money we had accrued meant we could afford decent lodgings although I hoped that King Edward would be paying for it eventually. Leaving Ned and Jack to sort out the stable and the rooms I took the despatches and headed for the castle. I had changed dramatically over the last couple of years. Before I had left Bordeaux, I had bought some good clothes and I now looked like a lord. The sumptuary laws were only recent, but I made sure that I wore no fur! My sword, scabbard and boots were of the finest quality and some people knuckled their heads as I passed. My father had always been angry if peasants did not show respect to him and I suspect that my brother was the same. It was immaterial to me for with or without my fine clothes I was the same man I had always been.

The sentry at the gatehouse did not recognise me and I was forced to wait until one of King Edward's household knights, Lord Basset of Drayton, came for me. The look he gave the sentry ensured that the next time I arrived I would be admitted immediately. "We heard that Lord Henry won two great battles. Is it true?"

"Aye my lord, and Gascony is now secure. When I left France, our army was encroaching upon the land of King Philip.

I did not add that had King Edward invaded then we might have had the whole of France!

"Then those despatches will inform our next actions." He seemed to notice my clothes for the first time. "You look different from the last time I saw you!"

"Yes, my lord, my men and I also had ransom and the Earl is a generous man."

His disparaging look made me wonder. I was not sure if he approved of archers who had coin.

The hall was full when we were admitted but a path was made, and I bowed and laid the despatches on the table. King Edward tore open the seals and almost devoured them. Prince Edward was there and he was now a youth who was on the threshold of manhood. Soon he would be the Black Prince due to the armour he had made but when he spoke to me, he was just the Prince of Wales and Duke of Cornwall. I had seen him before, and I think he knew me. That was confirmed when he spoke. "You are the archer who served with Captain Philip?"

I nodded, "I am, my lord!"

"He spoke highly of you and the fact that the Earl of Lancaster also thinks so much of you that he sends you as his messenger also makes me curious about you."

"Earl of Lancaster, my lord?"

"Of course, you did not know. His father died and he inherited the title."

King Edward suddenly jumped up, having read the documents, and exclaimed, "Not just one but two of the greatest victories English and Gascon arms have ever achieved. And you, archer, you represent the men who made this possible." He raised the parchment, "In less than half an hour our archers slew almost two thousand men!" He turned to his son. "We can leave for France as soon as the weather improves, and we can win another crown!"

Everyone in the hall cheered and I think I knew why. The King and his lords, not to mention his son, had planned on invading France. That they had not done so and yet Lord Henry had achieved so much with so few filled everyone with confidence.

The King and his son came over to me, "And you, messenger, Hawkwood, is it not?"

"It is Your Majesty."

"You will return to our service for Lord Henry tells me that it was you who was instrumental in the taking of three castles. You will continue to serve us. Where are you lodged?"

"The Miller's Stone, my lord. it is the inn which is close to the market square."

"Then I shall send monies for your rooms on the morrow. Enjoy yourself tonight, for this, is just the beginning!"

The inn was a good one and a roomy one. Campaigns to France often left England from Southampton and the size of the inn reflected that. The King had yet to make his summons and so we had it to ourselves. I knew that as soon as more men arrived the prices would rise; that was inevitable. The rest of the men shared chambers, often four to a room but I was accorded my own room. Ned knew of my treasure chest and he had guarded it. When I was taken to my room, he gave it to me, "This will not be a secure place for your chest, Captain. The innkeeper might be honest but there are others who work here, and they might risk the noose to become rich men."

I nodded. "I have a plan. You can tell the others that we are all employed, once more, by King Edward. He is pleased and this sojourn will not be a long one. We sail to France as soon as the weather improves but, for the while, we can rest." I knew that it would be months, perhaps even longer, before we could sail. Some of the army would be close enough to reach the muster in a day or two, we were not that far from London, but those who came from the borders would need a fortnight or more to reach us. "And how is Megs?"

"The stable boy seems to like the horse." We were both aware that was not always true. "When I gave him your sixpence, he seemed even happier!"

I went down to join my men. I knew that they would all be drunk by the end of the night. Gascony had good wine but archers, by and large, preferred beer and English beer at that. Besides, in Gascony war was always just a night away and here they would not be fighting. They could afford a thick head and queasy stomach after indulging too much. I never drank too much, and I was content after we had eaten to drink half the quantity of most of my men. I was quiet for I had much to think about. I had risen far higher than I had expected. I knew that my mother would have been proud that the King knew my name. My father would have hated it and both thoughts pleased me. I had my father's name and I was stuck with it, but I would never acknowledge him! I should have changed my name when I first came to London. When Megs and Stephen the Tailor had taken me in then would have been the time to do so but back then I was too honest. I knew that I had changed, and I had seen both treachery and dishonesty. Honest men were not always rewarded. I believed I was now a good man, having atoned for whatever faults I had once had, but I could lie. Even more, I knew that if I had to, I could murder, and I could steel. The battle of Auberoche where the French soldiers had been butchered had been murder, for many of those we had killed had not defended themselves and begged for mercy. I knew that if my position was reversed then I would fight until they hacked my sword from my dead hand.

The next day I rose first and the landlord, recognising me as the leader, fussed over me in the empty room in which they served food. He brought in slices of Wiltshire ham as well as a good cheddar and, best of all still warm white bread. Instead of a pat of butter, he brought in a bowl of local butter. It was as fine a meal as a man could ask for. The small beer washed it down beautifully. I smiled as he whisked away the ham, cheese and butter before the rest of my men appeared. They would have rye or oat bread and although they would be served good food they would not have the quantity which was offered to me.

I was surprised by the messenger who came from the King for it was his son, Edward, and he was accompanied by a knight I knew from Dunkerque, Sir John Chandos. He had received his knighthood for services in the Low Country. Although the Prince wore no mail he had on the royal coat of arms and the landlord almost fell over himself as he raced to bring out the fine food he had just whisked away! Had I not been so stunned by the status of my messenger I might have laughed aloud.

"My lord!"

The Prince dropped a purse on the table, "Here is payment for you and your archers for the next six months."

"Thank you, Prince Edward."

The landlord arrived and placed the food before the Prince and the knight. "Landlord, King Edward will pay the bill for John Hawkwood and his archers. Submit it to the castle where my father's steward will furnish the payment." The young prince stared at the landlord, "The request will be scrutinised and there will be no rooking!"

The landlord bowed but I saw the disappointment on his face. I would have less expensive fare from now on.

The Prince cut himself some bread, smeared it with butter and then added a thick slice of ham. The Prince was no fussy eater. Sir John Chandos said, "I saw you at Cadzand and I was right glad that we had your archers on our side."

"You too fought well, Sir John."

Prince Edward said, "I believe that archers are the key to winning back my father's French lands. Tell me, Hawkwood, how many arrows can you loose?"

"That depends upon our general." I saw him frown. "If we are ordered to then we can send twenty or thirty arrows in the time it takes to count to two hundred but if we did so then our rate from then on would diminish rapidly. If we released them steadily then a good archer can keep going for half an hour or so before he tires. Although we would have to change our bowstrings in that time."

"And at what range can you kill?"

"Every archer is different, my lord, but generally it is two hundred and fifty to three hundred paces."

"Impressive. I would like to see your men use the bow, would that be possible?"

I smiled and gave him an honest answer, "Aye, Prince Edward, but not this morning. They had a sea voyage which ended yesterday and last night they all drank too much." As if to prove the point Ned and Jack led half a dozen down and they stank of stale ale.

The Prince smiled, "Tomorrow then, let us say we meet at the common ground where the targets are set up. I would have you use war arrows and bodkins, not the prickshafts."

That showed me the Prince had already asked questions. Prickshafts were lighter arrows used to aim at the wooden prick in the centre of the clout, the canvas target. "Of course, my lord."

They left and Ned and Jack joined me. The innkeeper had not had time to whisk away the good ham, bread, cheese and butter. Ned and Jack still had an appetite and they fell upon the food. As they ate, I told them what the Prince had asked. "Have the men practise today for I wish to impress the Prince. I will go into the town and find this merchant, Basil of Tarsus. I wish my gold to be safe."

There was a town watch in Southampton and wearing my tunic with the red cross marked me as a King's man. I felt safe walking the streets with my small chest. Until forty or so years earlier I would have been seeking a Jew, but King Edward 1st had executed more than six hundred of them and had confiscated their money. The rest had been expelled. He had gained a substantial war chest as a result. When I found Basil of Tarsus, I realised that he was, in fact, a Jew. He was a Greek Jew and his clothes were not the traditional Jewish ones but there were signs I recognised in his shop. The first sign was the two huge bodyguards. Merchants were loath to waste money on such men but a Jew who needed his treasure protecting needed them. There were other signs too which I spotted as I spoke with him. I suspect that the authorities and even King Edward himself would know of his activities and his origins but as the Earl of Stafford knew of him, I guessed that they were pretending that he was no Jew.

"How can I help one of King Edward's archers? I am a simple merchant who imports dried fruit and spices from Greece."

Although a lucrative business it was also expensive and even I knew that he was lying but, like the Earl of Stafford, I ignored it. "I have recently returned from Gascony where I served with Lord Henry Plantagenet and Sir Ralph, Earl of Stafford. We did well out there and I have this chest!" I hefted the chest on to the table and opened it. I smiled as I saw the two bodyguards' hands go to their weapons in case I had secreted some device within.

His eyes widened when he saw the chest was filled, "You are indeed a rich young man but I fail to see how I can be of any assistance to you unless you wish to use this to buy dried fruits and then have me sell them, for a commission."

I saw what he was doing. He was giving me a way to have him protect my money and yet not reveal his true identity. "I travel a great deal and carrying such a large amount is a temptation to many men. I would have my pile of coins grow. Could you do that for me?"

He smiled, "Of course."

I did not like the smile. I closed the lid on the chest, "And of course it will be safe here." I did not look up at the two bodyguards, but I inclined my head, "But if you should decide to misappropriate my money or try to take it then these two lumps would not stop me taking all that you own." I heard one of them growl and I stood up to face the larger of the two, "I am an archer and I know how to fight when it matters." I nodded down and he looked at my rondel dagger which was pricking his testicles. "Basil, do you wish this one or both of them to be eunuchs, just say the word and it shall be so."

"Hob, Tam, go and make yourself useful. I will talk to this archer alone." When they had gone, he smiled, "There was no need for that, you know. I profit from my reputation and the great and the good all trust me."

"Then next time do not smile when you say my coins will be safe. They were not easily earned, and men died to gather me my wealth."

"Of course." He seemed contrite.

"It is likely that I will be away from England for a while, but I can write, and I can try to send you news if I am unlikely to return each year at about this time." I took a sealed piece of parchment from my tunic. "This is my will. If you hear that John Hawkwood is dead, then I ask you to open it and honour my wishes. Of course, by then I shall be dead, and it is perfectly possible that you will just take my money but as I shall not be in this world then it will matter not to me."

He became very serious and clutched some amulet, which I could not see, below his tunic. "But it will to me. I am a man of my word."

"Good." I stood and held out my arm. He clasped my hand and I squeezed. He nodded and smiled.

When I left, I was unconcerned, for I had lied to him. As far as I was concerned the coins were easily come by and if we were going to France then I would make even more coins next time. I had also decided that I would make the transition from archer to a man at arms. The main reason was ransom. Archers scoured the battlefield after it was over and picked up the leavings of the lords. A man at arms fought an enemy and could capture him. I had been impressed by the ransoms Lord Henry had acquired and I would try to emulate him. To that end, I sought out a weaponsmith. When I had last spoken to Ralph of Malton, he had told me of a good one who lived over the River Itchen in the village of Bitterne. Balin the Smith had a good reputation. Now that I was fully grown, I could have a hauberk and good helmet made for me. I had not given all of my treasure to Basil. I would go to France and fight as an archer but after that, I would equip myself as a man at arms and then I could, perhaps, ascend to the rank of gentleman.

Balin of Bitterne was so huge that he dwarfed me. However, whereas I was all muscle. Balin had a gut which acted as a barrier when he was at the forge. He almost dismissed me out of hand when his boy said I wished to see him. He glanced up and recognised what I was and went back to hammering the plate metal for a greave. "I do not add pieces of metal to brigandines! Find a blacksmith for it will be quicker and cheaper,"

I tossed a French gold piece on to his anvil, "I want a hauberk and a helmet."

He put down his hammer, "But you are an archer!"

"And one day I will be a man at arms. Call this preparation for a future yet to be born."

He looked at the coin, "You know that this will be neither cheap nor quick."

"I am a patient man and I can wait. Ralph of Malton said that you knew your trade and I trust his judgement."

He bit into the gold coin and put it in his apron pocket, "You are a King's archer?" I nodded, "Then you will be sailing to France. This may be ready before you sail but I doubt it."

"Then it will be waiting when I return. As I said, I am a patient man!"

"What is your name?"

"John Hawkwood."

"Well, John Hawkwood, let me measure you and then you can be on your way."

The next day we were at the common long before the Prince and Sir John arrived. We set up the targets and we practised. This was no bad thing for it was some time since we had drawn a bow in anger and that had been aboard the ship and not a good test. I knew that I was not the best archer; I never claimed to be. I was one who was a fair archer, but I knew how to lead and I knew how to fight. The Prince had brought some other young nobles with him. I came to know them when we went to Normandy. Only Sir John had his spurs and the four young men would be hoping to impress King Edward in battle and be given a knighthood.

I had my archers three hundred paces from the targets. That was probably the extreme range for my men. Prince Edward had prepared well, and he said, "That is too far away bring them back fifty paces as is the normal range. How many arrows can your men send in a minute?"

I answered confidently for this was one of our routines, "Fifteen, my lord, but that number of arrows might not be accurate."

He shook his head, "It matters not for even at a gallop it would take a horse three or four minutes to bring a mailed man close enough to strike at an archer. Make it two hundred and fifty paces." We all moved forward, and I saw grins on my men's faces. When we had an arrow nocked then the Prince came down the line to ensure that we were using war arrows. Satisfied that we were he said, "I want you to send ten arrows as quickly as you can, Loring here can count, and he will determine the rate." He nodded at me.

"Draw!"

The forty-one bows all creaked as we drew.

"Release!"

My men knew what they had to do and we each drew and released as fast as we could. Ten arrows were nothing and we all grinned when we had done. The young noble, Nigel Loring said, "Thirty-eight, my lord, I counted to thirty-eight!"

"Then let us see how accurate they were."

We had set up ten targets. Only one arrow had not hit the target and I saw a shamefaced Job of Tarporley. All of my archers knew who had missed for we each knew our own arrows. Three arrows had hit the prick and Prince Edward said, "Captain, whose arrows are these three?"

I looked at the flights, "Ned the Wanderer, Walter of Barnsley and Robin Goodfellow!"

The Prince took out three florins from his purse and shook his head. He tossed the coins to the three archers, "Sir John here said I would need more than one florin. I have learned much today. You are my father's archers but when we cross to France it is my banner you will follow, Hawkwood, and you will fight under my command. Is that clear?"

Who was I to argue with the future King of England? However, I also knew that if King Edward ordered me to fight in his division then I would do so. The Prince was the cub, but King Edward was the lion. I nodded. The Prince and his companions watched my men for a while longer and I overheard some of their conversation. I had learned to keep my ears open for information was like gold and could be used in many ways. Thus it was that I heard that the Earl of Lancaster, in Aquitaine, was being threatened by an army of over twenty thousand men and had sent for help. Lord Henry would not seek help unless he was in danger. That confirmed that we would be leaving sooner rather than later for King Edward would not risk all that Henry Plantagenet had gained for him. He would act.

We did not see him again until we embarked but five days a week saw us at the targets. I now had an idea what he wanted of us and so we practised until our arms and backs ached as though we had been hewing in the mines for a month. It was worth it for by the time we sailed to France, there were no archers in the whole army as well trained as mine!

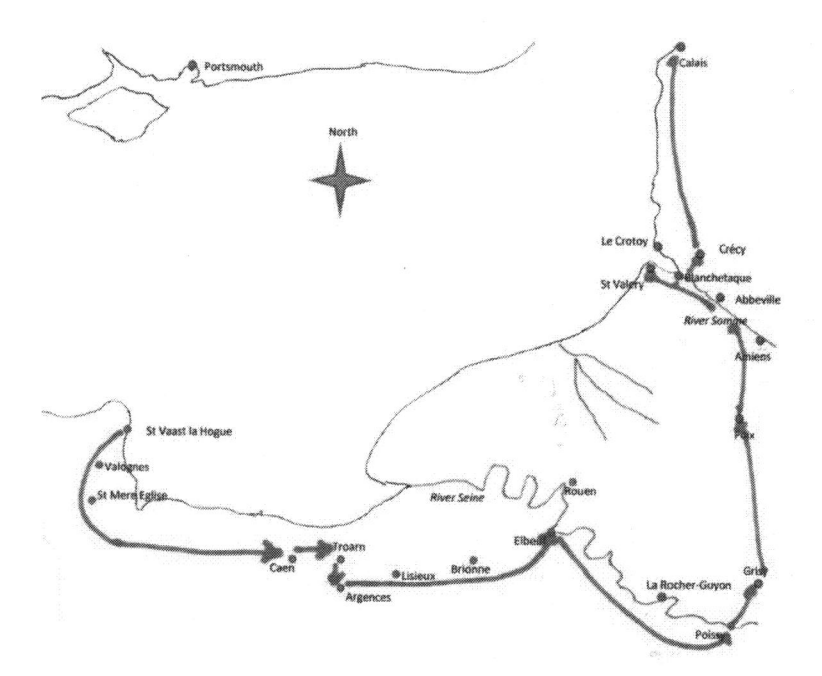

**Route taken by King Edward's Army 1346
Author's Map**

Chapter 10

We sailed for Normandy in July. This time the King had secured the largest fleet I had ever seen. There were more than seven hundred vessels of varying sizes and the King had more luck than the previous year. It was a relatively smooth crossing and we landed safely and together at Saint Vaast la Hogue in the Cherbourg Peninsula. My company of archers had not travelled with Prince Edward but, as he had promised us, we were in his division, the vanguard. Prince Edward had been so impressed by our exhibition that he had almost three thousand of us with him. Not all of us were mounted and, as the horses were brought ashore, I was summoned to meet with him. The King had given his son some experienced generals: the Earls of Warwick and Oxford, Count Godfrey d'Harcourt, Sir Thomas Holland, Lord Stafford, Lord Burghersh and, of course, Sir John Chandos.

There was a strange event on the beach for King Edward tripped and bloodied his nose on the beach. Rather than dismaying the King, he took it as a sign that this was his land! As soon as they were all landed King Edward gathered his knights and, in a very symbolic ceremony, knighted his son and gave him his spurs in front of the whole army. It was cleverly done as this was his first action in France and he was making a statement. He was telling King Philip that this was his land. He also gave Prince Edward the honour of being the vanguard, the scouting division of the whole army. It was an honour for the Prince and showed all of us the faith he had in his son. Of course, that put more pressure on my company of archers for we would be the advanced guard. The Low Countries had given us a reputation and Prince Edward would use our skills to facilitate our passage through Normandy.

After he had detached himself from the congratulations of his peers, the Prince came directly to me, "Hawkwood, we are going to move along the coast, first to Saint-Lô and thence to Caen. It will take some time to unload our ships. Before the French know that we are here I would have you take your men and gather as many horses as you can. Take William Jauderell and his mounted archers too but I want you to command. I need as many of my archers mounted as possible!"

Even though he was just sixteen Prince Edward had presence even then!

I did not know the country but as the sea was on our left it seemed to be a fairly simple proposition and by keeping the sea in that position I would not become lost. I had heard of William Jauderell. He was one of the best archers we had and like me was a vintenar. He readily agreed to follow my lead, not least because any failure would be laid at my door and yet he and his men would all benefit from the profits of what was, in essence, a huge chevauchée. The horses we took would be for Prince Edward but all else would be ours and I was known to be fortunate in that regard. It was about forty miles to Saint-Lô and as Normandy was famous for horses, I deduced that there must be many horse farms in the land twixt our camp and St Lo. Although knights' horses might be kept in castles the majority of the other horses, sumpters and palfreys, would be kept in fields. I had William Jauderell take his men to Valognes to ravage the area around that town whilst I took mine to Sainte-Mère-Église. Even as we set off the town of St Vaast la Hogue was being burned and other parties spread out to raid the nearby farms. Ships from our fleet paralleled our course and even as we rode south, I saw ships attacking the French boats and burning them. This was a chevauchée the like of which France and, indeed, the world, had never seen before.

William and his men left us a few miles from our camp, and we hurried on. I spied a farm and a small hall just five miles after parting from the other archers. I saw horses grazing in the fenced fields and I did not bother to scout it out but just waved my sword in a circle, the signal to surround the farm. The few men who came out to stop us were quickly slain and the women and children fled across the fields. I had Jack take four men and collect the horse herd. While they found halters and saddles the rest of us looted the farm for gold, weapons and food. We sent the thirty horses back to the main camp with the four men. They knew that they would be given a share of any loot. By late afternoon we had captured a total of eighty horses and so much loot that we had to keep six of the horses just to carry it. We reached Sainte-Mère-Église just before dark and the French were not expecting us. The burning farms we had left should have given them an indication that something was wrong, but they appeared to have ignored it.

This was the largest place we had found, and I contemplated waiting until the Prince arrived with his division. I only had thirty men with me; the rest were still on the road returning horses to the Prince. On the other hand, the longer we waited then the fewer horses there would be for us to collect. In the end, the decision was taken for me when William Jauderell and twenty of his men arrived. We had taken so many horses on our way south that he and his men had had less to do. His arrival meant that I had an opportunity to use his men and to block any escape from the village.

"William, take your men around the village and dismount them. You can stop any men escaping from this village. We will ride in as though we are men at arms and when they flee you can take out their men."

He cocked his head to the side, "And the women?"

I smiled, "We let the women and children go. True, they will spread the word of our presence but the ships which are raiding the coast and the smoke in the sky from the burned farms will have already done so. The women will exaggerate our numbers and make more garrisons flee at our approach. Let us spread fear."

He smiled, "I bow to your superior knowledge." He mounted and led his men around the village which was centred on the stone church and had, so far as I knew, more than a hundred houses. Such a place might have as many as thirty horses.

I adjusted Megs' girth as I spoke to my men. "Jack, I want you to take five men. Tie your horses to yonder trees and head into the village. Conceal yourselves and work your way through; use your bows to slay any men. When we ride in you can eliminate any who try to escape. We will come in at dusk. Try to stop them from seeking sanctuary in the church. Tonight, I intend us to sleep under a roof and eat well!"

I waited until the sun was setting and then drew my sword. Pointing it forward I dug my heels into the side of Megs. With eight others I galloped down the road towards the town. The rest of my mounted archers would find other ways into the village. Surprisingly the sound of our hooves did not seem to alarm the villagers. Perhaps they thought that we were Frenchmen. As we neared the village, I saw two men standing by the first house. Before they could shout a warning, they were pitched backwards, and I saw arrows sticking from them. Even then there appeared to be little panic for most of the villagers were indoors enjoying their evening meal. As we passed the first bodies then a couple of heads emerged from doorways to see who came and that was when the alarm was given. They must have been terrified to see helmeted horsemen galloping through their streets and when a woman screamed so shrilly that it hurt my ears then panic did set in. Men rushed out into the street with whatever weapon they had to hand. Most of these were part of the local levy and had a short sword or an axe. Jack and his men did what I had asked them and all of those who threatened us were struck by an arrow. By the time we reached the church, there was a mass exodus of panicking villagers. A few ran towards the church. As I had ordered Jack and his archers were running amongst them and the men were slain. Leaving Jack to secure the church we pursued those who ran. I heard hooves ahead and knew that some of the men had taken horses which must have been stabled close by their homes. William would stop them.

As soon as I came across the first body with an arrow in his front, I raised my sword and shouted, "Back, and search every house and stable. We seek horses and booty!" I knew that William Jauderell and his archers had stopped the men. I wheeled my horse around and looked for large houses. Robin Goodfellow had attached himself to me and I headed towards a house, set back from the main road which looked larger than the others for it had a second floor and was the only one we had seen like that. It had a trough outside and that suggested horses. Tying Megs to a hitching post I drew my rondel as well as my sword and, waving Robin around to the rear, I opened the front door. I heard a noise from the darkened interior. It sounded like someone was digging and I knew immediately what it was.

Someone had buried treasure and they were digging it up. I heard voices too speaking French. The glow I saw confirmed that they had a light to help them see.

"Hurry or the God-Damns will be here!"

"I am digging as fast as I can, master, you buried it too deeply. We should have used the boy to help us!"

I heard the sound of a slap and then the digging continued. The sound appeared to be coming from the rear and that suggested a kitchen. I went down a narrow passage and saw the glow from a fire. The noise grew louder. Robin would be at the rear and he would prevent an escape in that direction.

The first voice I had heard spoke again and this time was excited, "There it is, quickly and we will escape before they arrive."

I stepped into the kitchen and saw a warrior. He wore a long mail hauberk and had a good sword on his belt. He was a well-made warrior and looked to be strong. His hair was cropped short in the Norman style. The other was also a warrior wearing a leather metal studded brigandine. He was bending over a hole in the ground and trying to pull out a chest. The mailed man sensed my movement and turned around. He had no spurs and that made him a Norman man at arms. He was not to be underestimated. He hauled out his sword and turned to face me as the other man dragged the chest out of the ground. He turned and headed for the back door. The Norman had drawn his sword quickly even as I slashed at him. I was right to be wary for he deftly blocked my sword and turned it to riposte at my body. If I had not had my dagger ready, then he would have skewered me. His sword almost shaved my hose. I punched at him with the hilt of my sword for the low ceiling prevented me from slashing down at him. The crosspiece caught his eye and he grunted in pain. Holding my dagger against his sword to stop him from striking again I pulled back my sword hand and punched at his face once more. This time I connected with his nose. As the bone and cartilage broke and blood-spattered, I heard a shout from the rear. Robin had taken the other one. The man at arms reeled a little and, losing his footing, stepped into the hole. As he fell backwards, I heard a snap as his leg broke and this time he screamed. I would take no more chances and I lunged with my sword and ended his pain.

Robin appeared in the doorway, his sword and dagger at the ready. When he saw me whole, he smiled, "I have the other dead outside. He has a chest!"

"And it was worth risking capture. Did you spy any other?"

He shook his head. "There are four horses in the stable and one of them is a courser."

"That would be the one belonging to the man at arms. They spoke of a boy. You search upstairs and I will search the rest of the house."

"There are several other buildings outside but none of them looks like they could hold a man. They look like animal byres."

There was a tallow candle burning in the kitchen and Robin lit another he found. He took the candle and headed up the stairs. I sheathed my dagger and used the other candle to search the rest of the downstairs. There was a large room, but the furnishings suggested a bachelor. I saw no sign of a woman. There was a shield on the wall and two spears in the corner which confirmed that this was a man at arms. A bascinet helmet sat on the table. The other room downstairs was a storeroom and had treasure we could use. I decided that we would use this as our home for the night. It was the spoils of war! I was seeking a boy. Boys could become men and could fight us! It was not something I enjoyed but I would have to find him and eliminate the threat. I stepped outside the kitchen door into the darkness. I saw the dead man and the chest, and I heard the horses neighing and shifting nervously in the stable. Holding the candle before me I confirmed that the buildings were animal byres or storerooms. I opened the first one and found a pig and her young. The clucking in the second told me what lay within before I opened it. The third door looked to be another pig pen but, when I opened it, I found the boy. He was no more than twelve or thirteen summers old, it was hard to tell for the dirt and dried blood, but he would soon be a man and I drew back my sword to end his life.

When he spoke it was in English, "Mercy, I beg you, master, mercy!"

I stopped the blow and jammed my sword into the ground. I put my hand in to help him out. "Come, for I am an English archer and serve Prince Edward."

He shook his head and pointed to his neck where was there was a leather collar, "I cannot for I am chained to the wall."

Anger filled me and I wished I had made the man at arms suffer more than I had. I went closer to the boy so that I could see better. As I did so I saw that he was dressed in rags. "Hold this so that I may see more clearly." I handed him the candle. There was barely enough room to crawl in and I smelled human waste; the candle showed some of it smeared on what passed for breeks. The boy had been kept here and treated worse than an animal. There was a tale here! I could see that there was a chain which held the leather collar. "I will have to cut through the leather. This may take some time."

The boy said, "So long as I am out of my gaol I care not, sir!"

I placed my hand between the leather and the boy's neck so that I would not cut him. I started to use my dagger to saw through the leather close to the metal ring which bound it to the chain. It was fortunate that I had placed my hand there for the dagger's blade suddenly cut through the leather and cut the back of my hand. It was nothing but had it been the boy's neck.... I stepped out and held my hand down. When he came out, I saw that he was thin and emaciated. He was shaking. I sheathed my sword and dagger and went to the dead man. Taking his cloak, I wrapped it around the boy's shoulders. I took the candle and was leading him back into the house when Robin arrived. He looked at the boy in surprise. I said, "He is English. Bring in the chest and whatever else this man has. "We will stay here this night, but this boy needs our care."

When we entered the kitchen, the boy saw the body of the Norman man at arms and he spat at it. "I hope you rot in hell, you bastard!"

I sat him on the chair and went to the pot which was bubbling on the fire. There was a stew of some sort and I ladled a bowl of it and, after finding a spoon gave them to the boy. Robin returned with the chest. "Get rid of the Norman and bring back his mail and whatever else of value he has."

"Aye, Captain."

The boy was eating so greedily that I knew he had not eaten well, if at all. Questions would have to wait. He finished his first bowl and I gave him a second before Robin returned. "Watch the boy and I will return once I have spoken with the others." I lowered my voice, "He will need cleaning up before the others see him."

"Aye, Captain. The poor bairn is in a bad way- how could a man treat another like this?"

"I know not but we shall find out!" The village was relatively quiet for all opposition had been eliminated. I went to the centre of the village and saw William, "Did you take many horses?"

"Fifteen and there are more in the village."

"If you set two sentries on the south road, I will put two on the north. Let us go and find the priest."

Even as we walked towards the church, we saw women and children helping some old folk and they were fleeing from the church. I saw Ned there and he was glowering at Rafe the Dull. Ned shook his head, "Sorry Captain, Rafe here is well named!"

Rafe was a huge archer who could release arrow after arrow without any sign of weakening but in all other matters, he was slow. Some of the archers said, somewhat unkindly, that he had been dropped on his head as a child. My other archers were, generally, protective of him and did not take advantage of him. If he had not been an archer, then I do not know what he would have done to live.

I had learned to speak to him as though he was a child, "Rafe, tell me what happened, and I will not be angry."

"Ned had told them all to leave the church and I was seeking booty when there was a movement behind me. I turned and struck out, Captain, I did not know it was the priest."

I sighed, it was an accident, but the villagers would spread the story of violent English archers who disregarded God and his priests. "To make amends you must take him and bury him in the churchyard. Make a cross for him and when that is done Ned will write the priest's name on the cross and all will be well."

Rafe's face lit up, taking my words for forgiveness and his task of burial as absolution, "Thank you, Captain!" With contemptuous ease, he slung the body on his back and headed out of the church.

William said, "Is he a good archer?"

"Aye, but he has the mind of a seven-year-old. Ask him next week of this and it will be gone from his mind as though it was never there. He is harmless, unless of course he aims his bow at you!"

William nodded and spread his arm around the interior of the church, "And this?"

I shrugged, "The sin is committed and if we do not take what is within then others will."

"You are right. I will see that you and your men have fair division."

That done I turned to Ned, "We have the large house at the south side of the village. Put two men on guard duty at the north end of the village and then join us. We have food."

He nodded, "Dull Rafe's mistake apart, this has been a good day, has it not?"

"That it has, and it bodes well for the rest of this campaign."

I made my way back to our temporary home. With the rest of the vanguard just a few miles down the road, we had no real fear of an attack, but four sentries would be enough to keep us safe. I knew that Ned would pick the two archers who had done the least during the attack. It would not be a punishment but encouragement to emulate the rest the next time we went into action. When I entered the kitchen, I saw that Robin had tried to clean the soiled breeks, but the boy needed a good wash. In a perfect world, we would have bathed him but this was war and we would have to do the best that we could. Robin stood and came over to me, "A sad tale, Captain and I am glad we killed those two Normans. His back looks like he has been a galley slave for twenty years or more!"

"I told the lads we had food on the go, get something sorted eh? That stew will make a good start."

"There is a ham and plenty of beans and greens. I will see to it."

I sat down opposite the boy. I saw that he was almost a youth. Perhaps I had thought him younger than he actually was; he was very thin. He reminded me of me when I had been an apprentice. "I am John Hawkwood, a vintenar."

"I know, Captain, I saw you at Cadzand."

I looked surprised, "You were there?"

Shaking his head, he said, "Not at the battle but I was with the army. My name is Michael son of William and my father was a man at arms. We were not well off for we had fallen on hard times, but my father was a good soldier. My mother died two years since; God cursed us when he took her for our lives were worse after that day. My father said we should have taken the cross to make up for whatever sin we had committed. We did not and he regretted that until the day he died. My father had no horse and so he often fought afoot. When the King held his tournament at Brussels, we were with the company of Sir John Hayley and there were just ten of us. Sir John had lost a wager at the tournament and we were heading for Dunkerque to embark for England when we were ambushed. Sir John and his squire escaped but the others fought to protect my father, me and the other man who had no horse, Roger of Lewes. I held the horses and they fought until they all died."

I saw him filling up. He was still young and so I poured two goblets of the wine Robin had found and offered one to Michael, "Let us drink to the bravery of brothers in arms who fought until the end. For a warrior, it is a good end."

He drank deeply and I gestured for him to continue with the tale. He nodded with his head at the hole in the floor, "The man you slew was Bertrand de Gisors and he was a man at arms. My father slew his brother before he was overcome. In retribution, my father's body was butchered like an animal and..." he shook his head unable to finish but I knew what they would have done to his body.

"I understand but you were kept like an animal, why?"

"Butchering my father was not enough for he wanted vengeance. He fed me just enough to keep me alive and he took pleasure in beating me each day."

Now I understood Robin's words. "Let us get you sorted out eh? My men will be coming soon when they have finished their work and we should make you presentable. There is water out the back. Go and wash the grime from you." I knew there would be lice and nits. "When you return Robin will give you archer's hair!"

Robin had been in the kitchen for some time listening, "Aye Captain, that I will, and I saw some lye soap. That will cleanse him. I will see to it." From that moment on Robin took a special interest in Michael and became a sort of big brother to him.

I nodded, "And I will find some clothes for you!"

Robin shook his head, "I have looked already, Captain, and there is nothing to fit."

I smiled, "We shall see!"

Robin was right but, when I examined the chests and cupboards, I found a good pair of breeks, some hose, a tunic and a good shirt. I also found some needles and thread in the kitchen. My apprenticeship might come in handy. Michael was naked and wrapped in a blanket when I entered the kitchen again, but he was clean and he smelled not of shit but of soap, it was an improvement. Robin had used his knife to remove the longest hair and now he had made a lather and was using his dagger to carefully shave Michel's head. They both looked at me curiously as I carefully unpicked the breeks.

I smiled at them, "When I was your age, Michael, I was a tailor's apprentice. This just shows that a man can change his stars if he chooses."

After his head was shaved, I tossed him the hose, "They will not fit well but they will be more comfortable than nothing."

By the time he had donned them, my men had come in and, after helping themselves to horns of ale from the barrel, they looked at me with interest. They also stared at Michael. After what he had been through such scrutiny did not worry him.

"Fill in the hole. I do not want any to fall in and then help yourself to Robin's stew!"

I finished sewing the breeks. Stephen the Tailor would have given me a clip for the stitches were not all the same size, but I knew that they would not tear. I tossed them to him, and he put them on. I began to unpick the shirt which he would wear next to his skin.

As I sewed, I spoke, "So, Michael, what would you do now that you are freed?" Ned gave me a questioning look, but Robin shook his head. He would explain later.

Michael was pleased with his breeks and he was grinning, "To be honest, Captain, I know not. I am now an orphan and all that I know is following the army around." He looked around him, "I could be your servant, Captain! I can fetch wood and I can cook and…"

I began to sew the shirt, "I am not sure, Michael, for we are the vanguard and we ride."

"I can ride, Captain, and the horses in the stable are mainly the ones that de Gisors captured from my father's friends. I know the animals!"

Robin butted in, "Captain, it is our Christian duty!"

I glared at him, "When I need a lesson in charity, I will ask for it, Puck! Fetch me some stew!"

He was not put out and said cheerfully, "Aye, Captain, and some wine to cool your temper too, eh?"

"I know not why I put up with you, Robin Goodfellow!"

As he ladled stew into a wooden bowl he said, "Because I can hide in plain sight and I am the third-best archer in the company!"

I bit the thread and threw the shirt at Michael, "Here, I will finish the tunic when I have eaten." As he finished dressing, I said, "There are a pair of shoes in the bedroom. If you pad them then you might be able to wear them until we kill a Norman your size."

He started to head upstairs and then stopped, "Then I can stay with you?"

"For the present, aye, but if Prince Edward needs your horse you will have to travel with the baggage and the carpenters."

Laughing he said, "And I have done that before."

He ran upstairs; all his hurts seemed to be behind him.

"That was kindly done, Captain."

"Aye, well, Ned, I hate cruelty to any child and his father died for England. We will keep him until we return to England and then see what we can do."

For some reason, the extra mouth we had to feed seemed to endear me further with my men. I knew not why.

One of the horses we had taken was little more than a pony and too small for any archer save, perhaps, Robin Goodfellow and so Michael rode with us. He proved himself useful by holding the horses of myself, Ned and Jack and he was right, he was good with horses. The next day was a repetition of the first except that we used Sainte-Mère-Église as a base and brought the horses and supplies we found there. Over the next few days, we scoured the land for twenty miles around the village and found many more horses. The other archers joined us on the evening of that day, and with more men, we were able to forage further afield.

It was seven days after we had landed that Prince Edward reached Sainte-Mère-Église with the rest of the vanguard. We now had eight hundred mounted archers and the Prince was more than happy with our work. If he noticed Michael, he did not say anything and, on the nineteenth of July as the rest of the army caught up with us, we headed to Carentan. We left Sainte-Mère-Église a burning ruin with just the stone church remaining. All trace of Bertrand de Gisors was eliminated. The Normans and the French knew that we were coming, the refugees had told them so but without a castle, the soldiers abandoned the town and headed to Saint-Lô. Carentan suffered the same fate as the other towns through which we had passed. Smoke towards the coast told us that the fleet was doing the same as we were. Saint-Lô was also abandoned and proved to be the richest pickings thus far. We found fine houses and all that the people had taken was what they could carry. Chests were dug up and we found fine clothes and garments. Michael could throw away the ones I had made for him and he was dressed as a young noble. Other archers and men at arms heard of his story. Many of the men at arms knew William, his father, and we had so many clothes for him that it was fortunate that we also found a leather case to hold them. There was no real problem as the only one in the army that they would fit was Michael.

Saint-Lô was burned and left in ruins, a testament to this policy of running from us. I wondered if the French would fight us at all. They chose Caen as the place to fight us!

Chapter 11

Caen had a castle. A very strong castle with a huge circular keep; it was the place where they had buried the Conqueror and, I suppose that they saw it as a place we could not take easily which was why they chose it to halt us. They had the river to protect it and a curtain and town wall. In theory, we should have been forced to fight for it over weeks rather than days. The difference was the seven thousand archers whom the King had brought. We had not had to draw bow yet in numbers and, as we lined up, three hundred paces from the town wall, we were eager to show the French what we could do. We knew that they intended to fight us for they lined their walls with men at arms and crossbowmen as well as spearmen and townsfolk. I guessed that the ones who had fled east would now be ready to fight us. They had abandoned their homes and would see this as a chance to rid their land of the God-Damns! We had been the vanguard and led by Prince Edward but now it was his father and the other leader, the Earl of Northampton who took the decisions. We had the town surrounded and there appeared to be no hurry, but the King had three ranks of archers lined up within hours of our arrival. Prince Edward's archers were the largest number of archers and we occupied the front line. Behind us were the Earl of Northampton's men and finally the King's. We each had two bags of arrows and could loose forty-eight before we needed to replenish them. As most of us had not used our bows since we left England, they would send an arrow further than the French realised and the three hundred paces might have seemed extreme, but it was not. The King was on a white horse and he rode down the line. It was a brave thing to do as the crossbows were in range although, as I realised, at that range and with the plate armour the King was wearing it was unlikely that he would be hurt but I admired him for his bravado.

"Archers of England, we are here to win back that land which is rightfully England's and belongs to my family. This land belonged to William Duke of Normandy and he became King of England. Today you shall make it English once more."

We all cheered and waited for Captain Harry, the King's archer, to give us our order.

"Draw!"

I had never heard so many bows drawn at once and it made the hairs on the back of my neck tingle for it sounded like a living beast. The creature we had become was made of many different parts, but it was though our hearts beat as one. Although we would all loose together each of us would be in our own world and rhythm. Every one of us would have our own target in our head and as we loosed and eliminated the target we would move on. I was closest to the gatehouse and I saw a man at arms standing close to a crenulation. There was a crossbow too, but the operator was hiding. Perhaps he had fought against us before and knew that in this battle there would be only one winner.

"Loose!"

It was impossible for every arrow to be sent at exactly the same moment and so the whistling noise, so reminiscent of birds taking flight, rolled on for longer than normal. Of course, I was already drawing a second arrow, but I watched my arrow smack into the shoulder of a man at arms. Even though it was a bodkin arrow it might not be fatal at that range for if the man had any plate on him it would slow the entry of the missile. With so many thousands of arrows being sent at the walls, it would have been a surprise if men had not been killed. We sent a dozen flights and then the Earl of Northampton sent in his division of men at arms with scaling ladders. The walls were small enough to be able to use them.

I had used a war bag of thirty arrows when Captain Harry shouted, "Archers, rest!"

I knew what was coming next and so I turned to Michael who was standing behind the third rank of archers. "Put my bow in my case and watch my arrows!" We would be storming the walls and archers had the dilemma of dropping a bow or slinging it. Neither was a satisfactory state of affairs and I saw Ned and some of the others looking enviously at me as Michael scurried off. He showed initiative, however, when he returned and ran up to Ned and Jack.

"Masters, I can carry yours too!"

He had just passed through the third rank when Prince Edward gave the order for the whole of the army to advance. The men at arms had scaled the walls for so many defenders had been knocked from it that they managed to gain the fighting platform over a large area in a very short time. I ran, not to the ladders but the main gate to the town for the first men at arms would open it. Unencumbered by bows and bags of arrows Ned, Jack and I easily outstripped not only the mailed men at arms but the rest of the archers. The gates creaked open when we were forty paces from them. I saw that two of our men at arms who had opened them had blood on their tunics although whose blood it was harder to identify. I drew my sword before we passed through the gate and then I held my axe in my left hand. The French had many men at arms inside the castle and almost every man we saw had a sword or a weapon in his hand. They were, however, defeated before they began for they had fallen back at every stage and we had been in Normandy for fourteen nights and this was the first time they had fought us. The three of us ran at some crossbowmen who had descended the walls and were trying to load their crossbows. Even though there were six of them and they were thirty paces from us the three of us never hesitated for a moment. If we had then one of the bolts would have struck us. I was the fastest and the most confident. I struck the middle of their line before they had even raised their weapons and I used my sword to sweep up and knock a crossbow into the air whilst smashing my axe into the skull of a second man. The head made a sucking sound as I pulled it out. The soldier whose crossbow I had hit had fallen and I used my sword to skewer him to the ground. I was amongst them now and after pulling out my sword I hacked across the brigandine of a third. I whipped my head around to look for another target but all six lay dead. While Ned and I stood guard, Jack stripped them of their purses.

The town was now filled with the English, Welsh and Breton army. I did not doubt that many were trying to flee through the other gate, but few would manage it for we pressed and chased them through the streets. Some men at arms and some archers entered the shops and homes to begin their looting sooner rather than later. I knew that there would be more to be had from the better homes and businesses closer to the keep and the river. The keep was a strong one, but our rapid attack had made the French flee without defending it. I did not think that Duke William would have been happy at such capitulation. My archers and I did not pursue all the way to the other side of the town for we had done our part and there was a town to be sacked. I have heard men, usually churchmen, speak of a chevauchée as a barbaric excuse for men to behave badly. That is not so. King Edward used it, as I would in later times, as a good strategy. True, we would take what we could and burn what was left but the people of the place we raided would be already dead or fled by then. We were simply diminishing the ability of a people to fight. Such raids encouraged kings and counts to do one of two things, either to bring an army to battle or talk of peace. We had not done enough damage to France yet and so there would be no peace.

It was that first day which saw the greatest slaughter. On the second day bodies were taken from the town to be burned and King Edward's clerks counted them as the carpenters and miners we had brought piled them and burned them. We saw little of that for we spent two days looting Caen. It was the second biggest city in Normandy, and it was rich. Once again, we profited, and I collected as much treasure in those two days as I had given to Basil of Tarsus for safekeeping. My men and I found a house to use while we were in Caen. It was close to the gates and most of our army had passed it and moved on. We liked to have a roof over our heads while we collected our treasure. We fetched Michael and our better horses for there was a small stable attached to the house. Michael had spoken truly, and he was a good cook. With a fine kitchen, he set to work to cook for my forty men and me. We found things he could use as we foraged for the next two days. I, too, was now looking for different sorts of things. If I was to be a man at arms, then I needed an aketon or gambeson; a padded garment to wear beneath my new mail. I found the stiffening body of a man at arms who had tumbled from the fighting platform. His mail had been stripped but he had a good aketon and the man was my size. The fall had killed him but left the aketon undamaged. Balin was making me a helmet but I found an arming cap on another body. This man had been hacked in two by an axe, but his head was undamaged. I had been too slow in my search to find plate, but I told my men that, in future raids, they should look out for plate. If they were curious then they were also wise enough not to ask me.

King Edward dismissed the fleet and sent them back to England with orders to return with supplies and reinforcements north of the Somme at a small port called Le Crotoy. He had grand plans. We left Caen a ruin, but we tarried too long there. I can see that now but, at the time, it seemed as though the French were beaten, and we could march all the way to Paris. For the next week, we raided and looted taking Troarn, Lisieux and Brionne in turn. Captain Harry had come to value my archers and often spoke to me when he came from the councils of war. We still travelled in our three divisions but when we took a town the King would gather his leaders and plan his strategy. Thus it was that I had more of an idea about the grand plan and I knew that King Edward planned to take Rouen which was the largest town in Normandy and the richest. With that prize then the King of France would be forced to sue for peace. Most of the army cared not about a peace for the wagons were laden with loot and many men emulated me and carried their treasure in money belts beneath their clothes.

We halted at Brionne and we were cooking a pig we had found, the first since Sainte-Mère-Église. The sow and piglets we had taken at our first halt had lasted us four days and had been good eating; I hoped this one would last as long. I was salivating as the flesh crackled on the fire when Sir John Chandos sought me out, "Archer, the Prince and his father would have a word with you."

Nodding a warning to Michael to keep some good meat for me I left and headed for the mayor's house which had been commandeered by the King. As I entered, I saw a French knight, Count Godfrey d'Harcourt. He was often seen in the company of the Prince. It was the King who spoke, "John Hawkwood, I want you to choose your best ten men and guard Count Godfrey. He goes to scout out the bridges across the Seine. You are to protect him at all costs."

"Yes, Your Majesty."

"You will leave this night for I am anxious to take Rouen."

My heart sank. The evening I had envisaged was now ruined and, at best, I would be eating pork on the back of a horse. The amphora of wine we had would be consumed by my men. "Yes, Your Majesty."

The French knight said, "I will bring my men to your camp."

I was dismissed. When I reached the house we were using, I shouted, "Ned, Jack, come here. Robin, I shall need you!" My tone did not invite tardiness and the three of them were there in moments. "I am to take ten men and scout. Robin, here are the nine men you and I will lead." I rattled off their names. "Get some of the cooked pig for we eat on the hoof."

Robin grinned for he was hard to dishearten, "Then that is all to the good, for we will have the choice of the best cuts and I, for one, like the fresh juices and fat dripping down my chin!"

He hurried off, "Ned, I leave you in command. My treasure box and that which I have taken are with the spare horse. Have Michael watch over it."

"Aye, Captain."

Just then I heard the hooves of the Count and the six men of his household. "Are you ready, archer?"

I stepped outside. I did not like this arrogant French Count for the tone he used was one of a master to a slave and if Prince Edward and Sir John Chandos spoke to me kindly then so should he. "I was asked to choose my men and I am doing so,"

"My lord."

"I beg your pardon?"

"I am a French count and you will address me as my lord."

I shrugged, "You are a Frenchman who has changed sides. You have no lands and your title means nothing to me."

"You are impertinent."

I smiled, "Aye, and I enjoy killing Frenchmen. Do not worry, I will protect you, Count Godfrey, but I am not one of your serfs and I will not be treated as one. I am a free man and a Captain of Archers."

Robin had arrived and witnessed the conversation. He tossed me a juicy piece of pork, "Michael knows his business, Captain. This is a lovely piece of meat. The lads are here, and we can go now!"

Biting a hunk of meat, I hauled myself into the saddle and, ignoring the red-faced French Count, rode to the head of my men. "We head for the Seine, Robin, you and Peter take the lead." Still eating I wheeled Megs and we headed due north from the town and rode towards the Seine. We rode through the night and I saw that we rode through a deserted land. The smell of woodsmoke was absent. The people had fled. Our attack on Brionne had sent them hence. More, I heard no animal noises. They had taken their animals too which meant there was nothing to forage. It was dawn when we reached the Seine.

Robin was waiting for us by the blackened and burned piers of the bridge which had been destroyed. "It looks like we aren't crossing here, Captain."

The French Count rode up. We had not spoken a word during the night. He viewed the burned wood. "We will need to ride to Elbeuf!"

I nodded. The horses would struggle but I would not give the Frenchman the satisfaction of admitting that. I did not have to as one of his men at arms said, "Count, we will destroy our horses. They need some water and at least an hour of rest." He glared at me, "Unlike these God-Damns, we did not eat last night." Even though he had insulted me I smiled.

"Then one hour only. Archer, ride towards Elbeuf and await us there!"

Perhaps he thought to anger me, but it did not work. "Right lads let us ride while these Frenchmen enjoy a rest. We are Englishmen and need it not!"

In truth we did but I would not give him the pleasure of knowing that. We rode until we were out of sight and then I said, "Dismount. We will walk and then rest for a short while. I would not hurt our horses either."

We walked, perhaps a mile and that helped to cool down the horses. We stopped at a small farm which lay close to the river and let the horses drink and graze. We examined the farm and saw that it had been stripped of all food. I looked at the fields and saw that the ripening crop of wheat had been burned. The French were trying to starve our army. We did not rest long and then we mounted and rode along the river. We were archers and knew how to conceal ourselves. We reached Elbeuf and I saw the French flooding across the bridges. They were also preparing to fire the bridge.

"Peter, ride to the Prince and tell him that the French are preparing to set fire to the bridges over the Seine."

Peter had a good horse; it was one we had taken from Sainte-Mère-Église and he was a lighter rider. "Aye, Captain." He would be able to take a direct route and meet up with the army much sooner.

I turned to the others, "Tie up your horses and string your bows! Let us see what mischief we can cause. We will try to hurt their soldiers and panic the civilians!"

We strung our bows and walked closer to the small town. I guessed that any soldiers on guard would be watching the road from the south and not from the west. I saw that there were men at arms shepherding the people across the bridge while other soldiers were packing faggots around the wood piers. We used the cover of the deserted houses, for those living closest to the river had fled first, and I waved at my men to spread out. If we could make them think we were a larger number than we were we might delay them. I nocked an arrow and aimed at a loud sergeant at arms who was ordering the people to hurry up. I drew and released. The others sent their arrows a heartbeat later. The range was less than two hundred paces and the sergeant fell forward with the arrow in his back. When the other arrows hit those with the faggots and the men at arms then panic set in and the steady movement across the bridge became a stampede and I saw people falling into the river as they were barged to the side while I heard the screams of those who were trampled underfoot. There were so many people crowded on the bridge that it was hard to hit just the men at arms and soldiers. That encouraged them and a dozen detached themselves and ran at us. I believe that there were many men in our position who would have panicked but not my men. We merely switched targets to the men at arms who were racing at us. We hit them all and wasted not a single arrow! It was then I spied a knight ride his horse across the bridge. He was carrying a flaming torch and was a tempting target but the men who ran at us were a priority. By the time we had hit some and deterred the rest the knight had lit the faggots seemingly oblivious to the people already on it. He turned and galloped across the bridge and more people were thrown into the Seine. As the flames around the Elbeuf side of the bridge rose so the ones who were trying to cross realised the futility and they headed up the river road towards Pont de l'Arche, the next bridge over the Seine.

I turned to Matthew, "Fetch the horses! The rest of you let us see if any of the men at arms are alive."

One was. He had been hit in both legs by two arrows. While Robin tended his wounds I questioned the man, "What is your King doing?" He set his lip and I nodded to Robin, "You wish to die? If this archer does not bind your leg, then you will bleed to death. I ask again, where is your King?"

As Robin tightened the tourniquet the man at arms winced and nodded, "He has gathered our men north of the river at Rouen and called the arrière-ban." I knew what that meant. Every able-bodied man had to be at the muster to fight for the King. "Your God-Damns and the Flemish are attacking from the north and we are stretched."

I smiled, "Good, that was not so hard, was it?"

By the time Robin had finished, we had stripped the other bodies of their valuables and begun to search houses for the paltry pickings that they contained. The French Count and his men rode up. "We were too late then?"

I nodded, "We could not have stopped them, and I have sent word to Prince Edward. The army will be here before dark."

"Then we should head to Pont l'Arche before they can destroy that bridge too."

I shook my head, "Your horses have rested and ours have not. You can go on this time and we will follow."

"I order you to come!"

I stood and put my hands on my hips, "I do not take orders from a French traitor and I will not waste my horse's life when I know that every bridge between here and Paris will be destroyed already! If the army had been here then we might, and I repeat might, have saved this one, but I doubt it. We will wait!"

Count Godfrey was no fool and he realised I was right. As we cooked some food in one of the houses Robin said, "You will be in trouble for this, Captain."

I nodded, "But they will do little about it for King Edward needs his archers and we will be the ones seeking food to feed the army. I will take my punishment."

It was evening by the time Prince Edward and the vanguard arrived. By then the middle section of the bridge had collapsed into the river and there were just blackened stumps remaining. The Prince rode directly to Count Godfrey. I knew that the Frenchman would be exaggerating both my words and my actions. I had kept the prisoner whose name was Gilles with us. Robin had done a good job and cleansed the wounds. Although the soldier would struggle to walk for a while he would at least heal as neither bone nor artery had been touched. My archers looked on as an angry Prince Edward strode over to me.

"Count Godfrey told me that you were not only impertinent to him you refused an order too!"

"I was not impertinent, Prince Edward, I just did not acknowledge his title. I was asked to guard him and not to bow and scrape to him. As for disobeying the order, what could I have done with a handful of archers, my lord? See here," I pointed to the dead men at arms and my prisoner, "I did what I could with my archers but the only way to prevent the French from burning the bridges is simple, send every mounted archer instead of a handful."

He turned, angrily, and looked at the Count, "You have a prisoner? The Count did not mention that."

"And why would he for he wished to portray me in a poor light." I pointed over the river to the northern shore, "King Philip has raised the levy and he has a huge army to the north of us. Although Flemish soldiers and some English are attacking from the north King Philip has sent to the Duke of Normandy to bring north the army which was attacking Gascony. In my opinion, a lowly archer, every bridge up to and including Paris will be burned or destroyed and he will try to trap us between his two armies."

Prince Edward was clever, and he grasped what I said and the implications immediately, "You are a clever man, I will give you that, but you have ideas above your station. I command you to show the Count respect."

I smiled, "Then it might be better, my lord, if you kept us apart for there is mutual dislike."

Snorting he turned and said, "Send the prisoner to my quarters! You are impossible!"

I knew, at that moment, that the Prince would, eventually, tire of me. I needed a future which was determined by me and not at the whim of a king or a count.

The King and his council heeded my words and eight hundred of us rode ahead of the army each day as we raced to find a bridge intact but it was as I had told the Prince, the French were trying to trap us. We found little food and no animals. I think that we were luckier than the rest of the army as whatever there was to be found, we took. When we reached Poissy on the eleventh of August, we were just twenty miles from Paris. Behind us we saw the villages burned by Prince Edward and we waited. A messenger arrived to tell us to scout out the outskirts of Paris and to see if there were any other bridges that we could use. I was named as the captain who should lead the scouts. I took just my men for I knew it would be a waste of time.

We left Poissy and followed the Seine. We had our bows slung for if we found trouble then I wanted to be able to hit the French hard before retreating. The next three bridges were all destroyed and then when we saw the towers of the churches of Paris, we saw guarded bridges. The sunlight shone from the metal of their mail and their helmets and they saw us. We had travelled more than fourteen miles and the horses were tired. We could have turned them around and galloped away but they were so tired that I could not guarantee that we would escape.

"Dismount! Horse holders!" I knew I was losing a fifth of my men, but it could not be helped. "These are mailed men so let us use bodkins!"

Although a bodkin could easily pierce mail, it was less effective against plate, especially at longer range. I did not draw but kept it at the quarter draw as I gauged the target and the best time to strike. I saw that they had sent forty mailed men at us and they had with them forty hobelars or lightly armoured horsemen. My decision to dismount was a wise one for the hobelars would have caught us and, I have no doubt, despatched us!

"Draw!"

The men at arms were two hundred paces from us and the hobelars were using the mailed men for protection. I saw as I drew back, that the leading men at arms had plate and that they must have been knights.

"Release! And nock a second bodkin!"

As we nocked, I watched the first flight of thirty arrows descend and strike. A couple of horses were struck but, more importantly, eight of the mailed men were hit. The sound of the bodkin arrows hitting and penetrating mail was a distinctive one.

"Release! Nock a war arrow and aim at the hobelars."

The horsemen were now less than a hundred paces from us and when our thirty arrows struck, ten men at arms were hit and six fell from their saddles. There were less than half of the men at arms now and some of those were either wounded or had wounded horses. I saw a plated knight turn and shout something.

"Release!"

The knight's command was now clear. He had ordered his hobelars to close with us. At a range of eighty paces every arrow which struck would either kill or seriously wound the French light horsemen who had a leather jerkin at best. I did not order the fourth arrow for all of my men saw the threat and they nocked, drew and released as I did when the hobelars were less than forty paces from us. Three riders escaped unscathed and they wisely retreated. I did not push our luck, but we stood our ground with arrows nocked while the survivors retreated to the bridge. The wounded men who could either crawled or walked back. Fifteen hobelars and eight men at arms lay on the ground and were a good measure of our success.

"Back to the horses."

We mounted and walked our horses west, back to Poissy. I kept glancing over my shoulder but there was no pursuit. I did not know it then, but our arrival and our attack had created panic. Riders were sent to King Philip and his army. They thought that King Edward planned on taking Paris. He moved his whole army north of Paris in order to protect it. We reached Poissy as darkness was falling and we arrived as the carpenters we had brought to build siege engines had begun, instead, to repair the bridge. The one at Poissy was at a narrower point than the others.

I reported directly to the King and the Prince who both nodded, "You have done well. We will cross here and head for the Somme and our ships. Was there food east of here?"

"We saw nothing, King Edward. They have burned their crops and slaughtered their animals. A horse can graze but that is all."

"Then if we wish to feed the army we must head for the Somme."

Prince Edward nodded, "I want the archers to swim the river tomorrow while we finish the bridge. You and your men can do that?"

"It is not easy, Prince Edward, but most of us can. If I might suggest we just take the confident archers rather than risk losing others?"

"Very well, but I want the bridgehead securing!"

He was less friendly since Count Godfrey had spoken ill of me. My time with the Prince was going to be limited. I would need another paymaster.

Chapter 12

Five hundred of us swam across the river but the Prince's fears had been groundless. There was no sign of the French and I think that was because of our action close to Paris. My men and I were sent further north to discover the whereabouts of the French army; it seemed my men and I were expendable. As on the previous day, we rode with bows slung and we rode cautiously. My hunting dog, Robin Goodfellow, rode well ahead for he seemed to be able to sniff out the French. We were just a few miles from Grisy when he found their signs. There were two broken wagons and the discarded crossbow bolts told us that it was the French army. They had moved east, that much was obvious. To confirm it we rode to the east and saw the baggage train of the French some two miles up the road and they were heading closer to Paris.

By the time we turned and reached the Seine again, it was dark and most of the army had crossed the completed bridge. After I had reported to Prince Edward and the King I headed back to my men. When we had scouted, we had been lucky and found a milking goat which had somehow been overlooked. It might have been able to outrun the French but not a war arrow and we would eat well. As we were cooking it I saw Captain Geoffrey who commanded the Earl of Northampton's men in his camp. He had once commanded King Edward's archers and so I knew him.

He waved me over, "Are the French gone?"

I nodded, "They headed east."

He grinned, "Then King Edward shows that he has the measure of this Frenchman. While you were gone a rider came from the direction of Paris. I am guessing your arrival there yesterday made them think we intended to attack. King Philip has invited us to do battle and King Edward suggested we meet south of Paris. The army has been crossing ever since. We will burn the bridge we have built and head for Le Crotoy."

That was clever for the French would head south and by the time they discovered we had no intention of giving battle we would be further away, and King Edward would be able to choose his own battlefield! "It is probably for the best. We all have full purses and more, but a man cannot eat gold, as King Midas discovered to his cost. We may not have won a kingdom, but we go home as rich men."

"Aye, if we can get home!" The Captain was obviously a pessimist.

The Captain was right and as the bridge the carpenters had built was burned, we headed north for Grisy. I had already told the King and his son that there was little to be had in that area and so the archers were sent out in groups of forty to forage far and wide for whatever food we could find. The army was starving! We took it in turns over the next seven days, as we headed to the Somme, to take the most dangerous place to forage, the east. It was the most dangerous because the French were closer there and it was a fruitful part of Picardy. We had that duty just after we left Troisserau. The army now stayed together far more, and it was only the eight hundred mounted archers who rode ahead of the ever-diminishing snake which was the Edwardian army. Men died, and it was not because of battle. There was disease as well as dysentery and desertions. They took hundreds of men; more than we had lost in battle.

My men and I found a nameless village to the east of Troisserau and my men spied a small flock of sheep. They were keen to rush in, but I counselled caution. Something did not feel right. The farmhouse had smoke coming from it and yet when we had approached no farmer had come out to discover who had arrived.

"Ned and Jack, dismount half of the men and have horse holders. Have bows ready. I will take the rest and try to capture this flock, but it feels like a Judas Goat to me!"

Other foragers had been attacked by peasants who were outraged by our presence on French soil. I drew my sword and waved my nineteen men forward. I was pleased to see that Ned had left me Rafe and Robin. Those two were the most reliable of my archers. I waved my sword to spread my men out for I wanted them as far apart as possible. First of all, it would help us to capture the sheep more easily but, more importantly, it would make us a smaller target!

I could see no shepherd and then I realised that I could not see a dog. No shepherd would leave his flock unattended. That made me look for small clues and I saw that the hurdles which surrounded the sheep were atop a rampart and that meant a ditch. This was a trap! As soon as I realised that I shouted, "Ride hard! It is a trap!"

These were shepherds and farmers. They were peasants who did not have the weapons to follow the Oriflamme! I kicked Megs hard and rode for the shadow that was in the blackberry bush. The Frenchman was not a warrior and instead of standing his ground and waiting for me to pass so that he could have a free strike at me, he stepped out and slashed at us with his billhook. I jinked Megs to the side and hacked into his neck. It was when he died that the rest attacked. There were at least sixty of them and many had been hiding in ditches and on the ground. Ned and Jack had my men send arrows into those who were further from us and that allowed those who rode with me to use their swords against unarmoured peasants wielding primitive and home-made polearms, daggers and, at best, hunting bows with hunting arrows. One such arrow hit my gambeson, but it did not penetrate. I leaned from my saddle to take the head of a farmer who had a short sword. I actually felt sorry for the peasants, but the army needed to eat and we needed this flock. Even as I hacked a peasant in the shoulder, I wondered how the other archers could have lost men for while we were outnumbered my men had the gauge of these men. Perhaps the others had ridden in blindly for Ned and Jack directed the rain of arrows so that the men we struck and killed were unsupported and, by the time we had reached the sheep, the resistance was no longer there.

I turned and shouted, "Ned, have the sheep collected and drive them back. We will pursue these men!"

"Aye, Captain!"

My men and I rode for two miles hewing and hacking at men who were terrified and desperate to escape us. It was not cruelty for if we did not kill them then they would come back, and they would kill us. We had two armies seeking us and if the local population joined them then all of us might die!

It was when we reached Poix, which lay south of the Somme, that we heard that the French army, now so great that accurate numbers were hard to estimate, was gathered at Amiens and they would deny us the crossing of the Somme. The fleet would be at Le Crotoy, north of the Somme and we pushed on, desperately hoping that the fleet would be there and could come south of the river and take us off the beach at St. Valery! If they did not, then we would be trapped against the sea with nowhere to go. King Edward wanted a battle but on our terms!

We moved quickly over the next four days as we had a narrower corridor to forage. The French did as they had done on the Seine and every bridge was destroyed. They had emptied the land south of the river and waited for us on the north bank while keeping their swords in the backs of our rearguard, the King. We had kept the bones of the goat and Michael made a stew which gradually became a soup. He added flavour by gathering wild greens, garlic and herbs as we travelled north and west. He was now an integral part of the company and I could not think of one who did not like him. He had an endearing quality which made all men take to him. I wondered what I would do when and if we ever returned to England. I did not want him as a servant for there was no dignity in that.

We were camped at Acheux which was just a few miles from St. Valery where we hoped to spy and signal the fleet when I spoke with him about his future. "When we get to England, Michael, you will have the pay you have earned with us. What would you?"

He shrugged, "I know not, Captain. Those months I spent chained in that byre, whipped so often I could barely feel it, made me just want to die. I think when you opened the door it felt like I was born again but as a youth! What did you do when you were my age?"

"I told you that first night when I sewed your clothes, I was an apprentice tailor. Had I not met Captain Philip then by now I might be a master tailor!"

He laughed, "Somehow, Captain, I cannot see that. You are a born soldier. Everyone knows that and I have followed the army long enough to recognise it too. It is not just that you are an archer, Robin tells me all the time of your quick thinking and your skill with all weapons." I shrugged for I was unused to praise and did not know how to handle it. Michael suddenly pounced, "That is it, Captain! Make me your apprentice!"

I shook my head, "You are too old to be trained as an archer." I tapped his chest, "This needs to be much bigger."

"I know but I mean training to be a soldier. You have skills with weapons, and I can not only cook but also keep weapons sharp. I could be useful to you."

There are times in a man's life when events happen which seem to be decided by some supernatural power. Our discovery of Michael had been an accident, or had it? I was planning a different future and now I saw a plan. If I was to become a man at arms, then I would need my own men with me. I could use the raw clay that was Michael to become the first. I nodded, "Very well but if the day comes that you tire of my grumpy ways then tell me and we shall part. I will have no man beholden to me because of a promise he made when he was young. There will be no indenture papers. It is your word and mine which will bind us!"

"Aye, Captain, and I am your man."

It was one of the best decisions I ever made.

The next day I was with the advance party and I had taken Michael with me. I had decided to begin his training immediately. Prince Edward also rode just ahead of us and, as we neared St. Valery, we all stared north to Le Crotoy across the Somme estuary. We gazed on an empty sea. The Count was with the Prince as well as the rest of Prince Edward's advisers. We dismounted and Ned and Jack joined us.

"Well, Captain, that is us buggered and no mistake!"

I smiled at Ned's colourful language.

Jack nodded his agreement, "Aye, with the French crossing the river at Abbeville and no crossings over the Somme we have to fight the French, and this does not look like a good place to fight them. I heard the French vanguard is closing with the baggage!"

Michael frowned and said, "What do you mean, Jack, no crossings?"

I think Jack thought that Michael might be like Rafe and a little simple, "The bridges, they are all destroyed."

Michael nodded, "But not the tidal ford at Blanchetaque."

His words gave me hope, "What? Speak!"

He pointed upstream, "At Blanchetaque there is a ford which can be crossed at low tide. You will get your feet wet, but it can be crossed."

"How do you know?"

"When we came back from the north, we came this way for it was the shortest way home."

I ran to the Prince. "My lord!"

Count Godfrey glared at me and the Prince snapped, "We are busy, archer!"

"My lord, there is a crossing of the Somme just a couple of miles east of here. We can cross at low tide."

The Prince turned on the Count, "Well?"

He shrugged, "I have heard of it, but I know not where it is."

I said, "Prince Edward, we can ride along the river and the boy we rescued knows the place for he crossed there."

Sir John Chandos smiled, "Prince Edward, it is a better choice than the one we face here. Your father needs to bring the French to battle but it is not here that he would choose."

"Very well, Sir John, ride to my father and tell him this news. We will follow the archers to this ford at Blanchetaque and hope that the boy is right!"

The Prince and his household flanked Michael and me as we led the vanguard along the swampy ground to the ford. That it was a ford became obvious when we saw a force of over three thousand Frenchmen guarding the northern bank. The Prince clapped Michael on the shoulders and then gave him a golden coin, "Well done!" Then he turned to me, "I want every archer in the river to clear the other bank! I can see the tide is still high but by the time my father is here with the baggage then I want us to command the far bank!"

I whipped Megs' head around and rode back to the archers. I was still just a vintenar and I told the four captains what the Prince intended. Captain William was the most senior archer and he nodded. "Every archer dismount and line up on the riverbank. Tell them that they will get their feet wet!"

I gathered my men and I took off my boots. There was little point in ruining a good pair of boots and being barefoot would give me a more secure stance. As we waited for the entire company of archers to assemble we all organised our bags of arrows and strung our bows. As some were still with King Edward and the Earl of Northampton we just had three thousand archers but, as I looked across the river, I saw that the majority of those who faced us, whilst they had shields had little mail. If they made a defence using the shields, then they would be packed into a solid block and the defence that presented was an illusion. The shields they had could not protect their whole body and as the French man at arms we had hit at Elbeuf had discovered, arrows in the legs were equally deadly!

Captain William led us into the water. It was icy and my feet immediately began to numb; that would pass. We all held our bows high. The tide was receding which meant we could steadily work our way across the ford as we cleared the bank. The French did as I had anticipated and locked shields so that we were presented by a wall of wood topped with helmets. Less than half of the French appeared to be warriors. They were the ones with good helmets and larger shields. There was a sprinkling of mail amongst them. The rest were peasants with smaller round or square shields and spears. Some had older helmets or leather caps. As soon as the order was given then three thousand arrows soared into the sky and even while they were in the air another three thousand followed and by the time the first flights had plunged into wood and flesh a third flight was on its way.

"Forward!"

As we marched a little further across the ford, I saw the damage that we had done. The mailed warriors had survived largely intact for we were using war arrows and not bodkins, but the peasantry had been halved.

"Halt!"

When we loosed this time, we were so much closer that the arrows took a greater toll and after three more flights the French broke. Prince Edward had two hundred hobelars and the lightly armoured men had their horses swim the deeper part of the channel to chase the French from the field. We tramped back to our horses and mounted. I donned my buskins. Even before the ford was visible the archers were able to cross for we could swim the deep part. When we reached the northern bank, we found the

French camp and the supplies they had left. As we were the first ones across, we had food and drink! We had our reward for a soaking.

It took an hour, that is all, for the whole army to cross the ford. The last wagons across, the ones carrying the carpenters, the gunners and their eight crude cannons and gunpowder as well as the wood, found the water was up to the top of the wheels for the tide had turned but they made it and we saw King Philip's vanguard as it neared the now impassable Somme. Their only option was to return to Abbeville and cross the river at the bridge there. That was more than twelve miles away. We had gained more than a day and that meant King Edward had time to choose somewhere to fight the French. We were starving and we were exhausted but if the King could find somewhere to fight then we had a chance.

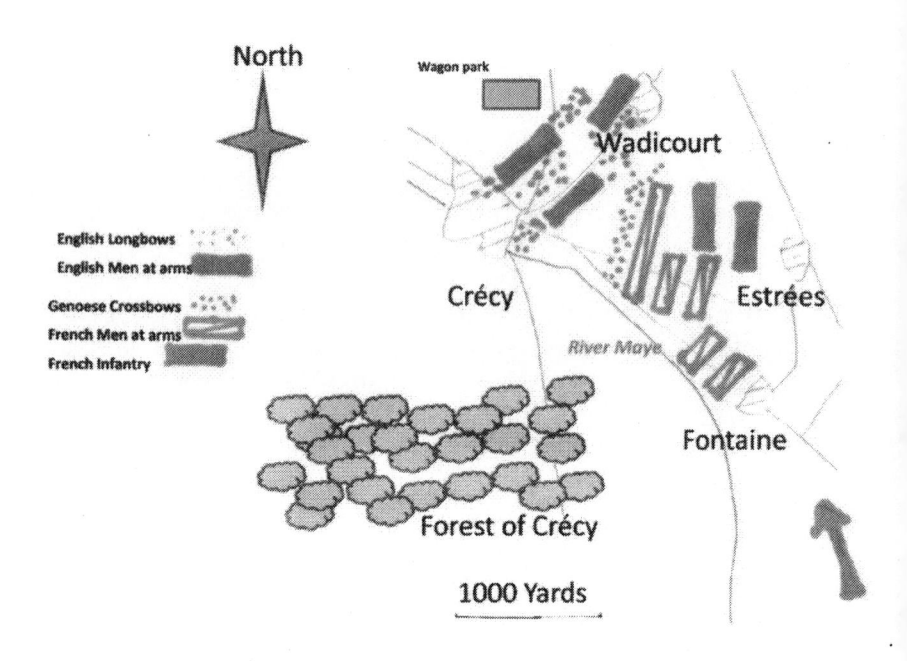

Battle of Crécy

Author's map

Chapter 13

We still had enough daylight to march north and when we saw the piece of higher ground and the long wood close to the village of Crécy-en-Ponthieu, then even Rafe the Dull knew that we had found a place to give battle. For archers it was perfect. There were woods close to a river and high ground so that we could loose our arrows over men at arms. The four villages and hamlets we saw would channel the French towards us for the main road from Abbeville passed along the river. We even found food for the French had not thought we would get this far and although the village was empty for the people had fled, they had not had enough time to take all of their food away. The village was within a mile or so of the three small hamlets, Fontaine, Wadicourt and Estrées where we found some animals and some food there too. We made camp and we waited. The wagon and horse park were on the reverse slope between the river and Wadicourt. King Edward used some of his mounted archers to head towards Abbeville to see where the French were while the rest of us were sent across the shallow River Maye to the wood of Crécy to cut down saplings and branches to make stakes. If we were to fight a battle, then we had to slow down the enemy and make them bleed before they got to us.

We had just gathered our wood, recrossed the river, and darkness had fallen when the archer scouts returned. They reported to the King and then spoke to us for we were all camped together.

"The French King is at Abbeville! We will not see them tonight and if they come tomorrow it will not be until noon!"

Jack asked the archer, "And how many are there?"

He grinned, "Let us just say that I hope the King has thirty thousand arrows for he shall need that number and then some! We may have to use our swords and bodkins tomorrow!"

With disease, dysentery and desertions I estimated that we had, perhaps, fourteen thousand men. We, the archers, were the largest contingent, there were five thousand of us but three and a half thousand of the men who would face the French were just spearmen without any mail and three thousand were hobelars. The French would have at least eight thousand men at arms and knights not to mention more crossbowmen than we had archers. It would not be an easy fight. Besides, they would have twenty thousand men mustered from the lands of Picardy and Artois. The night before the battle I gave Michael his first real lessons in becoming a warrior. He now had a short sword and a brigandine we had captured for him. There was also a helmet we had found which needed an arming cap but would serve him. We even had a shield taken from one of the men at arms from Elbeuf. We had scratched out the design. One day he would paint his own design upon it.

"You will stand behind me and use my body and that shield for protection."

"Will I not need to fetch arrows?"

"No, for we will have all that we need with us. We will each have two war bags and by each stake, there will be another four sheaves of arrows. If any of my men are hit, then go to them and tend them but use your shield for protection. If you survive tomorrow, then you will be well on your way to becoming a warrior."

I think he looked disappointed as though he expected to have to do something more glorious!

We were up before dawn and ate some of our food. We had enough for one more large meal and then we would be hungry again. However, just breaking our fast meant that men were happier with food in their bellies and they could face a battle better. We were then allocated our position. Prince Edward's division was given the place of honour for we were closest to the village and the river and on the lowest patch of ground. It was the place the French would attack but Prince Edward had the largest division and the greatest number of archers. The Earl of Northampton and the Bishop of Durham were to our left and higher up the slope with their flank anchored in the houses of Wadicourt. The King was on the highest part of the slope and in reserve. While the one thousand Welsh spearmen and one thousand men at arms dug pits before our positions, we archers, all three thousand of us, rammed timbers into the ground facing the south-east and then we sharpened them. The stakes were hammered in alternatively and offset from the archer ahead so that while we could stand in the spaces a horseman mounted on a large horse would not be able to make a direct approach. They would have to slow to a walk and twist and turn. The gunners then placed their eight cannons so that they had a clear field to fire their noisy machines. The last time I had seen such weapons they had been firing at me! When that was done, we stood in our three divisions and we waited. Scouts returned to say that the French had left Abbeville and were marching along the road. It was eight miles from the start of the column to the end! It was obvious that they would not be here soon and so we finished off our food.

Michael wondered at that, "Should we not save some food for after the battle?"

Robin laughed, "If we are defeated then we will be running for our lives and trying to swim back to England and if we win then there will be horsemeat aplenty!"

We ate well and then used old bowstrings and crudely fashioned hooks to lie in the sun and try to catch fish in the river. Ned just slept for he was an old hand. Surprisingly a few small fish were caught, and they were cooked there and then. Jack said, "Times past I have eaten them raw!" My company then began a heated debate about who had had to eat the worst food. It was banter and it passed the time. More importantly, it told me that the men were in good spirits.

When we saw, in the early afternoon, the French Royal Standard Bearer and another ten nobles ride up the road from Fontaine, the horn was sounded, and we left the river to take up our positions. I do not think that either before, or since, have I been so rested before a battle. We had to wake Ned up! Perhaps nature was on our side for, as we took our positions, the sun disappeared, and thick black clouds rolled in. I turned to my men, "Do not string your bow until the last moment, rain is on the way!"

King Edward, on the same small white horse he had ridden at Caen, rode down our lines, exhorting us to deeds of great valour for England and to guard his honour! We all cheered, the men at arms and spearmen banged their weapons against their shields and so the tactic was effective for he had inspired us.

The French nobles disappeared to be replaced, as the first drops of rain fell, by the French advance guard. They were Genoese crossbowmen and a few spearmen. As the Genoese formed their ranks the rain fell harder and then I saw the French men at arms appear. Unlike our men at arms, they had all retained their horses and within a short time, there were more mounted men at arms that we had in our whole army and I could see, trailing off in the distance, more banners arriving. The rain was bouncing as the Genoese tried to form ranks. Behind them, Blind King John of Bohemia and Count Charles of Alençon, King Philip's brother, formed the first battle. I estimated that there had to be over five thousand mailed horsemen preparing to charge us once the Genoese had weakened us.

The Genoese began to advance and soon we would have to string our bows. However, before we did so our eight cannons belched fire and stones at the Italian mercenaries. I was not impressed by these new weapons for they were full of sound and fury yet seemed to achieve little. The French horses, however, were a little discomfited and some of the Genoese seemed reluctant to advance but as there were more than five thousand of them the few dozen who seemed reluctant to advance did not seem to have an effect. I studied the Genoese and saw that their weapons were strung already, and the rain would make them slack. They would not be able to send their bolts as far as on a dry day. I glanced behind me and saw that the sky was beginning to clear. I heard the Earl of Northampton's archers ordered to string their bows. A few moments later Captain William ordered us to string our bows. The Genoese were still more than four hundred paces from us, and my men looked to me. I shook my head. When the Genoese were three hundred paces they began to slow and I said, quietly, "Right boys, string your bows!" My men did so efficiently.

The rain suddenly stopped and the clouds behind us broke. Shafts of sunlight shone into the eyes of the Genoese and nature was on our side! The forty-one bows of my men were the tautest of any and when Captain William commanded us to draw then the creak from our bows was louder. Some of the Genoese had launched their bolts early but I think it was in response to the eight guns which had belched flames again. The bolts were sent at the fearsome sounding cannons. They fell well short.

"Loose arrows!"

Every archer in the army sent their arrows high into the air as the Genoese gave their first half-hearted attempt to shift us. Normally the Genoese carried a pavise which they set up before them. It allowed them to reload without fear of being struck but they had none that day, and our arrows punctured and tore into flesh. Fifteen arrows were sent by every archer in the time it takes to count to fifty. The Genoese would be lucky to send three bolts back in that time. Some, myself and my men included, sent more. A few archers were down but they were the unlucky ones and we kept sending arrows while fewer and fewer bolts came in reply. It was too much for they were losing men and we were not. The Genoese broke. We did not stop our arrow storm and many Genoese died as they turned and ran. Before we could even cheer our victory, a French horn sounded and the huge line of men at arms rode towards us. I was dumbstruck for they made no attempt to evade the Genoese. The mercenaries were simply trampled under the hooves of the mailed men.

I shouted, "Bodkins!" These were mailed men.

Captain William and all the other captains were experienced, and no order was given to draw. The reasons were simple. The French were so keen to get at us that they were not in a straight line and as horses stumbled over bodies the disjointed line became even more ragged. The blind King of Bohemia was led into battle by six knights and honour dictated that no Bohemian rode before him. That section of the battle was behind Count Charles of Alençon. The last reason was that the closer they were to us the better chance we had of piercing mail. The French were one hundred and fifty paces from us when we were ordered to release, and we managed to send twenty arrows each before the order came to fall back to the flanks of our men at arms.

We each had an arrow nocked and, as we turned, sent it on a flat trajectory towards the first French battle. I saw my arrow slam into the chest of one of the King of Bohemia's bodyguards and he was thrown from his saddle. As I nocked another arrow, I saw that we had slaughtered many knights. Some riderless horses meandered around the battlefield. I even saw one drinking from the river. More Bohemians guarding their king died as they drew closer to us. We kept up a withering rate for we knew that soon only those actually next to the river would be able to use their bows for the French men at arms would be fighting with our own men at arms.

"Be ready to drop your bows and attack them with your swords!"

They cheered. That was their sort of fight for if you could kill a knight or man at arms then his armour, mail, weapons and purse could make you a man rich beyond his wildest dreams. While Captain William and the archers who were closest to the river continued to slam arrows into the sides of horses and men at arms, we dropped our bows behind the stakes and ran to our position next to the men at arms. After thinning the ranks of the French men at arms my men and I ran, and we found ourselves to the right of Prince Edward and his dismounted knights and men at arms. We were nimble and we managed to avoid the holes and the stakes. The French horses were not so lucky, and I saw several knights thrown from their mounts as they caught their hooves in the holes or were impaled on the stakes. King John of Bohemia was a brave man, but he had fewer wits than Rafe the Dull. He was down to one of his men leading him forward and he swashed his sword at invisible enemies. When his last protector was struck by an arrow the King rode directly towards us. He could not see us, but his horse took him in the same direction as the men led by Count Charles of Alençon. The horse did not run into the stakes, it was too well trained for that but when a Welshman, he must have been incredibly strong, hurled his spear at the blind king, then fate took over and the spear struck him in the face. He fell backwards over his horse. If he was not dead, then he soon would be as more mailed men on huge horses were charging towards us and they would not be able to avoid trampling the King.

The French knights, for the men at arms from the first battle had begun to withdraw, were fanatical as they urged their horses over dead, dying and soon to be dying men. Perhaps they could not believe that they were being slaughtered by peasants for, in their eyes, that is what we were. They forced their horses between stakes and they tried to skewer us with their lances. I had long ago worked out how to defeat them; an archer had to get close to negate the lance and to use daggers and swords to find spaces in mail and plate armour! I ran, not away, but towards the nearest man at arms. He was a knight and he pulled back his arm to skewer me with his lance. I almost laughed as I danced under his horse's head and hacked my sword into the side of his mailed leg. My sword was sharp, and my arm was strong. I felt my sword hit bone and, beneath his great helm, the man screamed. I used my dagger to slice through his girth and the knight slid from his horse. Harold of Sussex smashed his axe into the side of the horse's head, guaranteeing meat for my men that night! I jumped on to the knight who lay spread-eagled. I rammed my dagger up into his throat and, as horses rode to the left and right of me, I reached into his tunic and took his purse. Sheathing my own I grabbed his sword which was a hand and a half sword. I was strong enough to wield it one handed. His plate armour was also valuable but that would have to wait until the battle was fought and won.

    I ran back towards our lines. I saw Michael standing where I had left him, sheltering behind the shield. He looked terrified but he had obeyed me and that was a good sign. It was then I saw a French knight on a horse careering out of control towards Prince Edward. The Prince bravely slashed across the horse's throat, which killed it, but the momentum carried it forward and after it hit him then Prince Edward fell. I was amongst the French and I heard their shouts of joy as they saw the heir to the English throne knocked from his feet. The knights around Prince Edward seemed frozen with fear and, indeed, Count Godfrey ran! I was not a knight, I was an archer and I used the dead horse to spring into the air and knock from his saddle the knight who had his arm pulled back to skewer the young Prince. As we landed, I forced my dagger up under his helmet and into his throat. The richly decorated knight would have to wait until after the battle for me to strip him of his treasures.

    I leapt to my feet and shouted, "Hawkwood! To me!"

    Just three knights were standing close to the Prince and the French were heading for him. I needed men who could fight! I hacked my newly acquired sword into the side of the horse whose knight had filtered into the gap left by the knight I had killed. The horse reared in pain as my sword bit through to the bone. As the knight began to tumble backwards, I pulled at him to accelerate his fall and when he landed, I used my sword to hack through his neck.

The Prince was still on the ground. I reached down and hauled him to his feet, "Come, Prince Edward, it is easier to fight on your feet."

He grinned, "Impertinent as ever."

Sir Richard Fitzsimon, the standard-bearer who had also been knocked to the ground, picked up the Prince's standard and waved it high above his head to show the division that he was still alive.

Sir Thomas of Norwich ran to us, "Prince Edward, the King says he cannot send men to help you!"

The Prince shouted, "I asked for no help!"

Sir Thomas said, "Count Godfrey sent me."

He glared at the Frenchman who had fallen back a little. "We need no help! Lock shields and hold them! This storm will pass."

He might have been right for the Frenchmen from the first battle who survived began to head back but I saw the second wave ready to strike. "Prince Edward, I must lead my men and use our bows. Are you safe now?"

"I am!"

"Hawkwood, back to your bows!"

I stuck my new sword into my belt and leapt through the bodies towards the stake where I had left my bow. Four of my men were missing although I hoped that they would return. In the heat of the battle, it was easy to lose your place. They might be with other companies. I nocked a bodkin and looked over my shoulder. Michael was there but he had blood on his shield and his sword. He also looked a little pale. He had killed his first man!

I bellowed, for the blood was in my head, "Hawkwood, we can beat them! Aim true and trust in your skill. Our dead comrades' souls are just a little way above our heads. Make them proud!" It was rhetoric but it worked, and my men all cheered. "Michael, if you can get a spear or a lance it will give you better protection!"

"At the moment I am happy enough with the sword, Captain!"

Our cannons still cracked and whilst they killed few, I liked the way they upset the enemy horses. The second battle led by the Duke of Lorraine charged towards us, but they had an even harder task for the ground before us was littered with dead men and animals.

"Choose your targets well and go for the kill!" I had never seen so many knights and men at arms and, briefly, I wondered if we would survive. I had but thirty arrows left, and I saw a third battle preparing to charge. I drew back and aimed at the knight with the red surcoat and the gryphon on his shield. I aimed at a point just below the knight's neck. When a knight charged at you on a horse then even if you were incredibly accurate with your flight the movement of the horse could vary the strike dramatically. The arrow hit his chest and the arrow was well made and well struck. It pierced the plate and hit flesh. The lance dropped and only the cantle kept the rider in the saddle. My men were excelling themselves and men at arms and knights were hit, not all died but all were wounded, and a wounded horseman was easy prey to an archer. When the battle was just one hundred paces from us, I shouted, "Hawkwood! Fall back!" The battle had become smaller somehow. I knew not how the King or the Earl of Northampton fared. My battle was by the river and involved Prince Edward's division! As I dropped my bow, I drew my new sword and ran, following Michael! My apprentice was learning and the fact that he had survived filled me with hope!

The French battle almost stopped as it neared the bodies and the stakes. Prince Edward had recovered and was organising his men. We were better prepared this time and the French were beaten back, helped by the archers at the river's side who sent arrow after arrow into the flanks of the French! I slipped my dagger into my belt and used my hand and a half sword two handed. I was amazed when I sliced through the skull of a horse! The man at arms flew over my head to be butchered by the archers behind me. As I hacked at the next man at arms a third's horse knocked me to the ground. Michael stepped up and sliced through the man at arms' leg. He held out his hand to help me up. The apprentice was learning.

The combat was becoming confusing, but I could see that we had already killed many more Frenchmen and Bohemians than in the first charge and we appeared to have lost few if any! We had lost men but not as many as I would have expected. Our men at arms were no longer in neat lines and some spearmen and archers were intermingled. Michael, Ned and I found ourselves close to the Prince's standard. I knew that was always a dangerous place to be. The man who had led the first charge was still on the battlefield. Count Charles of Alençon, along with some of his household knights was looking where they ought to charge. Perhaps they had been resting blown horses or they had just returned to gain honour, I knew not the reason but they rode at the standard. The lances and spears the Prince and the men at arms had used at the start of the battle were now shattered and so they held their shields before them. The French, too, had to rely on swords, maces and axes for they had shattered their spears. They came at the trot, negotiating the pits and the stakes.

"Michael, stand behind the standard!"

Prince Edward was as brave a man as I had ever known and despite his youth, for he was only sixteen, he had skill and as Count Charles of Alençon rode at him, his courser snapping and biting, the Prince of Wales swung his sword around to hack, not at the sword but the horse's leg. Ned also used his axe to hack at the horse. Neither action would be considered chivalrous, but this was real combat and not the pretty war of tournament such as we had witnessed in Brussels. The Count flew from the dying horse and landed at the side of the standard. The household knights, enraged that their leader was lost, doubled their efforts to get at us. Robin had also run with us, but he had brought his bow. He found combat with a sword hard, especially when fighting horsemen because of his size. He sent an arrow into the chest of the nearest knight and he was so close that the arrow bit deeply. His fast hands sent another four arrows to kill the others too. Perhaps we would have all been better to bring our bows.

There was a hiatus and I was about to congratulate Robin when Michael shouted, "Captain! Behind you!" I whipped my head around and saw Count Charles of Alençon running on foot, not at me but Prince Edward. Prince Edward blocked the flailing sword of the Count and, with great precision pushed his own sword up into the mouth and skull of the Count.

Leaning on his sword, the Prince grinned, "I thank your foundling, Hawkwood, but it seems he values you above me."

I bowed, "I am not sure he knows how to address a prince, my lord."

Prince Edward looked up at the sky which was darkening as dusk approached, "Will they keep fighting do you think, my Lord Warwick?"

The Earl was also leaning on his sword and he looked south. The King of France was about to charge with the third battle. "I think so, Prince Edward."

Just then the Bishop of Durham and some men at arms arrived from the King. Prince Edward said, "My lord, it is good that you came but we are coping well enough here. How goes the fighting near to my father?"

"Much as here, Prince Edward, but we are helped by the slope."

I shouted, "Hawkwood, let us return to our bows! We have rested long enough!"

The Prince sounded sincere as he shouted, "Thank you, archer, I shall not forget the service you have done me this day!"

I sent four men for more arrows and we returned to our bows. I took a new string from under my hat and restrung my bow. I was tiring now, and I wondered if the French would simply use their weight of numbers to overwhelm us. As the Oriflamme standard came towards us I saw that this time all of the peasants and spearmen were joining in the attack. If the battle went on into the night, then the range at which we could use our bows would shorten. Would that affect us? King Philip was no coward and he rode at the head of his men. He was not making for Prince Edward but his father, the King. It gave us a better chance both to survive and to hit the royal household knights. I saw the King of France hit in the jaw by one arrow as another killed his horse. Would the battle end? A second horse was brought up and the King remounted. They charged on up the slope and we faced another wall of horsemen intermingled with spearmen and French farmers. I wondered, as I sent an arrow to hit a knight in the shoulder if we had enough arrows? The sun set and still the French came. This time we did not fall back when the horsemen closed with us for with the horsemen were men on foot and they could negotiate the stakes and the pits far easier than the horses. I used a war arrow to kill the first spearman and then dropped my bow and drew my two swords.

The stakes meant that the French could only approach one man at a time. That day taught me that I had more skill than most of the men that I was fighting. The spearmen held their long weapons in two hands and thrust them at my head. My left arm was strong enough to knock aside the spear and then slash down at the unprotected neck of the first Frenchman. In that way I slew eight spearmen and two peasants with billhooks. Now that it was dark the battlefield became a smaller place and ours shrank to the thirty or so paces that we could see before us. As I slew yet another spearman, I saw that there were no more men approaching. Were the French men at arms preparing another charge? I sheathed my swords and picked up my bow. Nocking a bodkin arrow, I listened for the thundering hooves of the French cavalry. There was none but I heard shouts from our front and the rattle of metal. The French men at arms were advancing, but this time on foot.

I shouted, "They come again but on foot!" The warning was for Prince Edward behind us. If mailed and plated men at arms were coming then, like the spearmen, they would be able to negotiate the stakes. The spearmen and the peasants had shown the French men at arms another way to fight.

I half drew my bow and stared into the dark. I was reassured by Michael behind me for he had shown that he had good eyes and sharp wits already. I was watching for the French to loom up out of the dark. When they did, I saw that it was the Count of Blois and his knights who were making this attack. I sent an arrow into his standard-bearer as Ned and Robin slew the Count himself. Rather than dismaying the knights, it made them more determined than ever to get at us. I think they felt that their pride had been hurt for we were just archers. Another picked up the standard and exhorted the others to avenge their lord. We were just thirty paces from our enemies and a bodkin could penetrate plate and mail at that range. We sent arrow after arrow into them yet still they came, and they threatened to overwhelm us.

I heard Prince Edward behind me shout, "Come, let us help our brave archers for these are men on foot!"

The men at arms and knights led by Prince Edward arrived just in time and they advanced through the stakes to meet the French on the ground before the stakes. We were able to send our arrows through the gaps so that even when one of our men at arms was struggling to beat his opponent an archer was on hand to end the Frenchman's life. The attack ended. I was amazed that, as yet, none had surrendered to us.

"Prince Edward, we need arrows, I beg leave to take my men and search for usable arrows."

"Of course, we will stay here until you return."

As I left I heard his standard-bearer ask, "Will they come again, my lord?"

Prince Edward shrugged, "I know not but so long as they keep the field then so shall we! I fear I need a whetstone!"

"Hawkwood, let us seek arrows! Michael, watch my back!"

I knew that my men would also take the opportunity to rob the dead and if any were alive to slit their throats. I retrieved twenty arrows, twelve of them bodkins. I also found several good rings and purses with golden florins in them. Michael discovered the greatest prize, at least in the eyes of the Prince, the Oriflamme, the sacred French banner lay in the blood and the gore of knights who had died defending it. When we returned, he gave it to Prince Edward who promised him a reward when the battle was over. We resumed our positions and we waited. Hours passed and it became clear that the fighting had finished for the day. I looked up at the sky and estimated that it was midnight.

The Earl of Warwick came amongst us and told us to rest where we stood. I unstrung my bow and said, "One man in three will stay awake. The rest get what sleep you can!" I turned to Michael, "You can sleep, you have earned your rest." I heard some men head to the river to drink. I had my ale skin with me and I took a swig from that.

I would not sleep. I peered into the dark and I listened. There were men alive out there for I could hear their moans. Such had been the press of men that there were knights and men at arms buried beneath piles of bodies. When we had searched the dead we had, quite literally, just scratched the surface! I heard other archers as they exchanged duties and men who had snatched a short sleep now watched.

I took out my whetstone and began to sharpen my swords. It was as I was doing so that the Prince and his standard-bearer approached. "When you are done, I would sharpen my own sword."

I rammed the swords into the soft soil and said, "I will do it for you, my lord. When I was an apprentice tailor, I learned the art of sharpening my master's shears!"

"You were a tailor?"

"Briefly, my lord, it was not for me."

Sir Richard said, "You were born to be a warrior and I, for one, am pleased that you chose this path!"

I looked at the sky, "Soon it will be dawn and I wonder what it will bring?"

Prince Edward looked thoughtful as I stroked the stone along his sword, "I know not but from the reports I have we have barely lost forty men so far."

I shook my head, "Surely that is wrong, my lord, for the enemy dead lie like a wall before us!"

"It is hard to believe but the men who counted the dead and the wounded were priests and have no reason to speak falsely. They have nought to gain from such a lie."

"Then we have won!"

"No, archer, for until they quit the field there is no result. If they keep the field, then we cannot leave for they will hunt us down."

Their blades sharpened, they continued their march around our lines, and I watched the sun rise. He was right, they had not quit the field and we would have to fight them again. After we had made water and ate what food we could find we prepared to fight. Then a horn sounded, and Prince Edward and his household knights left for a council of war. They returned a short while later. Mounted on his horse the Prince spoke to us all as he and the men at arms prepared to leave.

"The King has decided that we will make the French quit this field. Yesterday we saw them as they tried to break us. This day they will feel the full weight of English horsemen. When we drive them hence then the field is yours! Enjoy it, yeomen of England!"

The three battles formed up and they made a magnificent sight. There were two thousand seven hundred mailed men on horses which had rested for more than a day and a half. King Edward led them, and they picked their way past the dead Frenchmen before forming up. The French stood to and I wondered if we would be called upon to rain arrows upon them but the King had judged it well and as soon as the men at arms began to trot, panic set in and the French took to their heels! The rest of our army cheered and roared for a panicked army would be slaughtered. We heard the crash and clash as the first battle struck the last of the French men at arms and then, a short while later, they disappeared as they chased the army back to Abbeville.

We also took to our heels too but, in our case, it was to finish what we had begun the day before and relieve the dead of their treasure. We left their surcoats and their plate for the knights and men at arms would wish those as trophies. Besides, we had no means to carry back plate. We looked for coins and jewels. We sought swords which we could sell or use, and we looked for food.

It was the middle of the afternoon when the army returned, and they had with them prisoners for ransom as well as many horses. We had captured the French baggage and so the army would be well fed. We ate well that night and we heard the full extent of our victory. We had lost less than two hundred men and only two knights had been lost. The French lost four thousand French knights. Among the known knightly dead were two kings, nine princes, ten counts, a duke, an archbishop and a bishop. The ordinary Frenchmen had lost so many men that number was rounded and was more than sixteen thousand. In all my life I never heard of such a one-sided victory and yet, when we had been fighting, I was unsure if we were winning or losing. Such is war.

Chapter 14

The English fleet arrived as we were breaking camp and the King, his son and the Earl of Northampton rode down to the shore to speak with the lords who led the ships. When they returned it became clear that we would not be boarding the ships. Now that there was no longer a threat from the French the King had decided to take Calais! We had thought we would take the ships and return, richer men, to England. The King, it seemed, still had ambitions. Paris was just too large a bite for us to take but Calais might be a juicy morsel. We prepared to leave.

Whilst foraging the deserted camp we had found a couple of sumpters which had been abandoned and we used those for the Hawkwood company. As we were the first on the battlefield, we were also the first to find the dead horses and to butcher them. While we waited for the men at arms to return, we had cooked them. Now that we knew we were going to Calais we had enough food to last until we reached that port. It would be a siege and that meant the King would have to lay in supplies of food for us. We would forage for a while, but it would not take long for us to exhaust the land around Calais. I had raided around there and knew how little there was.

We raided and burned every town and farm as we headed north and then we came to Wissant. This was the major port for trade from north-west France and the King unleashed his army on the town like dogs of war! It was not only the vast warehouses which were pillaged but also the houses of the burghers of Wissant and when we finally gathered everything that they had to take we burned the town to the ground. If it was a message to the men of Calais to surrender then it did not work for as we arrived the gates were barred, and the town was prepared for a siege. Until the King's fleet managed to establish a blockade the French continued to supply the town by sea. By the end of August Calais was almost cut off but supplies still came in at night and it would be a long siege. King Edward could not feed his large army over the winter and some companies were paid off. I knew that mine, Hawkwood, would be one for I had offended a major ally of the King, Count Godrey. I suspect that Prince Edward was reluctant to do so but Count Godfrey had become increasingly vocal about what he called the peasant archer and his impertinence. There had been too many times when I had questioned his competence and he did not like it.

Prince Edward softened the blow by not only paying us that which was owed but also by giving each archer twenty pounds and to me, fifty. "I will need you again, John Hawkwood, and when I summon archers to follow my banner then I will expect you to be there."

I smiled, "And if I am a man at arms, Prince Edward?"

"Then I will be twice as pleased to have you serve me."

My forty men, Michael and myself, took ship and headed for Dover. I had money and I could afford to buy somewhere, the question was, where? As we disembarked at Dover I spoke with my archers. "None of us need to work but I, for one, will continue to try to seek employment. Prince Edward will have need of us again and, to be truthful, I did not relish a siege in winter. I think that we are better off in England for we all have full purses and none of us will starve. If I do not see you again then it has been an honour to lead you, but I hope that one day, you will follow me once more."

We clasped arms, as warriors do and the last to leave me were Ned, Robin and Jack. Ned and Jack were old friends and they would head back to London. Ned was a Londoner and had a sister who lived at Southwark. He said, "Captain when you were appointed over me, I wondered at that for you seemed so young. Captain Philip was right, you have the stuff of Caesar coursing through your veins. You know where to find me. My sister lives close to the Castle Inn. Jack and I will make ourselves known there."

"And I would have you in a heartbeat if I was asked to lead a company of archers!" I knew that men like Ned and Jack were rare. They were not only good at what they did they were good men and a leader liked to have his back protected by such men.

They left and I turned to Robin, who said to me, "Captain, I would stay with you."

I was touched but I needed to be honest with the archer. My plans were as vague as a morning mist. "But I know not where I will go."

"And that matters not to me for I have no plans and besides, I feel some responsibility towards Michael here. I will not be a burden."

I smiled for this was good news, "I am right glad that you wish it to be so. We will need horses but let us find an inn this night and celebrate our new union!" I do not know why but I felt enormously grateful to have two companions for I liked both of them and, more importantly, trusted them. Only Ned and Jack were the others who completely fitted that description. I felt obliged to pay for the inn, the food, the ale and the horses for Prince Edward had been more than generous to me. I now had twice the treasure that Basil of Tarsus kept for me. Even if he robbed me, I was still a rich man.

That evening as we ate the finest food in the inn and drank decent ale for the first time since Brussels, I began to formulate a plan. "I will not go to London for it is a cesspit filled with the worst of men. We will take a ferry and cross into Essex. Captain Philip lives in the north beyond the River Tees and I have never seen it. I would visit there."

The truth was that I was being less than honest with the two of them for by crossing to Essex I hoped to visit with my mother. I missed her and she had always treated me well. My sisters too would now be women grown. I intended to attempt to see them and then carry on north. "We will visit with Captain Philip and, perhaps, he may know where we can find employment for the winter." I knew that I would have to return to Southampton and the village of Bitterne to pick up my suit of mail for I still intended to become a man at arms. It struck me that a man at arms who could use a bow was three times as valuable as either an archer or a man at arms! The two of them seemed quite happy at that and I felt guilty. "Let us have an agreement, I shall pay you both the rate for an archer per day and you shall be part of my company, the Hawkwood company!"

The two of them had drunk more than I had and they happily nodded, "For me," said Robin, "I would follow you for nothing but if you are willing to pay then so be it! I shall be your man!"

Michael shook his head, "I should be paying you for training me!"

I laughed, "At Crécy you saved my life and I owe you. I am content!"

We left the next day and headed across the river. I rode hooded and I was a little more honest with my companions, "I go this way for I would see my mother, but I only wish to see her or my sisters. If my brother or my father is at home, then I shall ride on." Strangely they both understood that. "Robin, you will speak and say that you are archers who served with me at Crécy. If my father or brother comes to the door then we shall leave."

"Aye, Captain!"

My home looked quiet as we rode into the courtyard and I saw no signs of either my father or brother. I remained hooded as Robin dismounted and Michael held the sumpter which was laden with our gear. He knocked on the door and my heart soared when I saw my mother. They spoke briefly and my mother widened the door to admit him. He shook his head and spoke further, then she answered, and Robin dropped his hood. That was our sign that my father and brother were not at home. I dismounted and, heading towards the door, I handed my reins to Robin. I dropped my hood and my mother, now grey-haired, burst into tears and threw her arms around me when she recognised the man who had been but a boy when he had left.

Robin said, quietly, "We will watch here, Captain. Take all the time you like for you shall be safe!"

My mother sobbed and I felt her salty tears course down her cheek and my neck. I fought back the tears which would unman me. Eventually, red-eyed she pulled away. "All these years and not a word!"

I shrugged, "My father!"

She linked my arm and led me inside, "We have not shared a bed since the day you left. He keeps a whore in London and another in Colchester! I was cursed when I married him."

She led me to the family table which I remembered from so many years ago. "He will not return, nor my brother?"

She gave a rueful laugh, "They make money now and the two of them are too grand for here. They fancy themselves gentlemen but there is nothing gentle about either of them! Now it is just me for your sisters are married and have families of their own. I am a grandmother!"

It was then that I broke down for this was not right, "I will kill him and my brother! I am a warrior and have slain many of England's enemies. The two of them will take but a blow or two!"

She then became the mother who had chastised me as a child, "You shall not for that is a mortal sin and he is not worth it! I will fetch your food and have some sent to your companions who are so diligent that they watch over you! Then you shall tell me of your life for I can see a tale here!" She started to leave and then turned, "And tonight my son shall sleep under my roof. I will see to your companions."

I nodded, "Robin and Michael!"

She smiled, "They seem like good boys! I am pleased you have chosen your friends well!"

As she left, I looked around the room which seemed, somehow, smaller. This had been my home, but I had moved on. Despite my mother's admonition if the opportunity came then I would kill my brother and my father for the way that my mother, a real lady, had been treated. I had seen too much butchery and cruelty to believe that God actually cared about what we men did!

My mother returned and a short while later Robin brought in the leather bag with my clothes and treasure. He said quietly, "We are well looked after, Captain. Rest easy for I will watch over Michael!"

The food was brought in and my mother said, "I am pleased that you have found such loyal companions. Now, while we eat, tell me of your life since you were driven from your home!"

It took a long time to tell her what I had done. It was a sanitized version, of course, for she was my mother and a lady. It was the story of the battle sung, later, by troubadours and not the bloody butchery of reality! She poured some of my father's best wine, it was to punish him in his absence, and nodded to me as she touched my goblet with hers, "You are a great man already, I can see that and you will become greater." She laughed, "You will become the most famous Hawkwood and all of your father's money cannot diminish that."

I smiled and went to the two chests which Robin had brought in. I opened them and waved a hand over them, "There is a third as overflowing in Southampton. Take what you need and leave my father!"

She began to weep and kissed my hand. Shaking her head, she said, "I will not but this gives me such a feeling of joy that you cannot imagine. Your father believes you died in a gutter after you left for London and nothing could be further from the truth."

I closed the lids on my treasure and laughed, "If he goes to London then soon, he will hear my name. I would dearly love to be there when he hears my name lauded."

She laughed and then told me of my sisters and my uncle. They all did well, and my sisters held the same opinion of my father and brother as my mother and me. I now had nephews and nieces. By the time we had finished talking, it was almost midnight. She took a candle and said, "I will lead you to your chamber."

I took the candle from her, "Your son is almost a gentleman and I will escort you for I know where I shall sleep. I am sorry I left!"

"Had you not then you would have been dead for your father hated you!"

I stopped, "Why? What did I do to displease him?"

She began to weep, "That was my fault. There was a priest who used to visit us before you were born. I liked him for he was young and he made me laugh. Your father believed that the priest was your father." Before I could even think of asking the question she said, "I have given myself to only one man and that is the beast that is your father. He had the priest hounded from the village. I am sorry."

I embraced her, "At least I know the reason!"

When we departed, the next day, I left purses of coins for my uncle and my sisters. My mother would have none of it, but they would have some recompense for siding with me.

I felt as though a weight had been lifted from my shoulders as we headed up the Roman road to Northampton, then Lincoln and York. The journey north also helped me to formulate my plans. I was a warrior and a captain. I would hire my own company and pay them from my purse. We would hire out to the highest bidder. My only rule would be that I would never fight against the English. I knew how to fight, and I knew what kind of men I wanted. I would visit with Captain Philip and pick his brains. Winter in the north of England would be peaceful and give me the chance to become Captain John!

I had never been along the Great Northern Road for I had sailed to Scotland when we had been there with King Edward. Travelling the road at the end of September showed it at its best and its worst. We saw the richness of the land as the crops were harvested but then we had storms of biblical proportions. I had bought good horses for my men and a well-oiled cloak for Michael; we endured the storms. With so many men in France, there were fewer travellers upon the roads and the inns were reasonably priced. Word had yet to reach this part of England about our great victory, but men had heard of the Earl of Lancaster's victories and were keen to hear more of them. When we spoke of Crécy I think that they thought we were exaggerating. It did not worry me for we knew the veracity of our words. The further north we travelled the more the talk was of the Scots. There were rumours that King David sought to take advantage of the absence of so many English soldiers and planned to invade the north of England. An army was in the process of being mobilised at Richmond in North Yorkshire under the supervision of William de la Zouche, the Archbishop of York, who was Lord Warden of the Marches.

As we headed for the ferry at the Tees, Robin said wryly, "So much for being able to enjoy a winter of peace in the north. It seems that we have come to a conflagration and might just be singed a little ourselves!"

I feared he was right for as we crossed the ferry on the Tees, I saw mailed and armed men marching from the castle of Stockton and heading north. Hartburn was not far away and the picture there was the same. As we headed up the road, we saw men bidding farewell to their loved ones. I wondered if we had come too late. When we neared the village of Hartburn, we met a pig farmer, Cedric, who pointed us towards the farm of Captain Philip. "By your garb and your war gear I can see that you are archers, if you are here for the muster then it is further west at Barnard Castle for the Scots, it is said, are massing north of the Tweed. Captain Philip leads the archers of Hartburn."

"What of the Lord of the Manor?"

"There is none at the moment. The Bishop is busy, it is said, in London and in France. When time allows, he will appoint another, but Captain Philip is a soldier and he organises the archers. His farm is yonder and close to the two becks."

I frowned at the word for I had never heard it, "Becks?"

He laughed, "I can hear from your voice that you are a southerner. A beck is a stream. Follow the greenway and you will find the path which leads up the slope to his hall."

We crossed a small stone bridge to follow the roughly laid path between hawthorn and rowan to the small hall of Captain Philip. I saw that he had cattle and sheep in the field. I could not see the captain as a ploughman. Dogs barked as we neared the hall and by the time we crested the rise, the Captain and his men were there with weapons at the ready. I saw that the hall was an old wooden one and in some disrepair. I wondered at that but briefly for as soon as he recognised me Captain Philip's face lit up!

"Mathilde! We have guests!"

His wife came to the door and I saw that she was nursing a baby. She too smiled, "John Hawkwood, it is good to see you!" She hurried indoors and I dismounted.

The Captain said, "I fear that if you are staying the night then you will have to use the stable for my hall needs to be enlarged."

"Do not worry, Captain, we have endured worse. Michael, Robin see to the horses and our gear."

The Captain suddenly recognised Robin, "Robin Goodfellow! It is good to see you too!"

"I wondered if you had forgotten me, Captain." He waved a hand at the land and the hall, "The rewards for being a fighting man, eh?"

The Captain nodded, "Something like that! Although others might call it a pit into which a fighting man throws his hard-earned coins." He turned to me. "It is good to see you, John, but what brings you here? I would have expected you to be in France still with Lord Henry and Sir Ralph."

"I have much to tell you, but we came here thinking that we could spend some time with you for I have plans and I need your experience to sharpen them."

"Aye well, that may well have to wait for the Scots are abroad and up to mischief. They have realised that King Edward and the Earl of Lancaster are in France and Gascony and seek to come south. The Scottish King David has mustered a large army and they will come south soon. I am to lead the men of Hartburn." He put his arm out to lead me into his hall and he suddenly stopped, "Perhaps, John Hawkwood, God has sent you here." He lowered his voice. "It is rumoured that the Scots have an army of over twelve thousand men, and I cannot see the muster raising more than six thousand to oppose them. We might lose. It is not your fight and you would have no pay, but I ask you and your companions to come with us so that I may leave three of my men here to guard my family. I now have a young son. When any army raids there are those who are brigands and bandits. They seek to cause mischief. If I could leave three men here…"

I nodded, "I will have to ask Michael and Robin, but I would say aye. The pay does not worry me for I know my skill and even though it is piss poor Scots we fight, I will find enough coins and metal on the field to make it worth my while. When do we leave?"

He smiled and I saw the old crafty Captain of Archers I had first met in London, "The muster is to the west of here, but I will delay our departure until the Scots come closer. Your men and I will be the only ones mounted and having men tramp west to return east seems a little pointless. Hartlepool is a place that King David will wish to take for it was from there that Longshanks, the Hammer of the Scots, sailed to crush them and the land north of Stockton and south of Durham is rich farmland. He can feed his army and cross the river. Stockton castle is no fortress. The Scots will avoid castles if they can. They will come through the Palatinate and that is but half a day from here. We will wait." Robin and Michael approached, "And now let us go within and enjoy some ale. There is a good alewife in Hartburn, and I am anxious to hear your tale."

The hall was a cosy one but I could see that it needed work. Mathilde had a woman to help cook and a nurse for the baby, John. We crowded around the table but that only made it more convivial and comforting. I had always liked Mathilde. She had not been a young woman when she had married, and the baby was unexpected. The joy they both had in the child was touching. The food and the ale were good. We told the tale of the war, but we did not go into the detail of Michael's life too deeply out of consideration for the lady. However, she was a clever woman and I saw her piecing together the elements we left out.

I changed the subject when I saw tears forming in her eyes and asked about Hartburn. "The farm had been almost derelict when first we came. Almost all of the coins I had earned went in the first six months as we made it habitable. Prices were high this year and our animals yielded many young. If they had not then I fear we might have starved."

"Captain, if you need coins, I have two chests on my sumpter. I would have nothing but for you. If you need it then you are more than welcome to it!"

He shook his head, "That is more than kind, John, but I will not take your charity. A man stands on his own two feet."

"In truth, Captain, it is a burden for me. Consider it a loan. When we go with you to the muster, I shall have to leave the two chests here in any case."

"Then we shall watch over it for you." He raised his beaker, "A toast." We stood. "To brothers in arms who never forget and to the backbone of England, its archers!"

We enjoyed a delightful evening. Mathilde retired when John demanded food and the four of us sat and talked. We were able to go into greater detail about the battle and even Captain Philip was astounded at the small number of men we had lost.

Word reached us two days later that the Scots had invaded Cumbria and destroyed the castle at Liddell Peel, massacring the garrison there. The castle at Carlisle had paid gold for them not to head south and so the army had come east along the military road south of the Roman Wall. We prepared to leave but another rider arrived the following day to tell us that we were to head to

Durham for the Scots had ravaged Hexham Abbey and were heading south! Our peaceful winter in Hartburn looked like it would be a warlike autumn instead!

Chapter 15

After the numbers of men we had marched with in France, the twenty men Captain Philip led felt a little paltry. Half had bows and the other half had old swords, billhooks and spears. One or two had helmets and Michael felt like a veteran in his brigandine, helmet, riding a horse and with a good sword in his belt. We joined other local men as we headed north through Norton, Wulfestun and other tiny hamlets to head north to Durham. By the time we reached Bowburn just south of Durham, there were more than a hundred of us. Captain Philip's service as King Edward's archer meant that the other local leaders acknowledged him as their captain. We had heard, from refugees fleeing south, that the Scots were at Beaurepaire Priory just north of Durham. They were demanding money from the monks. At the same time knights came from the south and west to tell us that five hundred mounted Scottish men at arms under the command of William Douglas had been defeated at Merrington by Lord Ralph Neville. We were ordered to join the army in Durham itself. The war had begun and this time it was not French, Gascon and Flemish farms which were being burned, it was English ones and that made it personal!

When we arrived, we were directed to the west of the town walls where we would serve under the command of Lord Neville. The Scots, we were told, had headed for a piece of high ground known as the Saxon cross; it was north of the town. Captain Philip went to the council of war and we found somewhere safe for our horses. As we entered the camp, I estimated that we had some six thousand men. As the last report had said, the Scots had more than twice that number which meant that Lord Neville would be outnumbered by two to one. I did not know him but I hoped he was as good as Lord Henry or Sir Ralph! Some of the men who had come with us from Hartburn and Stockton were a little apprehensive about fighting these Scots who had destroyed abbeys and slaughtered farmers already.

Cedric the pig farmer laughed at some of the concerns voiced by the untried men, "The Scots make a lot of noise, but they are poor warriors. They fight in great banks of long spears called schiltrons." He nodded to me, "These archers will be able to slaughter them and if they try to get at these lads then," he patted his long axe, "we will show them that any one Englishman is worth two Scots!"

Walter of Whitton also came from Hartburn. He was not young, but he had not fought before, "Is it right master, what Cedric says?

I smiled, "I am not a master, Walter, I am a vintenar and the captain of twenty, but he is correct. We fought the French and they had many times our number. They were mailed lords and rode great warhorses, yet we defeated them. They died and we lost a handful of men and just two knights. If you will take my advice when this is over then put aside that spear and learn the longbow. It will take you some years to learn but Robin and I can loose a dozen arrows in the time it takes to have a piss! We may lack the numbers of the Scots, but Cedric is right, we are worth more on a battlefield!"

They were heartened and the mood improved. I saw now why Captain Philip had been so keen to have us with him. We were professionals and we would stiffen the untrained. When he came back, he told us that we were assigned to the men led by Lord Neville and would form part of his battle. The three battles had the same formation. We were to the left of Lord Neville's dismounted men at arms. We had two hundred archers with us but, on the other side were over a thousand Lancashire bowmen. They were considered the best left in England. Lord Percy and his battle were to our left and the Archbishop of York to our right. We slept in our formations. When dawn broke it was a misty morning. We ate where we stood and watched for the mist to clear. When it finally did, we saw the might of the Scottish army. We had heard it arriving in the night. King David had chosen his ground badly for although they had the high ground, before them was broken ground. Their strongest weapon, the long spear, needed flat ground for it to be used to best effect.

They would have to wait for us to attack or risk becoming disordered. I saw that the front rank of each schiltron had axemen to defend the spears. Their light horses and men at arms guarded their flanks.

Captain Philip nodded and appeared satisfied, "We can only hope that they try to attack us for if they do then we will slaughter them."

Michael asked, "Can we not attack them, Captain?"

"Attacking uphill over rough ground is never a good idea and so we will wait. The Scots are an impatient foe and they believe that they can defeat us. They will either attack or we will anger them and make them come! Either way, we can make ourselves comfortable."

This felt like Crécy all over for we sat and waited as the morning mist evaporated; we drank from ale skins and ate some of the food we had been given by the burghers of Durham. It was noon before there was any movement and then it was a summons from Lord Neville for his captains. When Captain Philip came back, he said, "John, I want you and Robin to come with us. I am to lead some of the Lancastrian archers to attack the Scottish right. We will see if we can stir them. We will collect your arrows first." The Captain's wound meant that he would not draw a bow but use his skills as an archer to direct the rest of us. We filled our war bags with fifty arrows, and each carried another sheaf of fifty. An archer could get through many arrows!

There were hobelars and Scottish archers on the flank we were to attack. The Scots did not use the longbow and their arrows were also not as good. Our one thousand archers took up a line one hundred and fifty paces from the Scots. Captain Philip was on his horse and he ordered, "Draw!"

I had not drawn a bow since Calais, and I felt it. I would have to practise more often or I would lose some of the power I had once possessed.

"Release!"

We each sent ten arrows in quick succession. It proved too much for the hobelars and archers whose numbers were thinned dramatically as our arrows rained upon them. Leaving almost half of their number they fled. I selected a bodkin for I could see that we faced the Earl of Moray and his men. Some of them were dismounted men at arms and knights wearing mail and plate. We sent twenty arrows into the battle and we had our reward when the Earl of Menteith led mounted men at arms towards us in an attempt to rid their flanks of the annoyance that was English archers. That day showed me the potential of archers. We should have been ridden down for we had neither stakes nor pits to protect us, but we did not flinch, and I emptied my second war bag as the Scots charged towards us. They had courage but courage alone is of little use. Our bodkins, sent at almost touching distance, meant that nearly every arrow brought down a man or struck a horse. The Earl was lucky and he made it to within ten paces of us before an arrow slew his horse and Captain Philip rode forward to capture him.

That proved too much for the Scots and as the survivors limped back to their rear King David ordered an attack by the whole army. Lord Neville had succeeded in goading the Scots into action. Captain Philip showed his skill as well as his poise, "The archers will fall back in good order. Release three arrows and walk back twenty paces and repeat!"

We were helped in our fighting retreat by the fact that the schiltrons were having to negotiate rough ground and were moving slower than we were. We were using a flat trajectory and Robin and I covered each other which made us even safer. I loosed and Robin stepped behind me. As I walked back, I nocked an arrow while Robin sent his arrow. In this way, we were able to hit the Scots who were closest to us. It helped that when the spearmen fell, they caused those behind to stumble and the whole, cumbersome schiltron slowed even more. Robin and I had almost emptied a second war bag each by the time we reached our men at arms and took our place behind them. Robin and I made our way to fight with the men of Hartburn. For this battle, they would be our brothers in arms. We had one war bag of arrows left and I gave that to Robin.

"I will stand in the line with Michael and the others." Captain Philip, having delivered his prisoner joined me. Neither of us had a shield nor mail but I was not afraid for the schiltrons which advanced towards us did not even have a brigandine!

I took my hand axe to use as a shield and held my hand and a half sword in my right hand. The bascinet I wore and the arming cap beneath, along with my leather brigandine were my only protection. Michael was next to me and he had his shield as well as a coif. He was too young yet to do much other than to protect my right side, but this would be a good experience for him- if he survived.

The Scots who had preceded the spears had all been slain by our archers so that all we had to do was to avoid the hedgehog of spears. The archers behind us had had their supply of arrows replenished and they thinned out the enemy as they approached. Some Scots managed to keep coming even though they had two or even three arrows sticking in them. They would succumb to their wounds eventually, but they looked like men determined to stay with their brothers! I admired that. The first spears were spread far enough apart for us to either avoid them or to chop at them with our swords. They were an unwieldy wooden weapon. Michael blocked two with his shield and I knocked a third up in the air before stepping into the gap we had created to ram my sword into the screaming face of a red-bearded Scotsman. I tore the sword out sideways and spattered the men next to him with blood, bone and brains. I quickly stepped back as a spear came from further back. I hacked at the wooden shaft with my axe and bit a huge chunk from it. Even as I rejoined Michael I saw an arrow, I knew it to be Robin's from the fletch, strike a Scot in the chest. The range was so short that it buried itself up to the feathers! The other archers were sending arrows into the sky and when they descended, they struck Scotsmen.

A Scottish man at arms, mailed from head to foot and with plated greaves advanced towards me. He had a war axe and a shield. "Michael, stand back!" This would be a hard fight for the archers behind me had no clear target and I could not allow the men of Hartburn to risk death against this warrior. I had to use my two skills: speed and strength. I feinted with my sword and made as though I would jab to his head. As he swung up his shield, I hacked my hand axe at it and bit a large chunk from the bottom of his shield. I quickly stepped back onto my right leg as he swung his own, longer axe. It barely missed me. However, the swing could not be easily stopped, and I brought my own sword down and struck his shoulder. He grunted as something cracked. I stepped forward and swung my axe at the centre of his shield.

An ominous crack appeared. I knew he was hurting for instead of swinging his axe at me, he tried to head-butt me, and I pulled my head back out of the way before he could connect. Knowing I had the advantage I swung again at his shoulder. He could not raise his arm and my sword slid along his mail and bit into his coif and then his neck. With blood spurting, he fell in a heap. The archers continued their arrow storm and the Scots endured it for as long as they could but, defeated they fell back.

As the men around me cheered I looked and saw that one battle, the one which had not engaged, now left the field. They had seen what we had done to one battle and were not brave enough to risk almost certain death. They would head north and plunder their way home! We now outnumbered the Scots!

Lord Neville shouted, "Archers, surround them and rain death upon them. Make the sky look like thunder and deliver England's wrath upon them!"

I grabbed my bow and a bag of arrows which had been brought up and I ran with Robin to stand with the archers of Lancashire. We sent so many arrows into the Scotsmen that we ran out and more had to be fetched. While they did so our men at arms entered the fray. Hitherto they had just watched but now they participated, and they attacked the larger number of Scottish knights and men at arms. When our arrows arrived, we picked off the Scots who were further back. I heard a Scottish voice order a retreat. It was what we had done so successfully at the start of the battle. The Scots did not have the same discipline and within a short time, the retreat became a rout as men tripped and fell. While the men at arms ran back for their horses, the rest of us ran after the Scots. This was too good an opportunity to spurn. Running, stopping and loosing arrows, we went on until we had no arrows left. I slung my bow and drew my axe and my sword. With Michael close behind me, we ran on catching and slaying the slower of the Scots until the mounted men at arms overtook us.

I raised my arm, "Now we can stop." I saw that I had most of the men of Hartburn with me. I smiled at them, "Today you all became warriors. When we return to the battlefield take what you need from the Scottish dead for that is the price they pay for failure and is your reward for courage. You will be better equipped so that if they are ever foolish enough to come south again, then you shall meet them well armed and equipped."

When we reached the battlefield Captain Philip was helping the healers to tend to the wounded. Walter of Whitton had had his arm laid open and he was being stitched. He had been lucky for a yeoman who lost a limb lost his livelihood. I went back to the man at arms I had slain. I stripped the mail from his body as well as the greaves and metal sabaton. His war axe would also be handy as would his helmet and coif. I knew that I had a helmet but having a spare as well as an extra suit of mail could not hurt. We were still on the battlefield, scavenging, when a wounded King David was brought in. His capture made the victory complete. We left the battlefield after dark and took the food the Scots had brought to cook.

Michael did not feel that he had done enough and so he insisted upon cooking. Many of the wives of the burghers of Durham also helped for we had saved their city! Robin and I were both happy. We had not been paid for our service, but the rewards had exceeded that which we might have been paid. We had no knights for ransom but the ones we had killed and whose bodies we had stripped had more coins on them than we expected. None of Captain Philip's men had been killed although there were wounds which might take until after Christmas to heal but all things taken into consideration, we had surprised even ourselves. With half the number of men at arms compared with the Scots we had not only defeated them but driven them home and they would not return in my lifetime!

After we had eaten Captain Philip was summoned to meet with Lord Ralph. We knew that most of the knights and men at arms were still pursuing the Scots as they fled north. The army would be disbanded, and Captain Philip was being given his instructions. He returned close to midnight; the cathedral's bells tolled it. He smiled at Robin and me, "You two must be a good luck charm." He tossed us each a purse of coins. "Lord Ralph gave ten pounds to each of the Lancashire archers and you two! For myself, I have twenty pounds and can now afford to buy materials which will allow me to finish my hall." He turned to the others, "We return home tomorrow. There are some captured wagons and horses. His lordship has given one to us for the wounded and the booty we take home. By this time tomorrow, we can all tell tall tales to our wives and sweethearts! We were at the battle of the Saxon Cross!"

The next morning, as we rode back to Hartburn, Captain Philip said, "And what are your plans now?"

"We came north for some peace and, as yet we have had none. I thought we might help you to rebuild your home. I need to work on my archery and your land seems as good a place as any. Of course, if we are in the way then…"

He laughed, "Believe me you will not be. I am grateful that you were with us. At the battle, John, you drew the Scots to you and not the farmers of Hartburn. I do not want you to think that you have to work. We will enjoy your company."

"And you know me, Captain, I shall not sit idly by while others labour.

And so, we spent two months working every hour in the ever-shortening days. Robin and I hunted in the woods of Coatham and Michael learned sword skills. We enjoyed playing with John, Captain Philip's son, and Michael picked up tips on cooking from Anna the cook and Mathilde. It was a perfect time. We stayed until Michaelmas and I enjoyed Christmas. Even when I had lived at home, I had not enjoyed Christmas despite my mother's best efforts for the looming presence of my father and brother had ensured that it was a miserable time for me.

I think that we would have stayed there for longer had we not visited Durham where the Bishop had returned. He spied us as we prayed in the cathedral and sought me out. "What are you doing here, John Hawkwood? I thought you would have been at the siege of Calais."

"We were sent home at the end of August, my lord, surplus to requirements." We told him of our part in the battle which was now known as the Battle of Neville's Cross for Lord Ralph had erected a new cross at the site of the battle.

The Bishop nodded, "Then you should know that as a result of that King Edward has sent for every archer in the land to meet at Southampton. Calais still holds out and he needs archers to take it." He then told us how Lord Henry Plantagenet had increased the English holdings in south-west France and that there was a hope that soon the French would capitulate.

Of course, when we told Captain Philip, he told us to go, "England needs you two and I would not sleep at night if I thought I kept you from this most complete of victories! We shall miss you, of course, but England's needs are greater than an old soldier who is now as content as any man!"

We left my chests of coins with the Captain for safekeeping. I told him to use any he needed to, but he said that the reward from Lord Neville and what he had taken from the field of battle meant he had the coins he required. I kept just enough from my chest to pay my way, I could always get more from Basil of Tarsus.

Chapter 16

With horses which had been taken from the Scots, we made the journey south to Southampton quickly. The winter weather helped for the ground was hard and we were able to travel faster than had it been wet and muddy. While Robin found us a ship, I went to Balin of Bitterne and picked up my mail. He had also made me a coif. The suit fitted perfectly, and I was also able to sell him the mail I had captured at Neville's Cross. Both of us were happy for we each thought we had had a fair deal and that, in my experience, was rare.

It took three days to get to Calais thanks to inclement weather and when we arrived, we reported to Captain William who now commanded the archers. "I am glad that you two are here for we need men with your experience. I would have you both as vintenars."

I looked at Robin and he nodded.

The Captain gave us the money which bound us to King Edward until released.

Things had changed since we had left and a spit of land to the north of Calais had been fortified which meant that the town was now completely cut off. Ships could no longer supply the garrison and they were starving; besides, our artillery could now batter that side of the town. We went to the camp to find the archers whom we would lead. As soon as I saw Ned and discovered that he, too, was a vintenar, then I felt happier. That happiness evaporated when I learned of the fate of Rafe the Dull. He had been hanged for the murder of a whore. Ned told me that it had been an accident. The huge giant had become overexcited when they had been copulating and she had died as he did not know his own strength. His slow wits hanged him for he could not explain to the court the real events; he did not have the words. Had King Edward not let us go then Rafe would be alive for we knew how to look after him. That was another lesson I learned about leadership; a leader looked after his men.

We learned, in the camp, that the French King was trying to bring an army to dislodge us. Until King Edward had built the fortification the French had been able to keep Calais supplied. Now that it had stopped the French tried to send their own raiders to disrupt our siege lines. The bulk of the new army was still in England and, one day in early May, King Edward and his son sent for me.

"Vintenar, we understand that you fought in these lands, towards Poperinge before Crécy."

I nodded, "Aye, my lord, I fought under Captain Philip and I have some idea what the land is like. It is flat and it is without any place to ambush!" I said that for I knew what he expected.

Prince Edward smiled at me, "And yet I know you, John Hawkwood. You have skills which we need if we are to win this land. I wish you to take fifty archers and harass any French army which comes near us."

"With fifty archers, my lord?"

"The fifty you take will make the enemy halt and that way you can send a rider to alert us. The time you buy will be sufficient for us to bring an army and meet them in the field. You may choose your own men! For this, we will pay you as a centenar."

"Thank you, Prince Edward." As I headed back to our camp, I knew that the men I led would be happy to be away from the siege works. Each day was monotonously similar to the day before. Unless we had the night watch we stood to and sent arrows at any Frenchman foolish enough to show himself above the parapet. As we had few targets we just peered at the walls of Calais.

My selection was easy. I took Robin and Ned as my vintenars. Michael would be my extra man. Since Crécy, he had grown, and I had had to buy him a larger horse. His pony helped carry our increasing war gear. Having bought the mail I wore that as I rode but I was aware that the days of Megs carrying me to war were over for I would be too heavy for her. To that end, Michael carried my spare sword in a scabbard tied to his saddle. He was becoming a squire to me although, as I was no knight, that was the wrong title.

It was as we were riding towards Poperinge that Ned observed, "You know, Captain, you no longer look like an archer. With that fine helmet and coif, not to mention your mail and greaves, you look like a man at arms."

"I have realised, Ned, that no matter how good we are as archers we will still be used as a tool to weaken the enemy before the men at arms end the battle and garner not only the glory but the treasure. After Crécy, we scavenged the field, as we did after Bergerac and Auberoche. It was the men at arms and knights who chased and captured the knights. The fifty thousand pounds captured by Lord Henry made him the richest man in England!"

Robin knew me well, "And that is what you wish, Captain, to be rich?"

"No, Robin, for the coins are a means to an end. If you have money, then you have power." I pointed to the north. "The Flemish army is there for they are allies of King Edward. If they were not, then he would have to hire them. I would have my own company of men and I would hire us out to fight for any who can afford us."

"Just archers, Captain?"

"No, Michael, for I have learned that you need a balance. Without men at arms to protect us then the archers are vulnerable and without English archers then men at arms cannot win battles. We showed at Crécy and Durham, that a small and well-trained army can defeat many times their number. That is what I intend." The winter had not been wasted and I had a better idea of how I wished to fight in the future after this war was over.

The burghers of Poperinge no longer feared the French and that meant that we were welcomed. Since King Edward and his army had arrived the Flemish had reclaimed some of their land and the effective border was further south. I intended to use that proximity to my advantage. I spoke with the council of Poperinge and we were allowed to billet ourselves in the town. The fact that I was mailed and attired as a man at arms seemed to make me more acceptable. We then spent each day patrolling the land to the south of the town. It was twenty miles to Saint-Omer which was the largest town still in French hands. Close by was the town of Arques and those two were the furthest extents of our rides. While Robin led some men to ride to Hazebrouk and Ned rode west to Bollezille, I took fifteen men to Saint-Omer. We headed through the forests which covered that part of France and we were able to rest our horses in the eaves of the forest to examine the town and its castle.

We dismounted and allowed the horses to graze and to drink from the small stream. I went with Walter of Barnsley and Michael to the edge of the woods where we sheltered behind the boles of some huge trees to spy out the defences.

"Captain, will we attack the town and castle?"

"No, Michael, but I want to know how many men are in the garrison. A small garrison means that we can come here regularly and not fear a foray from the French. It will also tell us when the French King arrives."

"Then should we not be closer to here rather than being at Poperinge?"

I looked at Walter who was smiling, "Every captain should have a Michael as a chattering magpie with incessant questions!" I looked at Michael, "It is good that you ask me such questions for it shows that you are thinking and that is always a good thing in a warrior. It is true that I believe they will come this way but, equally, they could choose to use the road further north. These forests are perfect for an ambush. You were not there but we used such forests at Bergerac when Lord Henry destroyed a huge French army. Now use your eyes as well as your mind and count the guards on the walls."

The gates were guarded by two men wearing liveried surcoats. On the gatehouse to the town were another four. There were wooden towers at the corners of the town, but none were occupied by soldiers. A single soldier patrolled between the towers. I could just make out the keep and spied six men there. All told I counted twenty men. I doubled that to allow for men on another shift and then added half again for the Lord of Saint-Omer and his personal retinue. That meant fifty or so men. Even if they came forth to discourage my men our arrows, as we had demonstrated before, would win us that battle. Satisfied I headed back to the others.

"We will ride back in an hour. Job of Tarporley, take a couple of men and let us see if we can steal some of the deer!"

The chance to hunt appealed and since the incident where Job had let down the company with his archery he had improved beyond measure. He was now the equal of Ned and Walter! We were just mounting our horses when they returned with two does. We slung the larger one over Michael's mount and the other on Job's. We would eat well for a couple of days. Although the burghers of Poperinge allowed us to camp they were not feeding us! The coins which the Prince had given to me might have to last a month or more.

By the time June came we had a familiar routine established and while we varied our other patrols one of us would ride each day to Saint-Omer. That we would be spotted was obvious for each patrol took the opportunity to hunt and any who visited the woods would know that. Although not always successful more often than not we managed to bring back something. One day Ned and his men managed to bring down a wild pig! That was a feast to be remembered. Although we had a routine, I was not complacent and each time I went to the edge of the forest I went as though I expected the French to be waiting for us. The month passed.

It was the last day of June and the days were as long as they were ever going to be. We had left after dawn and that meant we reached the woods relatively early and it was still cool. I had found the mail was too heavy and made me too hot and so I had not worn it on that day. As soon as Michael, Walter and I reached the edge of the wood I knew something was different. It was not just that there were now four men outside the gate but there was more traffic entering the town.

Michael was his usual inquisitive self and when he saw that my interest had been piqued, he said, "It could be market day, Captain."

"It is not market day for that is a Wednesday and those carts and wagons are laden. They are bringing supplies. Unless I miss my guess, an army is heading this way. Before I can send the news to Prince Edward and the King then I must confirm it. Walter, we will make a camp here in the woods. Send a rider back to Poperinge and have the others join us here tomorrow. If I am right, then I want to be able to move the company quickly."

"And if you are wrong, Captain, and the French are coming from a different direction?"

I smiled, "Then I will be the one in trouble. Do not worry, Walter, I know the consequences of my actions."

After he had left us Michael said, "He is right, Captain, you risk the wrath of the Prince and the King both!"

"I am Captain and I must make those judgements. If I am wrong, then the Prince will not use me again. I might even be dismissed." I grinned, "I do not think I am wrong!"

That night I placed two men at the edge of the woods as watchers. They were there to watch for any who had spied us but also to assess the defences at night. The fact that they kept a good watch at night told me much.

My men arrived the next day at roughly the same time as the French hobelars trotted through the gates of Saint-Omer. As I counted the two hundred or so horsemen I wondered if this was the vanguard of the French army or just men to rid the woods of us. Leaving Walter and Job to watch them I joined my men back at our camp. Ned and Robin rode in with our gear. I donned my mail as it was easier to wear it than to carry it on a horse.

"Is this the French army, Captain?"

"I think so, Robin, but until I see knights, I will reserve judgement. They have sent hobelars and that means we have to be wary. Hobelars were useful men to have if you were hunting archers!" We had to assume that we might be at the camp for some time and so my archers organised it while I went with Ned and Jack to rejoin the others watching the gate.

"Any more arrivals, Walter?"

"Not warriors, Captain, but there were wagons and they were laden. They were escorted by spearmen and a company of crossbowmen."

It was increasingly likely that this was the French army. I remembered that, before Crécy, the French army had been strung out over eight miles. If that was true here, then we would have to wait until the middle of the afternoon to discover if this was the French army. We were watching the main gate to the south and we knew that there was a gate at the northern end and one on the western wall. We were almost caught out, but I had Michael with us, and he had sharper ears and eyes than us.

"Captain, I hear horses and they are coming from the north."

In theory that could have meant English horsemen, but I knew that King Edward would send none until he heard from us. It had to be the hobelars. "Back to the camp and have the men stand to. I think that the French know we are here and the hobelars are coming to rid the woods of us." When we reached the camp, our sudden arrival alerted the men, "Stand to! Get your bows. I want horse holders with the animals. There may be French horsemen coming. Be prepared to mount and ride on my command." Turning to Michael I said, "Mount your horse and hold Megs as well as Ned and Jack's horse."

He had done this so many times that it almost felt foolish to give him the order. I strung my bow and nocked a war arrow. I could hear the horses now as they came through the woods. Our camp was in a clearing, but we would not have a clear line of sight. This would be as much a test of my archer's reactions as anything. One thing in our favour was that we had been coming here for almost a month and we knew the woods as well as any. Men found good places to stand where they had cover and as clear a line of sight as possible.

It was Robin who spotted the first hobelar. Riding small horses and with their leather jerkins, spears and round shields the horsemen could move quickly and change direction at will but Robin allowed for the jinking of the small horse and his arrow slammed into the hobelar's chest. It was first blood to us. Suddenly, the woods seemed to be full of the horsemen. My archers were good but the hobelars were coming from every direction. I sent an arrow into the shoulder of one Frenchman at a range of under ten paces so quickly did he appear. The power of the bow and the arrowhead knocked him from his saddle and, as he hit the ground, his neck was broken. I nocked and released another arrow which struck a hobelar in the side just as he was about to skewer Job. He dropped his spear and Job whipped the end of his bow around to tear across the Frenchman's face. We were winning the skirmish, but I saw at least three of my archers speared. They would not survive.

Then Michael shouted, "Behind you, Captain!" I turned and released the nocked arrow at the three-quarter draw. Even as the hobelar's spear struck me my arrow hit him in the shoulder and that, I believe, saved my life. Balin's mail helped but the spear dropped to the ground and I reached out my left hand and dragged the hobelar to crash at my feet, his horse racing off into the woods. I took an arrow and rammed it through his mouth. I pulled it out and nocked it, aware that the spearhead had penetrated one or two of the mail links and my aketon to prick my side. I sent the arrow, which had already killed one man into the back of another as the hobelars fled the woods.

I turned and saw a badly wounded hobelar; he had an arrow in his shoulder and what looked like a broken leg from the fall. His days as a soldier were over!

I went to him, "Where is your King's army, Frenchman?"

I had nothing to threaten him with, but I hoped that by using the word Frenchman in such a derogatory way he would be insulted enough to answer me with a curse. He obliged, "He is close you God-Damn! And he brings more than twenty thousand men to drive you and your men back into the sea."

I nodded and, taking my sword cut a branch from a nearby tree and threw it to him, "You might try to make this into a splint!"

"You will rot in hell you son of a whore!"

Ignoring the insult, I turned and looked around. We had lost few men and we could escape. "See to the wounded. Collect the weapons. Michael!" Michael rode over with Megs and I mounted, "Thank you for the warning. Come let us see where they go!" I hung my bow from the hook I had made for Megs from a crossbowman's spanning hook. "Ned take charge and when all is done bring the men to the edge of the wood, mounted and ready to ride home!" I drew my sword as we rode, following the fleeing hobelars. One, who was wounded already, fell as we neared the edge and his head, slamming into the bole of the tree, ended his life. We reined in and I saw the walls of the town lined with men. They had been reinforced and, as we looked, I saw banners and horsemen approaching. It was the French army.

The road before us would lead to Calais. Of course, we would have to ride through French land but that did not matter. Our patrols had shown us that there were few dangers on the road. That would now change. Ned and my men began to arrive. The dead archers were slung over the horses. We would bury them where the French could not despoil them.

"Ned, you and Michael lead the men towards Calais. Robin and I will be the rearguard."

The French knights and men at arms were two hundred paces from us as Ned and Michael led my men, like a flock of startled birds, from the trees and down the road. On the walls there was a shout of alarm and men began to load their crossbows. The French men at arms urged their horses to get at us. We were their avowed enemy, we were archers.

As Walter rode past me, he shouted, "I am the last!" and Robin and I rode along the road following the rest of my men. I saw that Robin held a hobelar spear in his hand. I should have thought of that too. I was riding on the left side of Robin when the crossbow bolt struck my shoulder. Once again it was Balin's mail which saved me from injury. The other bolts either missed or dropped short. The men at arms rode for, perhaps two miles and then stopped. We slowed and, when the others saw that we had slowed, then they did too. We kept up a steady pace all the way to Calais, but we did not push our horses. Leaving Michael to see to a very tired Megs I hurried to the house the King and his son were using as a headquarters.

The sentries outside recognised me, and I was admitted, "Well?"

"King Philip is at Saint-Omer, Your Majesty, and he has twenty thousand men."

Prince Edward nodded, "And we have more than thirty!"

"You have done well, Hawkwood." I was then ignored as the King turned to his son, "Have a rider fetch the Flemish and then ask Sir John Chandos to begin building ramparts and ditches. It will take a few days for King Philip to reach us, let us give him a warm welcome. We might kill two birds with one stone here. Defeat Philip and take Calais."

I left and headed back to my men. The armour had saved me, but it had been damaged and I paid the weaponsmith at the camp to replace the damaged links. It was not an expensive repair and I thought it was worth it. While I was without it, just a day, I made myself a surcoat to keep it covered. I was becoming used to my mail but I wished to keep it cleaner and so I managed to acquire some white material and, as I stood a watch, I sewed a plain white surcoat. I liked the effect and it meant it was harder for my enemies to detect that I wore mail.

The next day we were given the task of building a ditch close to the southwestern corner of our siege works. The soil was soft, and it was easy to dig the earth and pile it up behind us. By the end of the day, we had a ditch as deep as a man and a rampart which was four feet high. The next morning, we flattened the soil on the defended side of the rampart so that we had a solid fighting platform from which to loose our arrows. The French army took seven days to reach our position and that surprised me; I would have expected them to be speedier. By then we had a veritable fort outside our siege works. The French King rode with his senior lords to view our defences. He did not like what he saw for there was no attack for a day or two.

The French approached our ditches at the end of July, and I could see that they intended to probe us. King Philip had lost to us too many times to be bold. Caution was his new watchword and the wild charge of Crécy was a distant memory. I also saw that he was using mercenaries for his attack perhaps because he had lost so many of his nobles. He chose to attack the section of the defences which we defended. There were just five hundred men at arms spread along that part of the line and four hundred archers. The bulk of our archers were closer to the main gate. The French King used just five thousand men for his probe; we had time to count them as they approached. Two thousand were the Genoese crossbowmen again but this time they had their pavise with them. There were also mercenaries, men at arms. I recognised Swabian swordsmen as well as Italian and German men at arms. We had slain so many of his nobles that he had to hire elite warriors. These men would fight hard for their reputation lay in winning. If they lost and they were not dead, then they would never be hired again.

Sir Richard Elfingham, now Baron Elfingham, commanded the men at arms. He had done well in Gascony and was a trusted warrior. I was quite happy for him to command me. We had Captain Jack of Nottingham commanding our archers and I liked him too. All things considered, I was quite happy. I should not have been, but this was the first time I had fought against a completely mercenary force. I learned that they were not as reckless as a national army. The French knights at Crécy had been foolish when they attacked and not planned well. They had come in wave after wave. The Scots at Durham had been similarly affected by the red cross of St George and it had blinded them. They could have defeated us, but they were not well-led. These mercenaries were. I saw that they fought under a yellow banner with red chevrons. I did not recognise it. Their leader had a bascinet with a visor so I could not see his face. Many of the mercenaries wore that type of helmet. The Genoese had the kettle helmet.

The Genoese carried their crossbows on their backs and held their man-sized pavise before them. We did not waste arrows as they approached our lines. Behind them marched the men at arms. Although they had smaller shields than the Genoese, they had plate and mail armour. We could have hit them but the shorter the range the better the chance of stopping them. The crossbowmen stopped two hundred paces from us. We had the earth rampart before us and that would absorb many bolts. Indeed, it was so high that Robin Goodfellow could not even be seen from the other side. I wore my bascinet and my coif as well as my mail. It was possible that I could be hit but the Genoese who managed it would need to be incredibly accurate and hit my face. The Genoese set up their pavise and, effectively, disappeared as they used their spanning hooks to prepare their weapon.

"Draw!" We all pulled to a half draw.

The crossbowmen would need to either use their knee to steady their weapon or, more likely, rest the crossbow on the top of the pavise. As soon as they did so then we would have a target.

"Loose when you see a target!" Captain Jack trusted us.

I aimed at the nearest pavise and I began to draw back slowly to the full draw. Fighting crossbows behind a pavise was all about timing. When we had stayed in Hartburn with Captain Philip he had given Robin and I tips on how to fight against them. I had a bodkin arrow nocked and I saw the kettle helmet rise. I loosed a heartbeat before the crossbow came over the top. I nocked a second arrow, but this duel would be won by the more patient. I was fortunate for the arrow hit the crossbow close to where he held it and the metal there deflected it into his skull. The bodkin went directly through. As he fell forward his pavise collapsed. I drew my second and joined the others as we sent arrow after arrow at the Genoese. As at Crécy, our superior rate of release won the battle and also the fact that we knew exactly when they were going to release their bolts. We saw their crossbows rise. It is very hard to concentrate when you see the bodkin tipped shaft hurtling towards you. Archers did die but more crossbowmen fell.

The mercenary leader ordered the surviving Genoese forward and, surprisingly, they obeyed. The reasoning behind the order was clear. The men at arms were going to advance and close with us. They wanted to have to endure our arrows for as short a time as possible. Our own men at arms were fewer in number; if they could break through our barrier then the French army could exploit it and, perhaps relieve the siege.

Captain Jack shouted, "Choose your targets! We are better than these infernal machines for we are English archers!"

I chose a war arrow for the range would soon be close enough for me to aim at the nose, eye, any flesh, in fact, which I could see. We all drew and waited for the pavise to stop. They did so at one hundred paces range. They did not make a solid line of pavise and they left channels through which the men at arms could run. These were not the French knights who played at war, these were professional soldiers and soon they would be close enough to show us their skill and determination. When the pavise stopped I waited for the kettle helmet to disappear behind the wooden boards and I aimed. This would be a flatter, faster trajectory and the prick would be the centre of the crossbowman's head. I drew back to a three-quarter draw as I saw the top of the helmet rise. Obligingly the Genoese also lifted his crossbow at the same time and I drew to the full bow so that as he snapped up his crossbow and peered down it to aim at me, his death was already on the way for I sent my arrow to hit him on the top of his nose. I nocked another, a bodkin this time for I saw a Swabian, albeit briefly when the pavise fell. My arrow hit his left upper arm and the angle of the man at arms meant that it drove into his shoulder. His shield dropped and the Swabian wisely followed it to the ground.

I now saw, clearly, their plan. We were aiming at the Genoese and the men at arms were sprinting between them in a foot race to get to us. I nocked another bodkin, shouting, "Bodkins!" to my men. In the time it took to nock an arrow the first man at arms had covered almost half the distance to me and even though my arrow hit him in the chest a second was on his heels and by the time I had nocked an arrow was thirty paces from me. The arrow drove so deeply that only the fletch stood proud of the dead man's chest!

The next man had clambered up the ditch to the top of the rampart and was so close that nocking and releasing an arrow in time was out of the question and I dropped my bow and drew my sword as the Swabian swung his bastard sword at me. I used my hand and a half sword two-handed and the blades rang together; sparks flew, and the noise made my ears ring. I knew that the whole siege hung in the balance. Prince Edward and his father had not expected our lines to be breached and it looked like the French and their mercenaries had chosen their point of attack well. I knew that the Swabian would be the better swordsman and so I had to use my greater strength and my quick hands. I twisted my sword around as Ralph of Malton had shown me. I surprised him and I managed to push his sword over his shoulder. Before he could swing again, I pushed my shoulder at his knee, and he lost his balance toppling backwards into the stake filled ditch. He was skewered. I saw that although we had defeated the Genoese and the crossbowmen were fleeing, the men at arms had gained the ramparts and although our own men at arms were holding them until Prince Edward could send reinforcements, my archers would either be slaughtered or have to learn to fight superior swordsmen.

Michael was still with me and, as I headed down the line to where three mercenaries were hacking their way through my archers, I said, "Just watch my back for me. That is all! Take no risks for help will come soon!" I was not sure that I believed it.

Even as the three men killed Hob, one of my archers, I was swinging my long sword. Hob fell, almost hacked in two and my sword struck the mailed side of the swordsman who had killed him. He had been in the process of preparing to swing at Luke who was whipping his bow around to use it as a staff when my sword hit him, and it knocked him into his companion. I threw my axe at the man who had been knocked against the rampart and the head of the weapon struck him a ringing blow. Luke dropped his bow and, drawing his dagger leapt at the third swordsman. I think my sudden attack distracted the mercenary and Luke knocked the mailed man to the ground. I was on the two I had hit and I wasted no time, I slid my sword into the throat of the swordsman whose side I had laid open and even as I went to finish off the other Michael had beaten me to it. I turned and saw Luke drive his dagger into the eye of the man he had attacked.

"Luke, hold here. We will go to the aid of the others. Take yourself a sword."

Covered in the blood of the man he had slain he nodded, "Aye, the bastards will pay for slaying Hob, that I swear!" When men fought alongside each other then they were closer than brothers!

I reached Robin and Alan of the Woods as the two of them used their arrows to hit two Swabians standing atop the rampart. I helped Joseph who had been knocked to the ground to his feet and retrieved my axe. I heard the horn behind me and knew that help was on the way, but I could still see, further down the fighting platform, three swordsmen who had broken through. This time they had broken through a part held by our men at arms.

Alan of the Woods risked a look over the top, "They are falling back, Captain, and there are just those three left."

"Then stay here and Michael and I will deal with them."

"Be careful, Captain, these men have slain men at arms."

I laughed, "As have Michael and I. We can deal with them." I suppose it was arrogance, but I felt in no danger. Perhaps if I had been mounted on a horse fighting such men then I might have been, but this was almost like street fighting. The fighting platform was narrow and fine strokes meant nothing. It was a will to win and the ability to kill which counted.

I saw that the one who led the three wore a yellow surcoat. He was one of the household of the leader of the mercenaries.

The way the other two followed him confirmed that. They did for him as Michael did for me and it was the yellow surcoat which was hewing its way through our men at arms. Michael and I picked our way through the bodies which littered the fighting platform and it was a slip by Michael, who lost his footing, which alerted the two men guarding yellow surcoat. At the same moment, they turned and faced me. They both came at me and that helped me for the rampart to their right stopped them making a good swing with their swords. Until now the rampart had been their friend preventing the defenders from making clean strokes and now it helped me. Holding my hand and a half sword behind me I raised my short axe. The movement distracted the nearest swordsman, it was a heartbeat only, but it was enough for I used my legs to stride closer and swing my sword at him. He blocked it with his shield, and I hacked down with my axe. He stopped my blow with his sword but the axe head bit into the back of his hand. Michael lunged beneath my axe with his sword and it sliced through mail links to enter the mercenary's side. The other brought his sword around to take Michael's head. Robin's arrow slammed into the screaming and triumphant mouth of the mercenary. I finished off the man Michael had wounded and saw the last mercenary. He was ten feet from me and was about to skewer a man at arms. I hurled my axe and caught him squarely on the back of the helmet. He fell forward and, racing to him I sheathed my sword and drew my dagger to slit his throat. I pulled his unconscious body around and raised my dagger. I halted in mid-strike.

Michael said, "What is it, Captain? Finish him off."

I shook my head, "I cannot, I know him, he is my friend, Giovanni d'Azzo degli Ubaldini." Fate had conspired to bring us together. Behind me I heard a cheer as the last of the attackers was slain. "Quickly, Michael, take his surcoat from him and I will place the other two bodies on his."

It was as I was laying the two swordsmen on him that Giovanni's eyes began to open. He saw Michael first and then his companions. His eyes widened and his hand went to his belt. I said, urgently, "Hold Giovanni, it is John Hawkwood and I am trying to save your life. Feign death until dark." He had ever been clever, and he nodded. We dropped the body of the last swordsman across it as Robin came along.

"It is over, Captain, what goes on here?"

Robin was one of my men and I would not lie, I pointed to the discarded yellow surcoat, "It is an old friend and I would save his life."

Robin nodded, "Aye, for the King will have all mercenaries strung up."

"Michael you stay here. Strip the bodies of their treasure. The Prince will expect to speak with me."

Michael nodded and Robin said, "We will all watch. We lost men but these mercenaries carry full purses with them! They must have been paid in advance." He held up a jingling purse.

I left them and headed back along the top of the rampart for the fighting platform was littered with bodies. I counted six dead archers. The fact is that we had slain far more of the enemy, but the loss still hurt. I met the Prince and the King close to the place that the mercenaries had broken through.

King Edward nodded at me, "We watched you despatch those men at arms, Hawkwood, and we owe you and your men a great deal. We should have kept a better watch. Rid the fighting platform of the enemy dead and we will have you relieved before dark. You and your men deserve a night of rest for you bore the brunt of the fighting."

I nodded, "Aye, Your Majesty, and we will bury our own dead with honour."

I went back down the line and cupped my hands, "Hawkwood!"

My archers made their way to me. I saw that they were all laden with booty taken from the dead. We would mourn our own losses but this had been a victory for us. Every archer knew that this was their fate, one day.

"Throw the bodies across the ditch, when you have taken what you need. Then fetch the bodies of our own here and when our relief comes, we will take them hence to bury them. Robin, Michael and I will deal with these three mercenaries."

My archers left us, and we lifted the two bodies from Giovanni d'Azzo degli Ubaldini. He smiled, "You were always clever my friend. What now?"

"I owe you much and I will give you your life. Take off all that marks you as a man at arms. Keep your sword and your purse. Michael and Robin, fetch Hob's body and take off his cloak. Giovanni can wear it." While they were away, I said, "There are ships leaving our mole each day. You can take a ship, unless, of course, you wish to go back to Italy!"

He shook his head, "That is the last place I will go for they have a plague, the Great Death they call it, and it is sweeping the land. It will come here." He held his purse up. "With this I can start again. Perhaps I will go to England. The sea might keep it safe from the pestilence. It is a shame about the helmet and the mail but so long as I live, have my sword and purse then all is not lost!"

I smiled and helped him to his feet. Giving him a bow. I said, "You can keep your mail and your helmet. You will pretend to be an archer, take a bow and carry it. Hang your helmet and your mail from your shoulder. You will look as though you have looted the dead."

Robin and Michael appeared with Hob. I took the cloak and fastened it about the Italian's shoulders. When I pulled up the hood then he looked like an archer. I stuck Hob's hat on his head to complete the illusion.

Just then Captain William arrived with our relief. "Well done, Hawkwood, I am sorry that you lost men. Enjoy a night of rest. We will take over."

"Aye, Robin, you fetch Garth, we will take Hob." I slung Hob's body over Giovanni's shoulder; he was laden for the mail was over his other shoulder and his helmet hung from his sword. I had the purses from the two dead swordsmen, and I carried their mail. Michael carried their swords and helmets. We headed back to our camp looking like every other archer who had survived and was taking his booty back.

While my men tended to wounds, and after putting a bandage around the Italian's head, covering one eye, I left with Giovanni for the mole where supplies were embarked.

As we walked, I asked, "And what happened to your lord?"

He shook his head, "Your Lord Henry and his men killed him in Gascony. He was not a very good warrior, but I managed to take his mail and horse from the field of battle. I knew where he kept his treasure and I headed for Paris where I created the man at arms you see." He leaned in, "No one checks on a man's origins if he has money, mail, a horse and a sword."

It was outrageous, of course, but I now saw a way for me to become a man at arms. I knew that day was some way off but I now saw it. Meeting Giovanni had helped me, once again.

Even as we arrived a small cog had just finished landing some flour. We approached the captain, "I have a man here needs to get to England. Can you take him?"

The Captain was suspicious, "Is this authorised, vintenar?"

I pointed to the bandage, "He has lost an eye. Have you ever heard of a one-eyed archer?"

The sea Captain softened, "Come aboard, we leave soon."

I clasped Giovanni's arm, "Go with God my friend."

"Our lives are now bound, John, and not just by our names. We will fight together again, that I know. I owe you a life."

"You owe me nothing for we are friends!"

He stepped aboard and this time I knew that I would see him again, I just did not know where or when.

Epilogue

The siege ended a few days later. King Philip had gambled and lost. The mercenary attack had been the last throw of the dice. He and King Edward agreed for the Pope to arbitrate and it proved to be in England's favour. We kept all that we had taken and the jewel that was Calais was the greatest prize. We stayed in France until the end of October. I told my men of Giovanni for I wanted no rumours nor bad feeling amongst my men. They understood the bond and swore silence. We had little enough to do after the truce and King Edward was keen to pay us all off. In truth, we were keen to leave France for the pestilence which had struck Italy had spread through Genoa to southern France. Refugees were fleeing away from the disease, but the only safe place would be across the channel in England. God and nature would protect us from the disease which would be named, the Black Death. We were wrong but we did not know it then.

We crossed to England as rich men. We had our booty and the King had paid us in full. Calais had been a rich town. The French population was evicted and the ships which took us home brought English settlers keen to make money.

We reached England in November in the year of Our Lord, 1347. Our lives were about to change dramatically but as archers, the elite of England, with full purses, we did not care about our future. Robin, Michael and I headed for Southampton. I now had more treasure but instead of giving it to Basil of Tarsus, I intended to buy somewhere. I had a plan and the first part of that was to become a gentleman. I needed land and I needed training. I would become a man at arms and lead my own retinue. Robin and Michael were happy to be the first of my men! Gascony and Crécy had changed me and given me a dream. My future was in my own hands and I would mould myself into a warrior!

The End

Glossary

Fictional characters are in italics

Battle- a military formation rather than an event
Bastard Sword-One requiring two hands to use. The shield hung from the left arm
Brigandine- a leather or padded tunic worn by soldiers; often studded with metal
Chepe- Market (as in Cheapside)
Chevauchée – a raid on an enemy, usually by horsemen
Cordwainer- Shoemaker
Gardyvyan- Archer's haversack containing all his war-gear
God-Damns -derogatory French name for Englishmen
Harbingers- the men who found accommodation and campsites for archers
Oriflamme – The French standard which was normally kept in Saint-Denis
Rooking- overcharging
Spanning hook- the hook a crossbowman had on his belt to help draw his weapon

Historical note

John Hawkwood was a real person but much of his life is still a mystery. At the end of his career, he was one of the most powerful men in Northern Italy where he commanded the White or English Company. He famously won the battle of Castagnaro in 1387. However, his early life is less well documented, and I have used artistic licence to add details. He was born in Essex and his father was called Gilbert. I have made up the reason for his leaving but leave he did, and he became an apprentice tailor. It is rumoured that he fought at Crécy as a longbowman and I have used that to weave a tale. It is also alleged that he was knighted by the Black Prince at Poitiers. This first book in the series and, indeed, the second will be largely my fictionalised version of his life.

Those of you who are regular readers will know that I try to use the actual facts whenever I can and that is true here. I had never really read about the Gascon Chevauchée of Lord Henry. He deserves a whole series to himself for he was truly an amazing leader. The battles of Bergerac and Auberoche happened the way that I wrote them, and the Norman campaign of 1346 is also very accurate. The blind king of Bohemia being led into battle beggars belief but I can assure you I did not make it up! The casualty figures and the ransoms paid were also truly astonishing. The highest estimate of English and Welsh deaths at Crécy is 300 while most believe it was around 40. The French, in contrast, lost a whole generation of lords and knights. The next generation would fall at Poitiers. I could not resist having Hawkwood at Neville's Cross and Crécy. They both happened in the same year. Once again, the incompetence of the French was only matched by that of the Scots who managed to outnumber a scratch army of Northern lords and lose not only their knights but their King!

Who knows what would have happened if the Black Death had not reached England in 1348? The plague had struck England regularly but the Black Death, which had its origins in the east was something far more deadly. As I write COVID-19 appears to have much in common with the plague!

Griff Hosker
April 2020

The books I used for reference were:

- French Armies of the Hundred Years War- David Nicholle
- Castagnaro 1387- Devries and Capponi
- Italian Medieval Armies 1300-1500- Gabriele Esposito
- Armies of the Medieval Italian Wars-1125-1325
- Condottiere 1300-1500 Infamous Medieval Mercenaries – David Murphy
- The Armies of Crecy and Poitiers- Rothero
- The Scottish and Welsh Wars 1250-1400- Rothero
- English Longbowman 1330-1515- Bartlett and Embleton
- The Longbow- Mike Loades

Other books by Griff Hosker

If you enjoyed reading this book, then why not read another one by the author?

Ancient History

The Sword of Cartimandua Series
(Germania and Britannia 50 A.D. – 128 A.D.)
Ulpius Felix- Roman Warrior (prequel)
The Sword of Cartimandua
The Horse Warriors
Invasion Caledonia
Roman Retreat
Revolt of the Red Witch
Druid's Gold
Trajan's Hunters
The Last Frontier
Hero of Rome
Roman Hawk
Roman Treachery
Roman Wall
Roman Courage

The Wolf Warrior series
(Britain in the late 6th Century)
Saxon Dawn
Saxon Revenge
Saxon England
Saxon Blood
Saxon Slayer
Saxon Slaughter

Saxon Bane
Saxon Fall: Rise of the Warlord
Saxon Throne
Saxon Sword

Medieval History

The Dragon Heart Series
Viking Slave
Viking Warrior
Viking Jarl
Viking Kingdom
Viking Wolf
Viking War
Viking Sword
Viking Wrath
Viking Raid
Viking Legend
Viking Vengeance
Viking Dragon
Viking Treasure
Viking Enemy
Viking Witch
Viking Blood
Viking Weregeld
Viking Storm
Viking Warband
Viking Shadow
Viking Legacy
Viking Clan
Viking Bravery

The Norman Genesis Series
Hrolf the Viking
Horseman
The Battle for a Home
Revenge of the Franks
The Land of the Northmen
Ragnvald Hrolfsson

Brothers in Blood
Lord of Rouen
Drekar in the Seine
Duke of Normandy
The Duke and the King

New World Series
Blood on the Blade
Across the Seas
The Savage Wilderness
The Bear and the Wolf

The Reconquista Chronicles
Castilian Knight
El Campeador

The Aelfraed Series
(Britain and Byzantium 1050 A.D. - 1085 A.D.)
Housecarl
Outlaw
Varangian

The Anarchy Series England 1120-1180
English Knight
Knight of the Empress
Northern Knight
Baron of the North
Earl
King Henry's Champion
The King is Dead
Warlord of the North
Enemy at the Gate
The Fallen Crown
Warlord's War
Kingmaker
Henry II
Crusader
The Welsh Marches

Irish War
Poisonous Plots
The Princes' Revolt
Earl Marshal

**Border Knight
1182-1300**
Sword for Hire
Return of the Knight
Baron's War
Magna Carta
Welsh Wars
Henry III
The Bloody Border
Baron's Crusade
Sentinel of the North

Lord Edward's Archer
Lord Edward's Archer
King in Waiting

John Hawkwood
France and Italy **1330-1380**
Crécy

**Struggle for a Crown
1360- 1485**
Blood on the Crown
To Murder A King
The Throne
King Henry IV
The Road to Agincourt

Tales of the Sword

Modern History

The Napoleonic Horseman Series
Chasseur a Cheval
Napoleon's Guard
British Light Dragoon
Soldier Spy
1808: The Road to Coruña
Talavera
The Lines of Torres Vedras
Bloody Badajoz

The Lucky Jack American Civil War series
Rebel Raiders
Confederate Rangers
The Road to Gettysburg

The British Ace Series
1914
1915 Fokker Scourge
1916 Angels over the Somme
1917 Eagles Fall
1918 We will remember them
From Arctic Snow to Desert Sand
Wings over Persia

**Combined Operations series
1940-1945**
Commando
Raider
Behind Enemy Lines
Dieppe
Toehold in Europe
Sword Beach
Breakout
The Battle for Antwerp
King Tiger
Beyond the Rhine
Korea
Korean Winter

Other Books

Great Granny's Ghost (Aimed at 9-14-year-old young people)

For more information on all of the books then please visit the author's web site at www.griffhosker.com where there is a link to contact him or visit his Facebook page: GriffHosker at Sword Books

Printed in Poland
by Amazon Fulfillment
Poland Sp. z o.o., Wrocław
25 June 2022

e08b3bcf-91bc-4c3b-81b7-85cb89f9338aR01